KILBORN - SECOND EDITION

WAYNE HUGHES

~ The Jerrod Series, Book 1 ~

Books may be ordered from Amazon, through booksellers, or by contacting:

Wayne Hughes

jerrodcitizen@gmail.com

waynehughes.net

(806) 672 – 8286

~

ISBN: 978-1-7360367-1-6 (paperback)

~ Dedication ~

To Linda, who understood when the people on these pages
woke me at 3:00AM

Table of Contents

1

_____

"This is going to kill Zeke." Dan Baker pocketed the auction notice and was about to ask the volunteer at the hospital reception desk which room his friend was in. "Hey Dan, got a minute?" Ella Parker, one of the Jerrod Community Hospital nurses, walked up beside him.

"Sure, Ella. What's up?

She pointed to a small consultation room off the nurse's station. "Wanted to give you a heads-up before you see Zeke. Seems like everything is goin' wrong for him about now. Drake brought his dad in last night, saying Zeke's knee was hurting him. There are bruises." She too9k her phone out of her pocket, ran her finger down the screen.

"Zeke told the E.R. nurse he'd tripped after they had a little argument. You need to know all this before you go in. He's had trouble with his pacemaker, has had several big arguments with Drake. It worries me – worries me a lot."

"The pacemaker not working?"

"There are some problems with it, but I worry it may be something with the stents they put in last year. I hope I'm wrong, but he's acting like he isn't getting enough oxygen. I'd wonder if one or both might be clogged up.

"As for the pacemaker, it showed some irregularities. They put the remote reader on it and hooked up with Hedrick Memorial. We're hoping for results sometime this afternoon.

"Anyway, Drake came in, and things went to hell. They were arguing, and the monitor went crazy. I hustled in there, and Drake was leanin' over, poking his finger in Zeke's chest. Couldn't hear what he was saying, but it was the meanest whisper I've ever heard."

Ella stood and walked to the door and looked down the hall. "Dan, I pulled Drake away from Zeke's bed and aimed him out the door," she whispered. "He gave me a look like he wanted to do something bad to me. He narrowed his eyes to just slits. I'd never seen him do that before. It was spooky." She brushed away a piece of tape from her scrub greens.

"He may be my sister's boy, but ever since he came back here to help Zeke, he's been a regulation turd."

"You know, when we were growing up together here, I never would have thought about Zeke with gray hair and bruises in the hospital. I . . ." She pulled her buzzing cell phone out of her pocket. "Look, I gotta go. I'll keep a watch on this and let you know. Don't talk to Zeke about what I told you, all right? Tell Donna I said hello."

Dan followed her into the hallway and turned down the wing toward Zeke's room. He paused at the half-open door. He

rapped, waited for a quiet, hoarse "come in." He was stunned by what he saw.

Almost as tall as Dan, Zeke looked frail, skeletal. His right leg was propped up on several pillows. The livid bruise was visible on the right knee. It was a mixture of blue, black, and a greenish tinge. The

other knee's bruise was not as nasty but was about the same place as the left, as if he fell on his knees.

"Damn, buddy. What happened to you?"

Zeke struggled to sit partway up and looked down at his legs.

"Hey, Daniel. Me and Drake was having a little argument last night, and I stood up too quick and got all tangled up in my pajama bottoms and whack. I'm on the floor."

Dan leaned over and looked into his friend's bloodshot eyes. "Did Drake do this to you?" He could tell by the way Zeke looked there was something very wrong.

"Huh? On no, Dan. He did not. *Not at all*. An' I mean that. You hear me?" He laid back on the pillow and looked at the IV line running to his left hand and the blood pressure cuff on the right.

"I'd take all this shit outta me and offa me if I thought I could get away with it." He laid back against the pillow and stared up at the saline drip on the pole beside the bed. "But, they'd do it to me all over again. So, I got no choice but to wait."

Dan took his old friend's free hand. "Wait for what? What is the doc tellin' you?"

"Not much so far today. He muttered something about an unusual heart rate this morning and said he wanted to wait to hear from the boys in Abilene before saying anything more."

Dan looked at the monitor on the pole beside Zeke's bed. "Ella said Drake was here earlier."

"He was here all right. He busts in, not so much as a how-do-you do, wantin' me to sign a bunch of papers he had. Had to do with power of attorney or some such thing

"I said I wanted to look them over one more time, and he got all

huffy. I ended up tellin' him to leave the papers and come back tomorrow when I felt better. He grabbed the papers and stormed outta here real mad. That took a lot of nerve, considering I had to take care of his DWI fine right after he moved back.

"I think it was a mistake to get him back here. You know, he seemed happy doing what he was doing in Abilene, but I got no choice.

If he can't handle it, or if he screws it up, then it's all over. We got two spray planes sittin' out there. Number One is overdue for an engine overhaul, and the bank all but owns the other one. I thought he'd jump at the chance to keep the business runnin'."

Zeke shifted from side to side in the bed, held his chest as he coughed. "There are these GPS units you can put in a plane that show you a map of where you're spraying, what your passes look like on the ground. Those are fifty thousand each. If we could afford that, we'd get more business. But we can't afford it unless we get more business. I dunno," Zeke turned to stare out the window a moment, then threw the sheet off.

"Help me sit up."

Dan took Zeke's left hand and helped him pivot to a sitting position. "How's that?"

"Better. I get tired of layin' here, waitin'."

Dan could feel the weakness in Zeke's hand. It was evident from the tentative feel of his grip that his friend was losing strength.

Zeke paused, looked around to the room's solitary window, then back to Dan. "You know, the one positive thing coming out of Drake's decision to be here is Freddy Paz. He's a Cracker-Jack airframe and powerplant guy. It would be hard to justify having him full-time, but he brought some pretty good business with him.

"He installed all of the new electronic equipment in the sheriff's dispatch center and their vehicles. He's done some work on that kind of stuff for the school district and a couple of businesses. It's interesting to see the way he's blended into the community. Sometimes it's hard for an outsider – real hard for a Mexican outsider – to find their place here."

He looked around the room, down at the IV tube in his hand.

"What were we talkin' about?"

He lay back on the bed and pulled the sheet up to this chest, and stared at the ceiling. "You know, all this was so different, better all the way 'round when Bertie was here, but . . ." He faced away, toward the window, and was quiet for a moment. "I'm kinda tired, Dan." He spoke without looking back.

Ella was waiting for Dan in the hall. They walked together toward the reception desk. "You told me. Pretty bad. Ella, I don't like those bruises."

"Me neither, but there's not a damned thing we can do about it as long as Zeke sticks to his story. I told him the sheriff ought to know about the bruises if there was any possibility of domestic violence. Doc Chin also wanted to call the sheriff. But Zeke was adamant. So, we let it go." Ella looked down for a moment, wiped her eye with her index finger, sniffed, and looked up.

"You headed out?"

"Yep, gotta go do cotton stuff."

"I'll walk out with you."

They went down the corridor, turned left at the gift shop, through the double doors, out onto the lawn next to the parking lot.

Dan was almost in his Suburban when he stopped. He turned in time to see Ella reach the hospital's front door. "Hey, Ella," he shouted. "Wait a minute." He pulled the auction notice from his pocket and walked back up the sidewalk. Ella walked back toward him with a puzzled look on her face.

"You need to look at this." Dan waited for her to scan it. He knew she didn't have a clue when she gasped and put her hand over her mouth.

When she looked up, her eyes were moist, but Dan knew they were tears of rage. "That incredible asshole. How could he auction off Alberta's house? I mean, their house?"

"I thought you'd feel that way. I almost didn't show you, but there's somethin' not right about this. I don't think Zeke knows, and I don't think he'd agree to it. I think that was what Drake was getting around to when Zeke sent him away." Dan took the paper back from Ella and put it in his shirt pocket.

"What's going to happen, Dan?"

"Not sure. I've got to give it some thought. It's none of my business."

"But Dan, somebody's got to look out for Zeke's interests. Don't get me wrong. I'm family, and I'm gonna do everything I can, but he needs you. You guys have been best buds all your lives."

"Yeah. I'm gonna have to do a lot of thinking about this. I've got until next Tuesday to shake it out."

"What happens next Tuesday?"

"It's the deadline for ads for the paper. The ad proof came from Jack Knowles. I assume Drake paid for it, so Jack's obligated.

He turned to walk back to the parking lot. "Keep this under your hat for a while. I feel like I've gotta talk to Drake about all this. I don't know how I'm gonna do it. I've got to get it out of the way quick.

We're going to Fort Worth to meet Nelly's boyfriend two weeks from this Saturday. You know the drill. Everybody on their best behavior, sizin' the other guy up, decidin' whether to kill his ass or not," he said with a smile.

"Isn't Nelly close to graduation? She's still majoring in some kinda engineering, right?"

"Chemical engineering."

"What about her fella?"

"Of course, we hear nothing but good things from Nelly about him, couldn't expect otherwise. It sounds like he's pretty smart, microbiology, somethin' like that. He's some kinda Yankee. Pennsylvania, I think.

"You all right with holdin' off on this auction ad?"

Ella had finished dabbing her eyes and put the handkerchief back in her pocket. "But it's gonna be tough to look my nephew in the eye."

She looked away and then back, shielding her eyes from the midday sun. "To change the subject—and I don't want to shock you or anything—but I'm thinking about dating again."

"What?"

"Yep. There's life in the ole girl yet."

"Who?"

Ella pulled an imaginary zipper across her lips.

"When?"

"All you left out was 'where?' We're keeping it quiet right now."

"You gonna make me guess?"

"Guess all you want to." She looked at her watch. "Hey, it's time for rounds. I gotta go." She looked down at her phone, waved to Dan, and hurried back to the hospital.

At noon, Dan drove by the high school in time to see his wife LaDonna walking toward the cafeteria with a fellow teacher. She noticed him, waved her friend on. "What's going on, Danny?" She got in the passenger side of the Suburban.

"*Danny.*" That always brought warmth up his insides. She could read his worry from yards, even miles away, and knew the boyhood form of his name would give him some peace. It had been that way for their thirty years together. He handed her the ad proof.

"This can't be." The paper trembled in her hand. "What can we do? Can you talk to Drake? I mean, will you talk to him?"

"I don't see I have any choice. I showed this to Ella. She said the same."

"How long will Zeke be in the hospital?"

"Ella says he may be gettin' out tomorrow."

LaDonna checked her watch. "I've got to get to the cafeteria. Are you going to see Drake today?"

"Naw, we've got a shipment of tires comin' in, and I've got to go to a co-op meetin' at the bank. By the time I go out to the south place to check the center pivot, the day's over. It'll for sure be Friday. Maybe we'll know somethin' about Zeke by then."

"There's the bell. I'll see you later." She patted his hand, got out of the Suburban, waved, and headed for the cafeteria.

Dan watched her in his mirror as he pulled away. He turned the corner, passed the courthouse, drove by the Jerrod Citizen, turned toward D. Baker Tires. He slowed as he passed the shell of the movie theater. "Yeah, that's us, a burned-out little cotton town."

2

D rake and Archie Medders had taken the Kilborn Aviation flatbed
truck to Stangle's Safe Storage. Archie was a part-timer who got
work where and when he could. At times, he worked in the shop at D.
Baker Tires. Most of his time was spent doing odd jobs at the airport.
They winched the pallet holding a 250-gallon plastic container to the
truck bed, drove to Kilborn Aviation's hangar, and backed it in.

"We gotta be careful with this damned thing. I don't want another
spill. That lid doesn't seem to fit right. I can't stand to have the damned
Ag department breathing down my neck again. One violation this year is
enough." Drake climbed to the truck bed and twisted the lid.

The Kilborn Aviation mechanic, Freddy Paz, walked into the
hangar. "You want the lift?"

"Naw, Archie can do that. You get up here and help me scoot this
damned tote to the back."

Archie stood on the pallet lift and started the motor. He eased the
lift forward, so the forks went in the pallet and extended about six inches

out the other side. The hydraulics groaned as the weight was transferred. He began to ease backward, away from the truck bed.

Drake jumped off the truck bed. "Here, lemme do that." He pushed Archie aside and climbed onto the footpad of the forklift, spun it around. As he lowered the pallet, the inertia caused the load to slip off the forks, topple and hit the floor.

As it landed, the hook on one of the straps snapped. It bounced once, and the cap gave way, spilling the blue-grey liquid.

The tote grazed Archie's leg, knocking him on his back. He landed in the expanding puddle, some of which splashed onto his face and into his mouth. He spat the thick liquid out, lifted himself to one elbow. He managed to get on all fours and crawl toward a dry spot. He grabbed the truck's bumper and pulled himself up, brushing at his wet clothes.

Drake backed away, avoiding contact with Archie. "Archie, we gotta get that cleaned up. Now, let's get on it." Drake turned to Freddy.

"You help him. Get some gloves on."

Freddy dismissed the demand with a wave. "No way, man. That stuff's too dangerous. It ain't in my job description, Archie's either."
"I said for you to help him. You want me to fire your ass?

"Yeah, Drake, why don't you fire my ass? That's a damned good idea." Freddy took off his Kilborn Aviation cap and took a step toward Drake. "Then, I can tell the people who need to know where this came from and how you happened to get your hands on it. How about that? As Archie leaned down to right the half-empty herbicide container, the fumes filled his nose, his knees buckled. He slipped and fell back into the liquid, coming to rest on his side. Freddy rushed over to the corner of the hangar, grabbed a mop, extended the head to Archie, who grabbed but missed.

He tried to sit up but couldn't steady himself on the slick floor and fell on his back in the puddle. Hey." he shouted at Drake between coughs. "How about some goddamned help?"

Freddy pulled him up and helped him lean against the truck. Archie was trying to wipe away the sting from the side of his face, spitting to clear the taste from his mouth.

"Archie, Archie, Archie." Drake's tone a patronizing scold. He turned to Freddy. "Get the hose. We'll wash this down, so it doesn't stain the concrete."

Freddy retrieved the hose and handed the nozzle to Archie, who sprayed the mess, trying to push it out the door onto the asphalt. In his haste to finish, he splashed some of the dilute fluid on Drake's pant leg.

"Oh, that's great, Archie. Knock it off. The damage is done. Where's your pickup?" Archie twisted the nozzle to stop the jet of water and pointed past the hangar door and to the left. "Get it and back in here. I want to put this tote in your pickup bed."

"What am I supposed to do with it?" Archie eyed Drake and scratched at a spot under his left arm where the herbicide had penetrated his shirt.

"Don't care. Get rid of it. I'll make it worth your time. Look. Let's hose you down, so you don't get problems with this stuff all over you." Freddy had stepped away from the two, observing, staying out of the line of fire, hoping Drake's ire had cooled. It was essential for him to stay on with Kilborn Aviation.

Drake pulled a pair of clean coveralls out of the nearby wall locker. "Here. Get out of those clothes and put this on." Archie snatched it out of his hand and headed for the bathroom.

Drake went back to the locker and pulled a black plastic-wrapped bundle from the top shelf. He turned to see Freddy watching him.

"What are you lookin' at? You got nothing to do?"

Freddy nodded and walked toward the office door at the rear of the hangar. Drake watched him go inside, then took the package, went to

Archie's pickup, reached under the bed on the driver's side, and pushed it in place. "I'm gonna need this someday, momma. He won't know it's here. People are awful nosy. We know that, don't we?"

Archie came out of the bathroom dressed in the coveralls, carrying his wet, stained Levi's and shirt.

"Okay. I want you to take the rest of the day off. Load that container in your pickup and get rid of it somewhere. I'd get rid of them clothes, too, if I was you." Drake watched as Archie ran the pallet lift under the container and onto the bed of his pickup.

Archie climbed into his pickup, slammed the door, leaned out the window. "Ain't that shit kinda expensive? An' dangerous?" Standing outside by the Ag-Wagon Number One on its fuselage, Freddy made a mental note to include Drake's response in his daily messages.

Drake said, "We've gotta go back to storage tomorrow, the next day, and get one of those totes of *Adios* defoliant. That's the stuff I worry 'bout. We can't afford to handle that wrong. I don't wanna lose my applicator's license."

Archie coaxed the reluctant engine of his pickup to start one more time. Without a muffler, it made the corrugated sides of the hangar

Archie coaxed the reluctant engine of his pickup to start one more time. Without a muffler, it made the corrugated sides of the hangar reverberate.

"Thanks, man." Drake's tone was high-pitched, false friendly. "See you tomorrow morning."

———————

Dan pulled up to the hangar as Freddy was putting chocks under the spray plane's wheels. "How's it goin'? Drake around anywhere?"

Freddy nodded toward the hangar and walked to the tool shed. It had been a month since Dan had seen Drake. In that time, Drake had grown his hair longer, had gained weight. In the office, Drake opened a couple of beers and made small talk. Dan told him about Janelle's progress at TCU then talked about how worried Zeke was that Drake was about to auction their house.

Drake's mood changed as he stood up and paced the room, growing more and more agitated as the conversation continued. He told Dan they wouldn't even be talking if his mother was still alive. At the end of the conversation, he told Dan he was going to auction the house.

Later, Dan recalled Drake had made a point of saying they wouldn't be talking this way ". . . when Momma is here." He had corrected himself. "If she was 'still alive.' The conversation ended with Drake letting Dan know this would be the last time he'd discuss anything about his family.

He walked toward the office door. "One good piece of news, I guess. I gotta go to the hospital. They're lettin' my dad out this afternoon."

Dan stood. "Hey, that's great news."

Drake opened the door. "Yeah, I guess."

"What do you mean, you 'guess,' Drake? Aren't you happy 'bout that?"

Drake held the door open and stood still as Dan got in his car and headed for the rail crossing.

Archie had turned left and driven down the dirt road paralleling the tracks toward the Windy Acres Trailer Park. He had taken it slow, looking to the left and right, searching for a place to ditch the container rattling around in the pickup bed. The pain in his upper back flared again, and he decided to head for the trailer where he and Mazie and their son lived.

As he pulled up, Woof, the German Sheppard-Collie mix, began to yip, wagging his long, heavy tail and strained against a rope on his.

Mazie had been struggling to get six-month-old Harold Dean in the back of her aged Pinto. She was headed for her part-time job at Big Jimmy's, the time-worn drive-in. "What you doin' home this early? If I'd knowed you were comin,' I wouldn't be takin' H.D. to Mom's."

The infant spotted Archie, broke into a burbling wail, and held out his chubby hands, struggling to free himself from the car seat. Archie had started to reach in the rear window and comfort his son.

"Phew. Where'd you get them fancy coveralls? What's that smell?"

Archie held up his stained, dripping clothing.

She stepped between Archie and the car. "Don't be getting that shit on him. Hey. That's soppin' wet. What you been doin', playin' in the water?" Mazie had handed H.D. a much-abused stuffed giraffe, which he began to chew.

Mazie waved Archie off when he attempted to kiss her and molded herself into the Pinto, which groaned with her weight. She had filled

Mazie waved Archie off when he attempted to kiss her and molded herself into the Pinto, which groaned with her weight. She had filled the driver's seat with part of her bulk hiding the bottom of the steering wheel.

Archie untied the rope from Woof's collar and led him onto the porch. He sat for a moment on a stained, weather-beaten car bench seat. He draped his stinking shirt and pants on the porch rail.

Inside, he plopped on the broken-down couch with the mismatched cushions, poked the remote at the old TV. He rubbed Woof's long ears and scratched him at the base of his spine, stretched out on the couch. Woof licked Archie's hand, sat on his haunches. Archie closed his eyes and began to snore.

Woof scratched and settled with a soft groan. He rolled on his side, about to sleep, when he sensed a change pass in the room. He sat up, sniffed the air. He heard Archie take a deep breath, then felt the breathing stop. Woof sensed the quiet, nudged at Archie's forearm, sniffed his mouth, waited for the breath to come again. He stared at Archie's chest for a moment, at last content there was movement, lay down again, but not with any comfort.

3

———————

The previous minister of St. Anthony's Episcopal had been a bust. He'd resigned after nine months on the job. Dan and his fellow vestrymen were relieved to find Wyman Costley, who hit it off with the other church leaders, youth group members, and even custodial staff. His popularity extended beyond the church, to breakfast several days a week at the City Café and afternoon coffee in the Jerrod Citizens Bank hospitality room.

This Sunday, Father Costley's sermon centered on Christ's admonition about reaping what you sow. He worked his way to the importance of being a good steward of the soil by planting at the correct time, so the harvest can come at the right time to benefit most of

God's people. He wrapped up his sermon with a subtle reminder of the importance of tithing as the way to be a good steward of God's kingdom. "*Wyman, ole buddy,*" Dan thought, steward of God's kingdom. "*Wyman, ole buddy,*" Dan thought, "*you are slick today. Put in a fund-*

raising plug right before the plates are passed. Yep, slick, but a good
guy who doesn't take himself too seriously."

After the service, Dan waited in line to shake Costley's hand. He leaned in and whispered, "Got the old money pitch in there, your holiness."

"Keeping in practice. Planning on taking a 'love offering' from you on the golf course tomorrow." Costley put on his best smile for those waiting in line. He winked at Dan.

The following day over lunch in the clubhouse, the subject of wild hogs came up. Dan told Costley how domesticated pigs can go wild in a single generation. At the end of the conversation, he invited the minister to his farm to see for himself.

Late in the afternoon the next day, they drove to one of Dan's smaller fields, about fifteen miles from Jerrod. They drove by the cotton field and onto freshly-cut maize stubble. At one edge were a long row of trees and a cliff that dropped off 200 feet to a narrow canyon. He stopped close to the cliff's edge, took binoculars from the door pocket of the SUV.

"Yep, they're out there." Dan swept from left to right, back again, then stopped as he started another arc. "See those shapes right on the rim? Those are wild hogs." He handed the binoculars to Costley, who adjusted them for his narrower eye sockets.

"What? Oh yeah. I see them. What are they doing out here?" The binoculars felt like a brick in his hands. Wyman could see that Dan moved them left and right without effort.

Dan chuckled. "About anything they want to. Did you see the big boar? He'll sire enough pigs this year to be a great grandfather in two years. He's almost bullet-proof, real smart, downright vicious if he decides to take you on. He and his tribe can tear up an acre of farmland rootin' around in a few hours."

Costley looked again. "What can you do about them? Can't they be killed by hunters?"

"Yeah, they could. If we had an infantry battalion come through and everybody got a dozen hogs, that would cut the population in five square miles by about half until the next round of births.

Costley focused on the distant rim again. "Can you kill pigs with a .22?"

"Not a chance. It'd be like a wasp sting for you or me. It would only piss off *Don Puerco Grande*. He might decide to run you down for the heck of it. Very territorial."

"Sometimes it's hard to figure God's plan for a creature like that,"

Costley said. "Will they actually attack somebody?"

"If their sows and litters are threatened, or if they sense you can't defend yourself, they'll come at you full speed, even if you're minding your business, unaware of where they are.

"Last year about this time, I was out here at dusk to see if I could spot a shoat – a newly weaned pig – to shoot for a cheerleaders' barbeque. Those little pigs make good eatin'.

"Anyway, I was standin' on the hood of my old jeep with my thirty-thirty, waitin' for the boars to lead the herd up out of the canyon to feed. Then, I hear it. Behind me was a boar snufflin' and pawin' the ground, lookin' for worms or whatever and eyeballin' me.

"By the time I got the rifle to my shoulder, that damned pig had butted my left rear wheel twice, makin' the damn Jeep creak.

"By the time I got the rifle to my shoulder, that damned pig had butted my left rear wheel twice, makin' the damn Jeep creak. He backed off about ten yards, eyed me, pawed at the ground, headed for the breaks. I got off two shots. Never got close."

Wyman's mouth was half-open. "You think he would have killed you?"

"Hell, I know he would've. All I needed to do is get on the ground, and he would have run me down, regardless of how many shots I got off. You've got to hit' em in the chest or dead-on above the eyes to stop 'em. And if you kill one that big, there's nothin' you can do with it. Leave it where it falls, and the other pigs will take care of it before dawn."

Costley swallowed. "Take care of? You mean they will eat their own?"

"You bet. I've seen kill sites on other farms along this canyon where professional hunters downed as many as fifty in one night. They were all gone, except a few bones, in two or three days."

They got back to the farmhouse about six, as the sun was touching the horizon. They were greeted at the foot of the kitchen steps by Sniff, a rangy mutt with Labrador, Greyhound, and Irish Setter in his end of the gene pool. For the most part, he was LaDonna's dog, seldom making the rounds with Dan, but endeared himself to all visitors by sitting and offering his left forepaw.

"His name is Sniff. He wants to shake hands." Dan smiled as

Costley leaned over, took the dog's outstretched paw in his hand, moved it up and down three times. The dog stood, moved closer to Costley, began to sniff around his pants leg.

"Yep, that's *Sniff.*" Dan rubbed the dog's ears and gently shoved him toward the doghouse next to the steps.

LaDonna brought a large pitcher of tea and a plate of cookies and joined them at the table on the two-story farmhouse's wrap-around porch. Costley put his tea glass down and stared beyond the waist-high porch railing. He touched Dan's hand. "I need to ask you about someone. And you've got to keep this hush-hush. I'm sensitive about pastor-parishioner privilege. I'm not sure it applies here."

"Who?"

"Drake. Drake Kilborn. I assume you know him."

"All his life. What about him?"

Costley smoothed his grey hair back. "He came to me last week wanting to talk about what was going on with his mother. He talked about her like she was still alive."

Dan nodded. "He was always high-strung to the point of bein' reckless. He broke his arm tryin' to jump a creek on his bicycle at the bridge north of town but wouldn't let up ridin' until somebody found his mother. She showed up and damned near dragged him to the hospital. At the time, we excused it as being 'high-strung' - whatever that means.

"But that kid had a soft side to him. Sniff, for instance. Drake found him wanderin' around half-starved out in the breaks. He cleaned him up, took him to the vet, gave him to Nelly on her sixteenth birthday. She taught the dog how to shake hands."

LaDonna spoke up from where she was sitting on the porch rail.

"He wrecked one car after another, and we were afraid he was gonna kill himself, but our daughter seemed to see a lot of good in him, and they started dating. It got pretty serious by the time she was a junior, and he was a senior."

LaDonna exhaled. "There were times when Drake and Janelle would pop up as an 'item.' She always denied anything earth-shaking was happening. I don't know that I ever really believed that. Call it a mother's intuition. And, I also remember wondering if that feeling was stronger with him than it was with her."

LaDonna pushed at the tablecloth, then pulled it straight. "I hadn't thought about this for years, but I remember Drake in a creative writing class I taught. Regardless of the assignment, he always wrote about himself. That happened even when I assigned a neutral topic like describing the clouds or explaining how to build something. As I can remember, he never wrote anything about other people or their lives. He focused on himself. I remember wondering what Janelle saw in him.

"He got his pilot's license when he was sixteen and was learning crop-spraying. Zeke was real proud of him, and it looked like Drake had found somewhere to channel his energy. We were worried Janelle would end up flying with him.

"Janelle was number one, top of her class, all the way through school. Drake was usually on the other end of that spectrum. Plenty of the most eligible boys in high school tried to date her, but she always gravitated back to Drake. She didn't rebel like a lot of the other girls, but I think she picked Drake, so everybody knew she wasn't really Miss Goody-two-shoes.

Dan and I were determined to let her make her own choices about who she hung around with and didn't really worry about it. It all came to a head when a bunch of them were out at the bridge. There was beer, and then couples began pairing off. As Janelle told it, Drake was kinda 'handsy' and really got upset when she pushed him away. We were relieved when she felt comfortable telling us and even more relieved when she said that it was over between the two of them. She told us he apologized later, but they were only friends from then on."

LaDonna sat in the wicker chair next to Dan. "Four years ago, his mother, Bertie, died. He took that extra hard. She was the only one in the family who seemed to understand him and could calm him down.

He became almost a recluse. Then he would have these outbursts. He came close to being jailed for purposely running into the front of the laundromat. Zeke got that handled. They tried counseling, you name it.

Nothing worked. His behavior got darker and darker."

Dan stood and massaged his left knee, leaned against the railing.

"After high school, he decided he wanted to move to Abilene and fly for one of Zeke's friends. His job was haulin' oil field test equipment all over that part of Texas. Zeke and I talked a lot about the move. He told me how unhappy he was to see Drake move but hoped his behavior would change when he got away from Jerrod and the everyday reminders of his mother.

"That seemed to work out. Zeke kept in touch with his buddy in Abilene. There didn't seem to be any problems with Drake. Zeke started havin' heart trouble. He had a case of severe angina, and they finally rushed him to Hedrick Memorial in Abilene, where they put in stents.

"Zeke talked Drake into movin' back. He agreed to gradually hand over the flying business so he'd come home."

Costley thought a moment. "That explains a lot. Before he came to see me, I had a strange encounter with him. I had seen his father's name on the hospital list and went out there to visit. Drake was in his dad's room when I got there. We shared small talk, and I offered a prayer for his recovery. Drake took me by the arm and almost literally pulled me out of the room. I managed to pull away and shake Zeke's hand, and then out the door, we went."

"Drake almost pushed me down the hall. He really had a grip on my shoulder. I got the picture. I pulled away after we got outside.

"He really lit into me. He went on and on about how my predecessor had done—to use his exact words—a 'piss poor job' at his mother's funeral. I muttered something about how unfortunate that was. I decided then and there I wasn't going to make any headway with him. I wished him well and left. What gives?"

Dan rubbed the top of his head. "That's a tough one. It's not about the guy who preached the funeral or about the church. He can't seem to reconcile himself to her death."

"I know how he feels. I went through some pretty hard times when my wife died." Costley looked down at his hands. "But I had friends who helped me through it."

"I've seen that up close, really up close." LaDonna put her tea glass down and brushed her long red hair back. "When he came to town to visit Zeke, he had one or two dates with one of my fellow teachers.

You may know her, Mariel Ascencio." LaDonna leaned forward in her chair.

"When he was still living in Abilene, he found out Mariel and several teachers were there for an in-service day. He showed up as we were leaving and got in Mariel's face. He wanted to know why she had gone to Abilene without letting him know. He got louder and louder and grabbed her right there in the parking lot. I don't know what I thought would happen. It wasn't like him at all.

"A cop came and calmed Drake down. Because Mariel didn't want to press charges, he was released. Mariel said Drake showed up at her apartment a week later, and she threatened him with a restraining order. I guess that got his attention.

"Very few people in Jerrod know about this. Zeke is so popular that nobody wanted to complicate his life. It has been under wraps 'til now. Who knows what happens next."

"That explains a lot," Costley said. He drank the last of his tea and stood. Dan said, "Hey, why don't you stay for dinner?"

"I would, but I actually have a date tonight." He smiled and checked his watch. "Would you believe it? We're going to a steak place in Breckenridge. Long way to go for a meal, but with pleasant company."

Dan's eyes brightened. "Who? Anybody we know?" He and

Wyman walked down the steps to the driveway. LaDonna stayed on the landing.

"You probably do. We're keeping it quiet right now." Wyman got in his car and lowered his window.

"Will you tell us if we guess?" Dan cocked his head and smiled.

Wyman looked up. "Nope. Soon maybe."

Dan watched him leave, then went back up the steps and into the kitchen nook. "That's good news. I wonder who it is?" LaDonna looked at Dan carefully. "You know, don't you?"

"Nope. But I can guess."

"Guess."

"Ella. Ella Parker."

LaDonna laughed and punched his arm. "Come on."

"Wanna bet?"

As he was carrying the glasses in, Dan looked at LaDonna. "It would be good for both of them. But there's the thing about one of her relatives."

LaDonna put her hand to her mouth. "Oh my gosh. That's right. She's Drake's aunt."

"Could be interesting."

4

_____

R ob and Janelle waited on the bench outside Bigun's BBQ in Ft. Worth. They were staring at their cell phones when Dan and LaDonna drove up in the gaudiest car Rob had ever seen, a canary yellow 1961 Cadillac Biarritz convertible.

"Oh, there they are." Janelle squealed as she leaped from the bench and ran toward the knife-finned monstrosity. Rob decided to wait on the bench. He felt a nervous quiver in his hands. It was the uncomfortable sensation from his time as a cleanup pitcher in high school. Janelle motioned for him to come to the convertible.

"Dad, this is Rob Buchanan."

Dan's handshake made him wince. He prided himself in staying in shape. He worked out a lot, lifted weights, did a little MMA, but he was surprised by Dan's grip.

"Howdy, Rob. I'm Dan. Pleased to meet you. We hear lots of good things about you."

Rob was glad to have his hand back in its original condition.

Janelle took Rob's arm. "And this is my mom, LaDonna."

Random warning flags hoisted in Rob's brain. *Where do you find a big-assed car like that? Bright yellow? How does a woman that small end up with a giant like him? I wonder if he could break bones if he squeezed hard enough?*

"Nice to meet you, Mrs. Baker."

"Please. It's LaDonna."

"It's time to disappoint Doc Chin." Dan opened the door and motioned them into Bigun's. "Let's cholorestize."

Rob watched as Dan stooped and turn almost sideways through the door of the smoky miniature barn. *Will it be just a bloody nose when we tell him what we're doing? He's over six-foot-six. Gotta weigh more than two-fifty..*

When they finished eating, Janelle shoved her plate aside and leaned forward. "We've got some shopping to do. I'm going to ride with them. What are you going to do? You probably don't want to shop."

Dan leaned into Rob. "If you're like me, you'd rather have teeth pulled than go shopping. They'll have to put up with a couple of stops for me at tractor dealerships and supply houses."

"You got it." Rob could feel Dan's rock-hard bicep against his shoulder. "I've got to give a basic biology lab test to a bunch of freshmen tomorrow, so I better go back to campus this afternoon." He shook hands with Dan and turned to Janelle as her parents walked toward the car. "What's up for later?"

"Don't worry about it. It'll work out. Don't rush me." She wagged her finger at him,.

"Rush you? Let me remind you this was your idea."

"I know." She pressed her index finger to his lips. "I'll break the news to Mom. She'll bring Dad along. It's good you won't be there. There will be some gnashing of teeth. We should be back at the apartment around five o'clock."

"I hope you'll give me a heads-up if he decides to break my arm or something worse." Rob waved to LaDonna, who was standing beside the Cadillac, waiting for Janelle.

———————

As he walked into the apartment four hours later, he heard car doors slamming. He parted the Venetian blinds and felt a chill.

LaDonna and Janelle were coming up the sidewalk. Dan was still sitting in the convertible on his cell phone.

"God. Even sitting down, he's gigantic. Rob, my friend, you might have screwed up. You have to look up to make eye contact with him, and you're beddin' his daughter down? Better get ready for a butt kickin'." He was surprised at the raspy quality of his own voice.

He opened the door as Janelle and LaDonna reached the stoop. It was hard to read Janelle's face. It wasn't a frown. But something short of a smile. LaDonna scanned the tiny room and kitchenette. "I really like your apartment. It's a good place for both of you. Better than dorms. I bet those haven't changed from when we were in school."

Rob breathed half a sigh of relief and looked at Janelle. "Uh, what about your dad?"

"He's all right. He was a little pissed when I broke the news to him in the open convertible doing sixty miles an hour on 820, but he's over that now. I got him talking about what kind of maintenance my car might need. I assured him we were taking care of it. That was the end of any problem today.

"He's on the phone with his friend Zeke who owns the flying service at home. You might want to go out there and have a chat."

LaDonna surprised Rob by putting her hand on his shoulder.

"Don't worry about this." She swept the tiny living room with one gesture, stopping at the narrow staircase. "In college, we had to stay in the dorms for appearance's sake. We spent a lot of time 'hooking up' – is that what you call it?—at our friends' apartments.

"It all blew up when one of my high school friends—ex-friend— spotted us coming out of an apartment about sunrise one morning. She told her mother, who told her best friend who told our hairdresser, who told the minister's wife who told my mother she'd heard I was pregnant.

"Long story short, we're not exactly overjoyed about what y'all are doing. We're not going to throw a clod in the churn." She smiled at his reaction.

Rob cocked his head and smiled. "I can honestly say I've been here in Fort Worth for almost four years and have never heard that term."

Janelle laughed. "You'll hear more folksy stuff like that if you hang around my dad very long. Now, go out there and see if he is going to break your hand." Janelle glanced at her mother, who was stifling a laugh.

LaDonna pushed her glasses up from the tip of her nose. "You don't have anything to worry about from Danny. He's one of the gentlest people I've ever known, noisy sometimes, but mostly gentle.

He's over the 'noisy' for today. He's very protective of Nelly, though." Rob walked down the sidewalk as Dan was getting out of the car.

"Well?" he asked. It sounded lame.

Dan walked up to him, patted his arm with noticeable firmness.

5

_____

Two weeks later, Rob and Janelle made the four-hour trip to Jerrod from Fort Worth. They stopped at _Big Jimmy's_ drive-in before driving to the Baker farm. Janelle pointed to the long metal building next to the drive-in with _D. Baker Tires_ across the side.

"Dad's business." The grubby drive-in had attracted the usual crowd of high schoolers in their dualie pickups, gunning their engines. Laughter. Shouts. High-pitched giggles. Moths circling the gaudy neons of the faded canopy over the parking spaces with the bleached-out menu display on the driver's side.

Rob rolled his shoulders forward and back, feeling the tiredness sinking in. "Big day tomorrow?"

"Yeah. I gotta . . ." Her cell phone interrupted "Lo? Hi, Mom.

We're at _Big Larry's_. No, that's okay. Should be about thirty minutes.

What? Oh no. What's goin' on?" She listened for a bit, then put her hand over the phone.

"Zeke Kilborn, one of dad's oldest friends, is in the hospital," she told Rob. "He's got big heart problems."

Rob nodded. "You want me to order?"

Janelle held up one finger. "Mom? Wait a minute."

Rob stared at the menu lit by a single flickering fluorescent tube. "What do you want?"

"Burger. Mayonnaise. No pickles. Tea."

He ordered the same when the adolescent voice squawked on the speaker below the menu.

"Drake— Zeke's son—is living here. He called mom asking if I was going to be in the Cotton Carnival parade."

"Yeah? And?"

"We dated in high school. He was a year ahead of me. Had a good time. Nothin' special. His mom died four years ago, so he moved back here from Abilene right as I started TCU. When I would come home for holidays or summer, he would get me to go out with him even though we were just friends.

"It was okay at the start. Then he got weirder. He would have these cryin' spells and would be angry and belligerent. Always talking about Bertie, his mom. It got to be spooky, so I finally had to tell him to leave me alone. I didn't say anything to my parents because they – dad for sure – would have been real upset."

Rob turned to face her. "You worried about him doing something at the parade?"

"Naw. I don't think so. My grandma and my mom were in that parade. I wanted to come home and keep it going. My mom and his were in it at the same time. That's all." She pulled a Kleenex out of the console and sniffed hard.

They ate in silence. Janelle handed the basket with the half-eaten hamburger and soggy fries back to Rob. He flashed his lights, and the pudgy carhop came ambling out, swatting at moths exploring her purple-streaked hair. She leaned in Rob's window.

"Hey, Nelly girl. I thought that was you. What you doin' in town?" Mazie Medders took Rob's tray and waddled over to the passenger's side as Janelle lowered her window.

"Came for the Cotton Festival. Gonna ride in the parade, I guess."

Mazie leaned in a little farther, smiling at Rob. Her large chest filled the bottom half of the open window. "Who's this you hangin' with?"

"This is Rob Buchanan, my friend from TCU."

"Welcome to Nowhere." Mazie giggled and started to the kitchen. She stopped and walked back to Janelle's side of the car.

"Drake was through here a few minutes ago. He was kinda looking around. Don't imagine he's trying to pick up a high-schooler." Mazie smirked and winked.

"It's good to see you, Mazie." Janelle stared into her compact mirror. She wanted the conversation to end. Mazie made little fluttering gestures with her pudgy fingers as she walked away.

"Her boyfriend, Archie, works for Dad part-time. That's his baby mamma. We all went to high school together."

They headed west out of town, back into the moonless night. Rob tried to count the blurring telephone poles as they slipped past the edge of the headlights. He happened to glance at Janelle as the Kilborn Flying Service sign flashed by. She had turned to look over her shoulder, then faced the front.

He poked her gently in the side. He was hoping to bring some spirit to the surface. "So, good lookin', what are the sleeping arrangements tonight. Huh? There someplace quiet for us?" He poked again.

She perked up. "We have to see about that. There's the Grandma

House."

"The what?"

"Dad built a little bungalow for his mom out by the pool. She was too sick to move in before she died. It's a kind of a guest house, living room- kitchen combo, full bath, queen bed. We call it the Grandma House.

"Slow down a little. Turn next to the sign. That's our place."

There was a large yellow sign with "Baker" and a pointing finger.

Dan Baker dropped the hood on the gleaming Cadillac as they pulled up. "Hey, Nelly." Dan opened the Camry's door, lifted his daughter off her feet, spun her around in a rotating bear hug. He put her down and extended his hand to Rob.

"How was the drive?"

Rob remembered Dan's handshake from their first encounter.

Again, he winced slightly and pulled away. "Good. How are you, sir?"

LaDonna came down from the porch at the rear of the house, followed by Sniff, who sat and offered his left paw.

"You'll have to forgive him. He's the resident greeter." LaDonna hugged Janelle and brushed an errant curl from her daughter's forehead.

Rob leaned over and shook the dog's paw. The dog sniffed at Rob's pants leg. He glanced at LaDonna, scratched behind his ear, went to his igloo-shaped doghouse.

Rob had forgotten she was more than a foot shorter than her husband. Petite to his massive. He was about to take his luggage out of his car when Dan reached past him.

"Hey, lemme do that." He pointed to the steps going up to the kitchen entrance. "I'll put this stuff in the Grandma House."

They sat around the oak dining table for half an hour, making small talk.

Dan laid his beer bottle on its side and twirled it. "I've got to go over to the other place to get ready for defoliation Sunday morning."

"Defoliation?" Rob asked.

"The cotton plants."

"Why do you do take the leaves off?"

"We want the leaves off right after the bolls open. We get a cleaner pull to the gin if we don't have leaves cloggin' up the harvester and holdin' moisture we'll be penalized for. Some farmers wait for the frost to take the leaves off, but it looks like the frost is comin' late this year, so we have to strip so we can gin the crop before Thanksgiving."

"How do you put the defoliant on?"

"Airplane. My buddy Zeke has been sprayin' it for me for several years. Some guys use ground applicators. I think we get better coverage from the air."

Dan looked at Janelle and softened his tone. "Zeke's back in the hospital. He was there a month ago, havin' trouble with his pacemaker. Now he's back in." Dan stared at his huge hands as he rubbed them together. "Til he got those stents in January, he'd hardly ever been sick. Dan poured himself a second cup of coffee. "What are you guys up to tomorrow?"

Rob rubbed his eyes. "I've got to do some practice MCAT exam modules on the Internet in the morning. They're on-line Saturdays and Fridays."

"I'm afraid we don't have very good Internet service out here," Dan said. "You'll probably have to go to the library."

LaDonna had been listening to the conversation. "Med school? That's a long row to hoe."

Rob looked at Janelle, questioning. "Oh, yeah, it is, I guess. I'll give it a try if I can get in." He noticed Janelle's exaggerated yawn. Another signal to wrap it up.

LaDonna leaned forward. "I've heard that's a pretty tough test."

Rob glanced at Janelle. Her eyes were almost closed, the *knock it off* signal. "I understand it's about the toughest postgraduate entrance test you can take." He stood, sliding his chair up to the table. "Guess it's bedtime. *We* need to turn in. Long day today."

Three-count silence; Dan glanced out the window, LaDonna stared into her coffee cup, Rob and Janelle looked straight ahead. LaDonna and Dan broke the silence and stood. "Okay, you guys, in the mornin', then." She kissed Janelle on the cheek and stood aside as Rob walked to the door.

———————

Rob and Janelle were sitting naked in the queen-size bed after showering together. "Kinda awkward there at the last."

Janelle rolled to face him. "Couldn't be helped. I'm still their little girl." She smiled and poked him in the ribs. "They had to watch one of them damned Yankees take her away."

"Not far away."

"Far enough."

"Gotcha. So, what exactly are you expected to do in the parade? beside ride on the back of that yellow whale?"

"Oh, it's very complicated." Janell sat up very straight, threw her shoulders back. "Now watch carefully." She raised her right arm shoulder height extended her forearm up, cupped her hand.

"Elbow, elbow, wrist, blow a kiss, repeat." She repeated the move several times. Having seen enough, Rob pulled her hand down.

"Please, no more. I may be ill."

"They expect it. I remember practicing it after seeing a queen in the parade when I was in grade school."

Rob rolled his eyes and fluffed his pillow. "Good. I'm so proud of you."

Janelle waited for Rob to say something more but heard only his familiar snore. She turned off the lamp on the side table and snuggled up to him. A coyote called in the distance, and Sniff gave a half-hearted answer. "It's all good. Really good," she whispered.

6

———————

Janelle and Rob joined LaDonna for breakfast at eight-thirty. Dan had left earlier. They talked about the parade, LaDonna reminded them of the party at one of their friend's house afterward. The small talk tapered off when Janelle got up from the table and began to clear the dishes.

Rob and Janelle went back to the Grandma House and coordinated their day. Janelle would drive the Cadillac to get her dress for the parade altered. Rob would spend his time in the library doing his MCAT review. They would meet for lunch at Thrasher's Barbecue.

———————

At noon, they ordered and sat facing on square stools at Thrasher's long communal picnic table. They had started to eat when Drake Kilborn walked in.

He paused at the door. After looking at Rob, he walked over to Janelle.

"What do you know? Look who's here." He sat beside Janelle and started to put his arm around her. She moved away and hunched, trying to make herself smaller.

"What are you doin' in town, sweet thang? It's good to see you." He leaned toward her as if to kiss her. She shrugged his arm off and moved to one side. Rob glanced toward Janelle, then at Drake, who was sizing up his six-foot-plus frame and broad shoulders.

"This is my boyfriend, Rob Buchanan. She pointed at Rob, who had moved his stool back and was standing. "Rob, this is Drake Kilborn." She looked from one to the other, motioned palms down, asking for calm.

Rob pushed the stool under the table.

Drake locked eyes with Rob for a moment, then leaned toward Janelle. "Hey, I saw the Caddy. You're in the parade."

Rob walked down the table, stopped at the end.

Janelle wiped her hands on a paper towel from the roll on the table, pushed her stool back, her tone flat. "Yes, Drake, that's why Rob and I are here. I wanted him to meet some of my friends, see where I grew up."

His tone icy, Drake turned and looked at Rob, now standing at the end of the table. "Howya doin'?"

Rob glanced to Janelle, then back to Drake. "Don't we need to be going?"

Drake turned to walk to the end of the table, eyes still fixed on Rob. "You not in any hurry, are you, sweetheart? We need to catch up on old times."

Rob moved to Janelle's side of the table, raised his right hand, moved his watch around on his wrist.

Drake looked at Rob and cocked his head to one side. "So, you plannin' her day for her, are ya?"

A blush rose around Rob's neck as he tensed his shoulder muscles. "We got things to do. We're going." He took his glasses off, put them in his shirt pocket. It was a habit from grade school when he had walked through the sneering, cat-calling gaggle of bullies following him from his bus stop to the front door of his North Philly high school.

Ernie Thrasher was trying not to be too obvious as he looked past a customer at the cash register. Sensing the rise in tension, two couples hurriedly finished their sandwiches, cleared their end of the table, and moved toward the front door, avoiding looking at the two men. As they shut the door, it opened again.

Freddy Paz stood in the doorway. "Drake? I been callin' you."

"What do you want, Freddy?" Drake's smile was thin. He looked at Rob and turned to Freddy.

Freddy took two steps forward, acknowledged Janelle with a nod, stepped close to Drake. "We need to talk."

Drake squinted and turned to stare at Rob again. "Busy."

"Right now." Freddy grabbed Drake's shoulder, pulled the door open, pointed outside.

Drake shrugged Freddy's hand away, held up his hand and motioned to Janelle. "How long you stayin'?"

Rob lowered his voice. "We're going back to TCU tomorrow."

Janelle stood, walked to Rob, put her hand on his arm. "Tomorrow. We're leaving tomorrow."

Drake winked and smiled, walked past Freddy, paused in the open door. "I'll see you at the parade." He motioned Freddy through the door ahead of him. It slammed, making the rusty John Deere thermometer and the two pictures of John Wayne bounce on the wall.

Rob and Janelle stood at the front window of Thrasher's, waiting for Drake to pull out of the parking lot in his bright red Mustang.

They walked to the Cadillac, Rob holding the door for Janelle. He was shifting from one foot to the other, clenching and unclenching his fist.

"Rob?"

He looked down at her. "Yeah?"

"Rob, *nothing*. We're going to do *nothing*. We'll be gone from him in less than 24 hours. Let's not leave a mess behind."

Rob looked up and down the street as if expecting the Mustang to reappear. He took his glasses out of his pocket and put them on. "Okay. I feel like a real punk letting him get away with that. What's your dad going to think about me?"

"He's not going to think anything. This is over. There's not going to be any more trouble. Rob, we're going to the farm right now. Right? We're going?"

Rob closed her door. "Yeah." He got in his car, followed her out of town.

———

Later, Rob, Janelle, Dan, and LaDonna sat around the table on the wrap-around porch after finishing hamburgers. "You guys are awful quiet."

"Hum?" Janelle looked at Rob, who was staring past her at the open prairie land bordering the house. "We're both pretty much bushed with mid-terms and all, and the drive here. Yeah. Pooped." He rubbed his forehead and looked at her. "Yeah. 'Pooped.'" Janelle exhaled. "Look, let's get this stuff cleared off, Mom.

We've got to get ready for the parade."

They stood, cleared the table, went to the kitchen.

"Beer?" Dan pointed to a small refrigerator at one corner of the balcony. "My stash. You like *Dos Equis*?" Dan popped the cap on the bottle and handed it to Rob. "I guess Janelle has told you 'bout Drake?"

"Yeah, a little. I met him when we were eating lunch."

"Bad news, that guy. I hope y'all don't have to mess with him while you're here. He turns up like a bad penny."

Rob put his bottle on the table and brushed the water droplets from the side. "It's already happened."

He explained the confrontation at Thrashers and Janelle's insistence on moving on. "I felt like a real pussy when he was standing there. Looked like he was waiting for a fight."

"Rob, the worst thing you coulda done was square off with him. You know that old sayin' that the most dangerous enemy you can have is the one with nothin' to lose? Drake Kilborn has less and less to lose. He's about at the end of his road. You were smart not to take it any further."

Rob stood. "I need to get a shower. This is between us, right?" He looked toward the kitchen. "Janelle didn't want you to know it happened."

Dan stood and collected the bottles. "Yeah. We'll have fun at the parade tonight, go to that party afterward, and it will all be okay. Don't worry."

Dan and Rob rode to Jerrod in the Cadillac, top-down. Janelle, dressed in her Cotton Queen gown, every hair in place, rode with LaDonna in the Suburban.

They stopped in the courthouse parking lot where Dan helped Janelle sit on the soft top storage boot, her feet tucked in the back seat. They stopped in the courthouse parking lot where Dan helped Janelle sit on the soft top storage boot, her feet tucked in the back seat.

A parade volunteer taped hand-lettered signs with Janelle's name and year as Cotton Queen on both front doors. Dan got behind the wheel and moved in line behind the high school band.

Rob and LaDonna watched as the parade went by. It circled the courthouse square, snaked through the parking lot, reversed course, retraced the route. Dan slowed as he passed them, and Janelle did an exaggerated version of the wave. Rob gave her a thumbs-up, Janelle threw kisses and made an exaggerated show of elbow, wrist, wrist.

They didn't see him, but Drake Kilborn began shadowing the parade as it completed its second loop.

Back in the courthouse parking lot, Dan helped Janelle from the Cadillac, and she walked toward Rob. Drake moved his Mustang between them and Dan's Suburban.

He got out, stumbled while he pulled on his black Stetson, moved toward Janelle. "Ain't we purdy?" He pushed his hat back. "You and me got a party to go to." He extended his hand as if expecting her to take it. Rob grabbed his shoulder and spun him.

Drake leaned forward and swung. Rob ducked, stepped to the side, punched Drake in the ribs. Drake stumbled, grabbed his chest, went to one knee. He was struggling to get up when Rob drew his fist back without saying anything.

Drake raised his hand. "You got me this time. We ain't through yet." He stood, bracing himself on his car's right fender. "Momma is with me in the car. She told me not to do this. Okay. This time . . ."

Dan grabbed Drake's coat collar, pulled him to his feet. Drake attempted to turn, but Dan held him by one arm, pulled him close, and whispered in his ear. "Drake, that skinny little kid standing next to Janelle there? He won't be as easy to push around as your dad. His knees won't be banged up, neither."

Drake gave Dan a blank look and tried to wriggle free. Dan

tightened his grip and pushed him to the driver's side of the Mustang. Drake's voice was strained because of the way Dan had twisted his collar. "Momma, he's pushin' me around."

Dan opened the Mustang's door and shoved Drake in. "Bertie's not here, Drake, but I'm sendin' you on your own way because she wouldn't want you hurt."

Drake looked to the right. "Mommy . . ."

Dan leaned in the window. "Damnit, Drake. Get your shit together. Your momma's nowhere around. Now stop it. Drive out of here. Now." He leaned up, pointing to the street.

Drake looked up at him, reached for his mirrored aviator glasses, put them on, started the car. "We're not through." He burned rubber out of the parking lot, leaving black marks and scattering pea gravel over Rob and Janelle.

7

_____

After Rob and Janelle left for Ft. Worth, Dan drove to the farm. As he was passing the cotton gin south of town, his cell phone rang. *E. Parker* on the display.

"What's happening, Ella?"

"Good news. Doc Chin released Zeke a few minutes ago. I'm gonna drive him home."

"So, is this good news?"

"Sort of. The fact is the Doc doesn't know what else to do. His pacemaker is doing okay. All his vitals are all right. He's in a real blue mood."

"I hope he's gonna be okay. I'll try to get by there later to see him. They're gonna defoliate my cotton this mornin'." He turned down the dirt road to his cotton field. "Thanks for callin'. Let me know if you need anything."

He stopped at the edge of the field, got out, waded about fifty yards through the cotton crop. He was always amazed at the hybrid plants, uniformly waist-high, the white clumps of half-open bolls stretching to the horizon.

He pulled leaves from a half-dozen plants and saw they were ready to drop. He'd talked to Ronny Joyce, one of Zeke's pilots, and arranged for this field to be defoliated beginning about one o'clock. He checked his watch. Twelve fifteen.

Archie was supposed to be at the field setting flags for the pilot to use in his defoliating passes. Dan scanned the horizon in all directions looking for Archie's pickup.

His cell phone buzzed. Ronny.

"Dan? You heard from Archie?"

"Nope, did you talk to him Friday?"

"Yep, he said he would be out there right now. He was supposed to call me when he found you. Guess you haven't seen him. Freddy Paz's car should be on the south side. He said he'd be there about now."

Dan took binoculars from under his seat. "I can see him from here. Looks like he's got his radio out."

"Last I heard of Archie was yesterday. He was at the tire shop." Dan stepped out into the dirt road and shielded his eyes. Looking both ways, he spotted a pickup about a mile away. It was hard to tell with the late morning heat rising from the road, but it didn't look like it was parked—more like driven partway off the shoulder before stopping.

Dan climbed in his Suburban, holding his phone. "I think I may see his truck. I'm gonna check it out. I'll call you as soon as I know anything. Why don't you try callin' him again?"

It took less than a minute driving the dusty road to confirm what he thought he'd seen. Archie's ancient brown Ford 150 with the banged- up passenger door and faded yellow fender was sitting at an odd angle in the bar ditch. Archie was behind the wheel, head back on the rear window, mouth wide open. Dan honked, banged on the hood, but Archie didn't move. He felt a cold chill. He walked to the open driver's side window.

There was a thin rivulet of blood-stained saliva trailing down his chin from the left side of his mouth. His breathing had a liquid sound. His lips were blue.

"Shit, son, what have you gotten yourself into?" He reached for Archie's left wrist and felt for a pulse. It was a weak .He called Ronny.

"Hey. I found Archie. He drove his pickup in the bar ditch on the southeast corner of the field."

"Is he okay?"

"I don't think so. He's passed out, and there's a little blood comin' out of his mouth. I'm gonna call 9-1-1 right now."

The white and red Jerrod EMS ambulance found them fifteen minutes later. Archie's breathing had quieted, but he was still on the edge of consciousness. The two EMTs extracted Archie's limp form from the pickup, got him on the stretcher and into the ambulance's rear door.

Dan had trouble bending to get inside, where Archie was being strapped in. He leaned down and put his hand on Archie's chest, listening to the ragged breathing. He put his mouth next to Archie's ear.

"Archie, hang in there, buddy. You're in good hands," he half-whispered. Dan was surprised when he felt Archie's fingers grab one of the suspenders of his overalls.

"Mazie. Tell Mazie." His whisper was faint, almost inaudible.

"Sure. The ambulance guys probably have that covered, but I'll make sure." Dan looked at one of the paramedics, who shook his head.

Archie swallowed hard and then sneezed a reddish liquid, spraying the ambulance's overhead light and oxygen console. He motioned for

Dan to move closer. One of the medics reached in front of Dan to put an oxygen mask on Archie. Dan pushed the attendant's hand away, held up a finger, signaling one more thing. He leaned close to Archie's quivering mouth.

". . . rake," Archie bubbled. Seeing Dan's confusion, he sputtered again and mumbled, "that goddamned," swallowed hard and coughed again, " . . . rake," and closed his eyes.

"We gotta go *now*," the tech shouted, taking Dan's arm. He gently nudged him so he could put the oxygen mask over Archie's face. Dan moved back and out the door, slamming it as the ambulance sped away in a fog of dust, emergency horns bleating.

Dan watched it go and wondered aloud, "Rake? What about a rake?" He walked around Archie's ancient pickup. None of the tires flat. No apparent damage. He glanced in the bed and saw the large plastic container on its side. A slimy grey liquid had leaked from the tote and pooled at the gate of the pickup's bed.

He closed his eyes for a moment, took a deep breath. "Drake, you sonofabitch. You're havin' Archie doin' your cleanup. Wonder what else the poor kid was exposed to."

He moved the collapsed tote around, trying to get it away from the liquid when Freddy Paz drove up in the Kilborn Aviation truck.

Freddy joined Dan at the back of Archie's pickup. "Hey, what happened? What's going on with the ambulance? I guess they took Archie? We not spraying today?"

"I called Ronny and waved him off. I don't know when we'll do it. It's gotta be before the end of next week. I called the ambulance. Archie was in a bad way when I pulled up," Dan replied.

Paz was pulling a glove on his right hand. "What was Archie doing?"

"He was barely conscious, bleedin' at the mouth."

"Hmm. He say anything?"

Dan leaned on the pickup. *Why ask that? Why did he need to know?* He decided to hold back a little. "Didn't say much. Mostly coughin'."

Paz looked at Dan, then turned and poked at the tote. "Wonder why Archie was carrying that around with him."

Dan thought it was strange the way Freddy tapped on the container. *Only one finger? With a glove?* He was staring when Freddy stepped down and pulled his glove off, tossed it into the cab of the Kilborn truck. Freddy met his gaze, smiled, rubbed his hands together, ran his fingers through his thick, black hair.

He looked up and down the dirt road. "I better get to the hospital. Archie and I have gotten to be pretty good friends. I need to see if I can do anything for him." He got in the truck and was about to shut the door.

"Is there a way you could move Archie's pickup to your place? You know, for a few days? As soon as this is straightened out, I'll come get it, or maybe Ronny could. Would that be a lot of trouble?"

Dan stared at Freddy for a moment. "Okay. I'll move it. When can you get it?"

Freddy climbed up into the Kilborn truck cab, shut the door, started the engine. "Day after tomorrow, I'd guess. Meanwhile, if you hear anything, Mister Baker, would you let me know about an investigation? I'm curious." He put the truck in gear, waved at Dan, and headed for Jerrod.

8

D an was in the cramped waiting room of Jerrod Community Hospital for a half-hour, alternating between sitting and and standing to relieve the pressure on his knee from being in the plastic chairs. He also changed position to avoid accusing glances from Mazie, who was holding H.D. Her mother, Alice Faye—Mazie plus a hundred pounds—glared at everybody in the tiny space.

When Mazie spotted anyone in the hallway who looked like a hospital worker, Alice Faye huffed and puffed herself up, cornering them. She demanded to know what was happening to her son-in-law.

The inquisition varied, the questioning amounting to "Kin you tell me 'bout Archie? That there is his wife"--pointing to Mazie—"and little 'un. We need 'ta know somethin', Goddamnit."

No one, not the food service worker pushing the tray cart, not the janitor with the mop bucket satisfied Alice Faye. She cut off their attempts to calm her by jabbing her pudgy finger in their face and shouting "Lahr. Lahr." at the top of her lungs. Having heard enough, Mazie put H.D. in the lap of the person sitting next to her, waddled into the hall, snagged her sweating, cursing mother by the pendulous slab of fat under her arm, guided her back into the waiting room.

After several confrontations, workers were scarce, except for a nurse or lab tech who, warned about the ambush, ran past the waiting room.

Alice Faye renewed her protest at full volume, revisiting her dislike for being treated like a twelve-year-old. Then sat with a loud grunt, grab her wide-eyed grandson, whose high-pitched wail Dan felt sure could be heard three blocks away.

In between these diatribes, Mazie and Alice Faye turned to him, insist he disclose new information about Archie. Though he had not left the waiting room for the last thirty minutes. It did no good to deny any special knowledge. He, too, was a lahr, lahr.

He had gone to the bathroom twice, once to escape Alice Faye's protestations and once because he couldn't think of any other way to pass the time. The ambulance volunteers had left and couldn't be of any help. So, it was his lot to wait too.

The monotonous, noisy tension was broken by the rumble of his cell phone. He pulled it from his pocket, walked out of the room, observed by Alice Faye and Mazie.

"What's up, Ella?" he half-whispered as he walked down the hallway, turned at the reception desk, went out through the doubleglass doors. "What's goin' on with Archie?"

"It looks like he's all right . . . for now."

"Good. When will you break the news to his wife and her mother? They're causin' a lot of problems in there."

"Believe me, we heard. Doctor Chin's trying to decide what to tell them right now. I expect we'll call them into the small consultation room in a few minutes."

"You said Archie looks okay for now?"

"That's a way of saying the Doc doesn't know what's going on. He wants to send Archie to Hendrick in Abilene. Archie's on oxygen. Doc thinks it's respiratory."

"Have you called the ambulance back?

"Doc Chin wants to talk to Mazie first."

"Good luck with that, 'specially if her mother is anywhere around."

"I know. Look, I gotta go. Where are you gonna be?" "I'm in town for a while."

"You might get a call from the Sheriff."

"Sheriff? Why?"

"Overheard the Doc talking to him. I've said too much. Talk later."

Dan stared for a moment at his cell phone. *What's the sheriff got to do with this? No point in messing with this until I have to. Guess I'll just wait to hear from him.* He checked his watch: two o'clock. He wasn't all that hungry, so Thrasher's BBQ would do. His phone rumbled again.

"Hey, hon', how's it going?"

Dan brought LaDonna up to date about Mazie and her mother, the cryptic comment from Ella about Sheriff Mose Britten questioning him.

"The only thing I can think of is what Archie said to me when I was with him in the ambulance. He said somethin' about 'that damned rake."

"Yeah, I remember. Danny?"

"I'm here. Wait a minute. Was Archie tryin' to tell me somethin' a minute. Was Archie tryin' to tell me somethin' about Drake?"

LaDonna's voice was hard to make out because of road noise. "Oh, Danny, that doesn't sound good."

"Hey, let's not put somethin' where there's probably nothin'. I'll talk to Mose when I see him. What are you doin'?"

"Headed home."

Dan pocketed his phone, got in his Suburban, pulled out of the parking lot into the street when he saw the Kilborn Aviation truck turn behind the hospital building. *What's he doing back there?* Dan turned right from the lot and drove to the staff parking lot. Freddy was going in the side door.

Maybe he wants to know about Archie's pickup. Dan decided to pull in behind the truck. He got out of the Suburban, walked by the Kilborn truck, and up the wheelchair ramp to the entrance when he glanced in the driver's window. He knew he'd seen Paz throw the glove through the driver's side window. It should have landed on the passenger side floorboard, but it was in the seat, zipped up in a large sealable plastic bag. Most of it was covered by a copy of *Aviation Maintenance Magazine,* but it was clear to Dan, even at a glance, a small detail that he knew would hang in his thoughts.

He realized Sheriff Mose Britten was standing at his elbow. "What are you looking at Mr. Baker?" He moved up next to him, so they both were looking in the truck cab.

Britten, a retired Texas Ranger, brought all the trappings to his county job—khaki pants, starched, white long sleeve shirt, grey Resistol cowboy hat, low-heeled black Ropers, matching pistol belt.

There was .320 Sig-Sauer in the holster, radio with the mic clipped to the left shirt epaulet.

He had a reputation for a no-bullshit approach and strict professional demeanor in his second four-year term, including no first names.

"Look, I need to ask some questions about what you saw when you found Archie Medders passed out in his pickup next to your field this morning."

Dan knew the slight squeeze of his arm was more than a friendly gesture. He was being led away from the truck. He pulled away as they sat on the bench where the few hospital staff who still smoked came for their breaks.

Britten pulled a spiral notepad out of his hip pocket, clicked his pen, wrote as Dan described the scene. He talked about finding Archie semi-conscious, calling the ambulance, Archie's mumbling.

"Rake? He said something about a rake?" Britten wrote 'rake' and circled it. "What do you think that means?"

Dan stretched his left leg out as far as he could. The hurt was back. "Huh? Oh yeah. Damned if I know. 'That damned rake.' That was all I got out of it. How'd you hear about that?"

"Ambulance guys said he kept saying it over and over on the way here. They thought it was kinda weird, so they had the staff call me." Britten closed his pad. He held his ballpoint up close to his left eye, tip up, squinted as if he was looking through a gunsight, smiled, pocketed it. He stood and brushed himself off, extending his hand to Dan.

He pulled Dan up from the bench. "What's happening with your knee?" Any other time, Dan would consider the assist something a friend would do, but it was different now. Dan felt like the man was gauging his physical limitations. He moved away from the grip as quickly as he could.

"Little present the Army gave me." Dan sensed Britten trying to lighten the mood. It seemed phony, out of place. *Is he really trying to be my friend? You don't have to 'try' to do that.*

"If you can think of anything else, will you give me a call?" Britten fished around in a small case from his right shirt pocket and produced a crisp business card.

Business cards were rare in Jerrod. Dan took note of how heavy the paper stock was. "Sure. You might think about asking Archie's common law and her mother. They're in the waiting room right now.

Maybe Freddy Paz too, the airport mechanic."

"We're gonna be talking to quite a few about this," Britten rubbed his jaw. There was that smirk of a smile again. "Thanks for your time." He turned toward the emergency room side entrance.

Freddy Paz came out and headed for the Kilborn truck. Dan was tempted to ask him what he'd heard, but Britten deliberately stepped in front of Freddy, his back to Dan.

"Freddy, can I take you out to my place, so you can get Archie's pickup?" Dan raised his voice as if trying to penetrate Mose Britten's broad back.

Britten turned his head to the left and spoke over his shoulder. "Got a few questions for Mr. Paz. Can he call you?" Britten had his pad out again.

"Sure. Freddy, give me a call." Dan imagined the short Mexican having to look up into the sheriff's sunglasses. *Must be tough to worry if you'll be jailed, even deported if you dare to talk to a lawman. And, Sheriff, I'm gonna put you in my 'phony file' for the time bein'.*

As Dan backed out, he noticed Britten putting the pad away and looking from side to side as he talked to Freddy. *Hmm*

He decided to check in with Zeke and pulled up at the curb at his two-story brick house. Zeke's pickup was in the driveway, Drake's red.

He decided to check in with Zeke and pulled up at the curb at his two-story brick house. Zeke's pickup was in the driveway, Drake's red Mustang was parked at the front curb. He decided to call on his cell before going to the door.

Three, then four rings and a "leave a message" recording. Dan had decided to come back later and was about to go when his phone chirped.

"Hey, Dan. Couldn't get to the phone fast enough." Zeke sounded more up-beat, but his voice a little husky.

"What's going on, young man? How you doin'?"

"A lot better. Got a clean bill of health from the doc this mornin'. He said I should come home and rest. All that pokin' and proddin', and it turns out I got a low blood count. Whatever that means. Is that you down there?" Dan saw the curtains being pushed aside in the upstairs bedroom.

"Yep, it's me checkin' in."

"Look, why don't you come up for a minute? Drake is here."

Dan's throat went dry. *What to say?* Zeke sounded happy. Perhaps Drake had said nothing about the confrontations.

"Dan?"

"Oh, look, I better get goin'. I need to go grab a bite and then check in on Archie again at the hospital."

"Hospital? What's goin' on with Archie?"

The phone line became muffled. Dan could hear Zeke talking to someone in the room. It had to be Drake.

"Drake says he doesn't know anything about Archie bein' in the hospital. He said last he knew, Archie was suppose'ta to spot for Ronny when he did your spray this morning."

"The spray didn't happen. It might be a good idea to look in on Archie."

"What do you mean, didn't happen. Did we mess up? Here—Why don't you talk to Drake, Dan?"

Mouth dry again. Dan swallowed. "No, I need to get goin'. I'll check in with *you* later." He closed his phone, hoping his old friend wasn't put off by his abruptness.

Dan was about to pull away when Drake opened the front door, jumped off the porch, got in Zeke's pickup. Dan stared at Drake. *If you're going to the hospital, why are you taking that truck?*

Drake met Dan's stare, looked away, put his aviator glasses on, glanced over his shoulder, backing out of the driveway.

Asshole. I wonder what you see in the mirror. Dan opened his phone, looked through the log, and found Ella's number. Three rings and to voice mail. "Hey, Ella, heads up. I stopped to see Zeke. Drake was there. He left in a big hurry after he heard me and Zeke talkin' 'bout Archie. He's probably on his way to the hospital."

Dan had lost his appetite for anything from Thrasher's, so decided to head home. A block from the highway intersection, he glanced toward Stangle's Safe Storage. At the end of the row of overhead doors was Zeke's pickup. Dan let his car coast. He could see Drake and Freddy Paz transferring a large plastic container in a metal frame to a storage unit. *Big hurry to mess with that kinda stuff on*

Friday, right Drake? Lots'a worries about Archie in the hospital.

"Not much I can do about that." He realized he was muttering and grinding his teeth as he turned at the next block and headed for the highway. LaDonna always made him sit down on the porch swing and brought him a beer when he muttered.

She was sitting on the porch when he drove up. He shouted out his window, "Hey. Come on. You gotta take me over to the south place so I can get Archie's pickup and bring it back here." She walked around to the passenger's side and got in.

"Why do you have to do that?"

"I don't know what to think. Seems like some of Archie's people would come and get it, but Freddy Paz specifically asked me to do it.

He said it would be a few days, then he'd come get it. Something doesn't fit here."

"Why's that Freddy guy involved in this?"

"He's a friend of Archie's. That's all I can figure."

During the twenty-minute drive, Dan went over the events of the last twelve hours, trying to sort out who fit where. He was getting the uneasy feeling of being worked into a corner but didn't say so.

It took Dan ten minutes to start Archie's pickup. He had to clean off the corroded battery posts and run jumper cables from the Suburban. Dan could tell from the gradual slowing turnover of the engine the battery was almost gone. As he was about to give up, it jerked and snorted to life.

Pulling into the driveway, he could feel the container shifting around in the bed. He left the pickup running, opened the doors of his seed shed, cleared away pieces of scrap metal and wood from the floor, and searched through a workbench until he found a roll of heavy-duty trash bags. He tore one away and walked back outside.

"What are you going to do with that?" LaDonna had parked and was halfway up the kitchen steps after stopping to shake hands with Sniff.

"I'm gonna put this over that container. I don't want that stuff leakin' when I get inside."

"Stuff?"

"Defoliant."

Why would Archie have it in his pickup?"

"Good question. We've got a lot of those kind of questions floatin' around today."

9

A rchie's dead." Dan's voice was flat, almost matter of fact. A sound from LaDonna's phone sounded like it was being kicked around in a pile of rocks. "Wait. I dropped my phone. Now, say that again. Archie's what? What happened?"

"Dead. Heard from Zeke. He said Ella called. Doctor Chin decided Archie needed to go to Abilene for some toxicology tests."

"Toxicology? Why? Isn't that about poisoning? I thought he was havin' trouble with his breathing."

"Zeke said she didn't go into detail. All she knew was he died in the ambulance. The EMTs couldn't revive him, and the deputy who was escortin' them couldn't do any good either. They were takin' him to Hedrick Med Center."

"What happens now?"

"Zeke wasn't sure. I guess we'll hear more over the next day or two. He didn't know if there would be an autopsy."

"Autopsy? How could that be an issue?"

"Ella told Zeke the sheriff had been asking a lot of questions." Dan felt a buzz in his cell phone and held it back from his ear. "Hmm. Speakin' of the sheriff, that's him tryin' to ring in. I'll talk to you later."

"Dan Baker."

"Hello, Mr. Baker, this is Mose Britten."

"Mornin', Sheriff."

"Remember when you were tellin' me about Archie Medders' pickup and the container in the back?"

"Sure. I put it in my feed barn. I figure Archie will be needin' it after he gets out of the hospital." *Let the sheriff be the one who tells him about Archie, not the other way 'round.*

"Mr. Baker, Archie died on the way to the hospital in Abilene this morning."

'Course, you already knew about that, didn't you?"

"Uh."

"Let's put it this way. I have been in my business long enough to know how a lie sounds, even if it's a little white one. Okay?"

Dan fidgeted, almost sure the sheriff could see the guilty look on his face through his phone. "Sorry."

"No need. Small town folks protect confidences. I've got no problem with that. So, about the pickup. When can I take a look at it?"

"When do you want to? I'm on my way to town now. I'd prefer not to have to turn around and go back out to the farm after bein' this close. Could it wait until right after noon?"

"I'm out of town myself right now. I should be back there by, let's say, two. Would that work?"

"Two, I guess. You know where my place is?" *Silly thing to ask. Of course, he does.*

"By the way, is that container you told me about still in the pickup?"

Dan cleared his throat. "Yeah. I stood it up and put a heavy-duty garbage bag over it before I put it in my barn."

"That's good. Now, before I let you go, I've got a favor." He made *favor* sound like *order*. He didn't wait for Dan's response. "Without going into any detail, I'd like to rely on you to not repeat this conversation we've been having and not tell anyone about the pickup."

"Of course, Sheriff. Of course."

"Good. We're all settled in here. Thanks for your help, and have a pleasant morning."

Does he realize how unpleasant this has made my morning? No. Dan started his Suburban and pulled back on the road. As he passed the airport railroad crossing, the Kilborn Aviation truck sped by, turned off the highway, disappeared behind the big hangar.

He decided to skip breakfast and drove to the tire shop. On his way in the door, JerriSue glanced up from her *Soap Opera Digest.* She pushed her rhinestone cat's-eyeglasses down her nose. She rarely acknowledged him when he walked in.

"Guess you heard." She pulled out a fresh Lucky Strike and lit it from one still smoldering in an overflowing saucer beside her monitor.

"Heard what?" He didn't want verbal sparring or knowing looks this particular morning.

"Yep, you heard."

He stood in the front window, staring out to the street.

"What do you want?" JerriSue's voice interrupted his thoughts.

He didn't bother turning around. He knew she wasn't looking at him, anyway.

"What do you mean, what do I want?'"

"You got the fidgets. You wanna know what's goin' on with

Archie's death, call Ella Parker. She knows everything that goes on in that hospital."

Dan turned to face her. She was still looking at the magazine but was pointing a bony index finger down at the cradle phone on her desk. She lowered her finger and tapped the handset three times with a black lacquered nail without looking up. He went to his office and pulled out his cell phone. "Ella, can you talk?"

"Wait a minute." There was a rustling sound, then silence, then street noise. "I had to come outside. I was in the ER waiting area."

"Heard about Archie. Don't wanna go all morbid on you, but what do you hear about what's goin' on with Archie's body?" It felt odd to Dan, talking about a person he'd last seen in the back of an ambulance, struggling to survive.

"Overheard a conversation between the doc and somebody at Hedrick. Best I could make out, there's going to be an autopsy sometime this afternoon."

"You mean Mazie gave permission?"

"I don't think she had any say in it. Best as I understand, the trauma chief at Hedrick thought Archie's death was 'due to suspicious circumstances.' I think that's all it took.

"Speaking of Mazie, she and her mother are sitting in the emergency waiting area right now, waiting on Doc Chin. I don't know what they need from him. I kinda got the impression they don't know what to do next. I'm going to suggest he have them call a preacher.

"I feel sorry for them. They have that baby to deal with, momma is very needy, and Mazie, well, she's really not up to this. She doesn't know it. And, they don't have a dime to their names."

"Hang on." Dan could hear Ella telling someone something about the waiting room. "That was Freddy Paz. He was a friend of Archie's, I think. He was asking about Mazie. Maybe he can help her and her mom. I better go."

"Ella?"

"Yeah?"

"I suspect Mazie and her mother are going to need grief counseling. You might call Reverend Costley – you know, Wyman Costley – and suggest he come to the hospital."

Long pause. "Okay, I'll do that, Dan." She said his name slowly, almost reproachfully. Then she chuckled. "Goodbye, nosy. Tell LaDonna hello."

"Hear there's a good place for steaks in Breckenridge."

"Who told you?"

"You did, right now." He chuckled. "Talk to ya later."

Fifteen minutes later, he pulled into his driveway and walked to the seed barn. He was about to open the door when Mose Britten drove up. As the sheriff stepped out of the SUV, Freddy Paz got out of the passenger side. Freddy's "so good to see you" smile was missing today.

Britten walked up to Dan, his hand out, but he could see Dan was focused behind him. Dan gripped the sheriff's hand and continued to look at Paz, who made a show of looking down at his watch. "What was all that about keepin' this between us?"

The sheriff smiled broadly for the first time Dan could remember. "I ran into Mr. Paz at the hospital. He reminded me he was a friend of Mr. Medders, so I thought I'd bring him out here to drive Archie's pickup back to town.

"I'm going to ask Mr. Paz to wait out here while you and I take a look at the pickup. Then, if it's all right with you, he'll drive it to Mr. Medders' trailer."

Dan slid the doors open. He and Britten stepped inside. As they were walking to the back of the pickup, the sheriff held up his left hand, a clear signal Dan should wait right where he stood. Britten opened the driver's side door, got in, sat, tapped the horn, turned the engine over.

It sputtered and coughed a few times and came to life, filling the small barn with blue smoke, causing Dan to step backward to the outside. Britten put the pickup in gear and drove it onto the parking area.

He left it running, got out, and motioned Freddy over. "Mr. Paz, I think you know where Mr. Medders' trailer is. I'd like you to drive this there. I'll catch up with you. I appreciate your desire to help the grieving widow out." He then stepped in front of Paz, as he had done at the hospital. It was clear to Dan it was meant to block his view. The sheriff pointed at the pickup and then pointed to the left and right.

Freddy nodded and walked away.

The sheriff turned and stuck out his hand again. "I want to thank you, Mr. Baker, for your cooperation with the sheriff's office and your long service as an auxiliary deputy. I hope you'll continue to keep our visits confidential, and that includes him being here to help us."

Dan was making a mental list. "Mister" Baker—check. "Sheriff's office, not "me" or "my office"—check. "Long service as an auxiliary deputy"—check. "Mr. Paz being here to *help* us"— check. *Wonder if the high sheriff of Holden County knows how silly he sounds. So, ole Freddy Paz requires confidentiality, too, does he?*

"I've got a question, sheriff. Is there gonna be an autopsy of

Archie's body? I understand the Abilene hospital people think his death is due to suspicious circumstances."

"Where'd you hear that, Mr. Baker?" It was clear to Dan that Britten's eyes narrowed.

"Oh, you know, confidence is a confidence."

"You know you can be summoned for a coroner's inquest?"

For a moment, they stared at each other. Neither moved. Dan cocked his head and smiled. "So, summon me." He was surprised at the way the words came out of his mouth. He was, after all, addressing the chief law enforcement officer of Holden County. But he was getting tired of playing games. He crossed his arms and widened his stance.

"Let's put it this way, for the time being, Mr. Baker. A confidence is a confidence."

The sheriff got back in his SUV, Paz got in Archie's sputtering pickup, and they left, headed for Jerrod.

———

It didn't take Freddy long to spot Archie's trailer at Windy Acres Trailer Park. Half a dozen pickups were like the one he was driving— several decrepit motorcycles, a four-wheeler. The rickety porch was crowded with hairy men ranging from bulbous to skeletal, all with a beer in hand. A gaunt, hollow-eyed, bearded specimen dressed in cutoffs and wife-beater walked up to the pickup.

"Who you?"

"I'm Freddy, Freddy Paz. I'm ah, er, was, a friend of Archie's."

The inquisitor leaned in the driver's window. The man's breath was deadly, and the gaseous collection of pizza, beer, and marijuana punctuated his speech. "This Archie's pickup?"

The man's breath made Freddy want to vomit, but he kept a neutral expression. "Yeah, wanted to make sure his *wife* got it. It was out on the farm where he was supposed to be spottin' for the sprayer."

"Goddamned crop-duster. That's probably what kilt 'im." The man stepped back, belched, and scratched his crotch.

Freddy got out and shut the door, doing his best to make himself seem smaller. He tugged at the bill of his Kilborn Aviation cap and pasted on a smile. He turned, fighting the urge to run down the line of trailers—instead, two steps.

The man stepped in front of him and put his hand on Freddy's chest. Freddy tensed and stood straighter. The man seemed to sense the change in Freddy's stance and dropped his hand.

"Whut's my sister supposed to do?" He pointed at the trailer, where Mazie had wobbled out onto the porch, drunk. She was leaning on the fattest of the mourners. "She has a right to see her man's body. Whut about their little boy?"

Freddy narrowed his eyes. He threw his shoulders back, making him seem taller. "Look, the sheriff will probably be here before long. He can fill you in." He had dropped his deferential Mexican field-hand accent. "I don't know anything about what's going on. He probably does." One step forward. "You understand me?"

The man almost stumbling as he backed away, both calloused palms at shoulder level. "Yeah, okay. That don't help us a lot."

"It's all I can do." Freddy glanced at the group on the porch. Mazie had collapsed into the arms of the large, shirtless fat man. There was a shriek coming from inside the trailer, then an infant's wail.

While the clan was focused on the sounds, Freddy began to walk – not run – hoping to put some space between him and the beer-soaked mourners. He turned right on the lane between the two rows of trailers.

"Hey Freddy, ¿*Que Pasa*?"

Startled, Freddy looked right and left, trying to locate the voice. Tomas Ascencio stepped off the wooden porch of one of the trailers around the corner from Archie's place. Freddy had become friends with Tomas, a supervisor at the cement plant across from the trailer park. Freddy had met his family at the Holy Saints Catholic Church when he'd moved from Abilene with Drake.

"Hey Tomas. *¿Que pasa mi amigo?*

"*Pues nada.*"

Freddy stepped forward to shake the tall, muscular Mexican's hand. "I dropped Archie Medders' pickup off at his place. You know Archie?"

Tomas smiled. "Archie is one good *hombre* – do anything for you."

"Yeah, I worked with him for a while. I know what you mean." He looked around, lowered his voice, moved closer to Tomas. "You know Archie died, don't you?"

"What?" The big man slapped the top of his curly head and pulled his hand down to his mouth, his eyes wide. "You kiddin'? So that's the reason for all that noise and those people at his place? What happened?"

"I don't know. Happened yesterday."

"Yeah, Archie talked to me a lot about that guy. Said he was always givin' Archie all kinds of shit work. He wanted to quit but had that crazy-assed little fat bitch and her mother to take care of. Would'a quit them 'cept for the baby. He loved that little kid. "Ah. Listen to me, talking about Archie like he don't exist no more."

"Cause he doesn't." Freddy took a good look into Tomas's eyes. He was going to risk it.

"Tomas, I need a favor. I don't like that damn Drake any more than Archie did. As a matter of fact, I've worked for the *cabron* since Abilene, and I can honestly say I've never met anybody who said they're his friend."

"Favor? What kind?"

"Look, he sold that pickup to Archie, more like one of them rentto-buy deals. I never thought that was fair because he could take it back any time he wanted."

"Hell. That's an asshole thing to do."

"For sure. All I'm asking is that you keep an eye on the pickup. If you see Drake snooping around it, trying to drive it off or take stuff out of it, would you give me a call?"

"Sure, absolutely."

"*Bueno.* Here's my cell number." He handed Tomas a Kilborn Aviation business card with his number hand-written on the back.

"Sure thing. Hey, where you headed? You need a ride?"

"Naw, man. Thanks." He glanced at his watch. "I'm suppos'ta meet someone on the road by the entrance in about five minutes. Hey, thanks for everything."

The two clasped hands and touched shoulder to shoulder. Freddy looked in Tomas's eyes and in a near-whisper, *"Nuestra palabra es nuestra hermandad."*

"Our word is our brotherhood. *Para la eternidad.*" He looked at Paz's card, put it in his pants pocket, went back to his trailer.

Freddy slowly jogged toward the trailer-park entrance. He had parked his car there three hours before riding with the sheriff to the Baker farm.

He started the car, pulled his phone from beneath the dash, pressed *power* and *messages.*

At the Medders' trailer, the mutt Woof was waked by the rising pitch of the voices and stomping feet overhead. He came from under the porch, dragging the rope no longer tied to the railing. He stretched, spotted Archie's pickup, started loping toward it, wagging his tail with happiness. He stopped at the front fender, walked around to the driver's side, stood up on his hind legs, put his paws on the door, sniffed at the open window. There was death there. He let his forepaws slide down the door, laid his ears back, tucked his tail, and ran-walked a short distance toward the plowed field bordering the trailer park, crawled under the bottom strand of barbed wire. He ambled ten yards, nose to the ruts. He turned to look at the pickup in the distance, sat for a moment, cocking his head from side to side. Then he stood, stretched, walked a few feet, looked back, wagged his tail twice, sniffed at the air, and trotted out of sight.

10

D an finished his second midmorning cup of coffee out of the gurgling, spitting, decades-old dented coffee maker, top held together with Gorilla Glue. Dan would swear the coffee tasted like glue. JerriSue never got around to buying a replacement, despite him insisting it could be paid for out of petty cash.

Deputy Marvin Harter, JerriSue's husband, knocked at Dan's office door frame. Harter held an official-looking envelope, SUBPOENA stamped across it.

"Mornin', Dan."

Every time Dan had seen him for almost twenty years, Marvin Harter was smiling and cheerful. He'd even gotten a couple of speeding tickets from the squat little deputy, who had smiled and joked as he wrote them out.

His shirt was partially tucked in, badge askew above his left pocket, weapons belt under his protruding belly. That look was why he'd never advanced beyond patrol duty and serving jury summons and subpoenas.

"Got you a little in-vite here. Inquest tomorrow." He offered the envelope to Dan. "You need to read it while I'm standin' here, sign it, and date it so I can show the boss you got it. And you need to initial beside your name there." He pointed at a line three-quarter down the page on the clipboard he was carrying.

Impressive cast of characters. He handed Harter the clipboard, followed him to the office door. The deputy paused at his wife's desk, slammed the clipboard down playfully. "Don't you work too hard, sweet pea."

After Harter left, Dan picked up his desk phone and dialed the justice of the peace office.

"Judge Akers' office." It was Cora Whittle, LaDonna's cousin.

"Hey, you good-lookin' thing. This is Dan. Is he in?"

"Yeah, he's in there. Say hi to 'Donna for me. Hang on."

"This is Judge Akers."

"Can't get used to the skinny little kid I used to drink with callin' himself 'judge.'"

"You should have by now, Hairless Wonder. You keep votin' for me."

"I think I need to buy you lunch."

"Lemme see if I can guess why. Couldn't be about our little party tomorrow, right?"

"You free about one?"

"Let's look. Yeah. I've got a probate hearing at two-thirty."

"Okay. I'll see you at the club, right at one. Park at the clubhouse."

He called the country club manager and arranged for a small private card room.

Defoliation. Dan checked his watch. Twelve fifteen. He decided to risk talking to Drake. He called the Kilborn number. Three rings.

"Hello. Kilborn Aviation." It was Ronny Joyce, the pilot. Dan dreaded the question. "This is Dan Baker. Is, is Drake there?"

"Nope, hasn't been in today."

"Okay." Dan was about to hang up.

"Can I help you, Mr. Baker?"

"Maybe. We were supposed to defoliate the twenty-eighth, but that all blew up."

"Yeah, I remember. Sorry, all that happened. We've been real busy sprayin' for other guys since. I think we're booked up the rest of the week. I figured we'd get back to you, but Drake hasn't said to call or anything."

Go figure. "Yeah, well, I want to reschedule. Can I do that with you, or do I have to talk . . ." Dan let the words hang in the phone line, waiting for Ronny to say something. Anything to make it comfortable.

"That's all right. I'll look at our calendar and talk to Drake. I'll call you back, or he will. You got any days in mind?"

"Whenever you can get to it. Sooner the better. Certain before Thanksgiving."

"Okay. Let's see. How much did we use last year? I'm thinking it was 300 gallons."

"I dunno. Yeah, probably. That sounds right."

"Tell you what. I'll talk to Drake first thing this afternoon. He's suppos'ta be here after meetin' with Archie's family. He said around two."

"Okay, good. Let me hear from *you* as soon as possible."

He hung up and exhaled from the bottom of his lungs. There was a sort of relief, a resolution. He'd get his defoliation scheduled and wouldn't have to speak to Drake. *Fat chance.*

11

D an drove to the rear of the country club and parked. As he was walking into the pro shop, he happened to glance toward the putting green. Drake Kilborn was working a bucket of balls spilled at the edge of the circle.

Dan headed for the club entrance. "Somethin' tells me Drake's the one who's gonna need help pretty soon," he muttered to himself. *I can see you're really helping out Archie's grieving family.*

He asked the club manager if Judge Akers was there yet. She pointed to the door to one of the small card rooms. "Right there, about five minutes ago. Y'all gonna need menus?"

"Yeah, I'll take 'em in."

He walked into the card room and shut the door behind him. Jimmy Akers stood.

"How you doin', young man?" They shook hands.

"Okay. Sorta okay, your honor."

They sat and took a moment studying the noon specials. Dan leaned back to the door, opened it, signaled to the club manager, placed their orders. "Sharon, we need some privacy. You haven't seen either of us, right?"

"You got it." She took the menus and pulled the door closed.

"Okay, fill me in. What happens in a coroner's inquest?"

"I've never presided at one like this, so I made some notes off one of the state's legal websites." Akers took a small memo pad from his pocket, put on his glasses, and started tracing the page with his finger.

"Here's what happened with Arthur Harold Medders . . ."

"That was Archie's name?"

"Yeah. Should have said that." Akers took out his ballpoint and made a mark on the page. "I need to remember that for tomorrow.

"Anyway, as you probably know, he died on the way to Hedrick Memorial in Abilene. The EMTs couldn't revive him, neither could Deputy Harter. So, they drove him to the hospital emergency room, where one of the trauma surgeons declared him DOA.

"That doctor did an examination, saw something out of the ordinary, and called another doctor, who agreed. It went upstairs to the hospital administrator, who called the J.P. for that precinct. She issued an order keeping the body from being moved until a pathologist could take a look.

"Luckily, the contract pathologist was in town and arranged to do the autopsy yesterday afternoon. I don't know what he found, but he filed a report with the county attorney saying the death was due to suspicious circumstances. The case should be referred to a coroner's inquest."

"You mean an inquest in Abilene?"

"Yep, it looked that way until that J.P. called me and explained what happened. She wasn't particularly anxious to handle an inquest for an out-of-towner but would if we didn't want to do it here.

"That would have been a pain for the family and everybody else to have to go to Abilene." There was a soft knock on the door. Dan leaned back and opened it. Sharon put their meals on the round table.

Akers continued to consult his notes as they started eating. "Dan, I'm not real sure I should be tellin' you all this, but it's gonna be out in the inquest, so I guess it's all right."

"I don't know why not." Dan pointed at the judge's notes. "Inquest? Abilene?"

"Oh, yeah. Anyway, I got Russ Jennings, our county attorney on the call, and the three of us agreed the inquest could be moved to

Jerrod. I called the pathologist, and he said he'd be available tomorrow, for a fee."

"Fee?"

"Yeah, he's under contract to Taylor County, so we have to pick up his travel expenses and pay him for his time."

"Okay. What's a coroner's inquest do?" Dan looked at his watch. *Already one twenty.*

"The short version, it's a kind of public hearing into the probable cause of a death. I'll be presiding.

"After all the testimony, I'll decide to turn the case over to the district attorney. She can recommend no action, which isn't likely. Or she can call for additional testimony or recommend the case be remanded to the county attorney, who may or may not refer it to a grand jury."

"How long you expect this to go on?"

"No way of knowing. It depends on the testimony. You're on that list. So's Doc Chin, the Taylor County medical examiner, Harter, and the EMTs who took him to the hospital."

Memory of the almost empty container of foul-smelling defoliant

came into focus in Dan's mind. He wished away that image. And he had
been trying to unsee Archie sprawled in the pickup cab.

"What, Dan?"

"Nothin'. A flashback." Another glance at his watch. One thirty.
"So is this deal public?"

"Yep, as public as any other preliminary hearing. Anybody can
watch, but only the witnesses and the county attorney can address the
court. I'm gonna start at nine and hope to be finished by noon.

"Under the law, I can't officially release the remains for burial until
the meeting is over. I plan to mention that the first thing to try to keep
order. I'm gonna want this done as quick as anybody else. The way to do
that is to keep it movin'.

"Medders' widow - I guess you'd call her a 'widow' – called me
this morning. She's pretty hot about the secrecy. Can't say I blame her. I
could hear some other woman . . ."

". . . Her mother probably."

". . . screaming in the background, yelling questions. I'm afraid that
may be a hint of what we have in store tomorrow."

Dan remembered mother and daughter demanding answers from
everybody at the hospital. "Isn't the body already in town?"

Akers finished his sandwich and picked at the banana pudding.

"Yep. I talked to Jim Logan over at the funeral home right before I
got here. He's going ahead with the embalming. State health rules. The
pathologist said it was all right."

"Anything about a funeral?"

"Nope. I don't know nothin', and that's fine. It ain't one of my jobs."
Akers looked at his watch and stood. "Oh shit. I gotta git. I've got a
probation hearing in twenty minutes. Look. You'll be getting a call from
Jennings. You know him?"

"Nope, not really. Met him once, I think. What's he want with me?"

"He'll have a few questions about what you saw when you called 9-1-1 about Archie. Basically, he's gonna walk you through the procedure for the inquest. No big deal."

Akers left the room after nodding to Dan, whose cell phone buzzed from its place on the table, the church number on display. He stepped into the lobby, waved the manager over, signed the check.

On the way out of the pro shop, he saw Drake still on the putting green. As Dan stopped to look, Drake glanced sideways at him. First, there was surprise on his face, then the slightest smile as he looked down at the few balls left on the green.

It took Dan a few minutes to drive back into town. JerriSue held up a Post-It Note sticking to her left index finger when he walked into the store.

Call Jennings7728285.

Call Costley

Her

Dan still couldn't fathom it. *Why is "LaDonna" so tricky to write down?* His office clock read two-thirty. She was still in class. Couldn't answer if he called.

"Russ Jennings."

"This is Dan Baker. Judge Akers said I should call you."

"Thanks for calling, Mr. Baker. You're a witness in tomorrow's coroner's inquest, right?"

"That's what they tell me. Frankly, I'm a little spooked about this."

"No need. It's a simple process."

"Yeah, with the whole town watchin'." "I can't tell you there won't be a crowd." "So, what happens?

"After you're sworn in by the judge, you'll go back to the jury room. You'll be called back into the courtroom when your name comes up. I think you're first on the list. I'll be asking you the questions."

"What kinda questions?"

"All I want to know is what you saw when you found Archie on the road last Friday. You have all those facts clear in your head? I can't talk to you ahead of time about your answers. Mr. Baker?"

"Yeah, I'm here. Thinkin' it through."

"As I said, Mr. Baker, I can't discuss the questioning with you. I will say you should only respond to what I ask you, nothing else. Don't volunteer anything. Is that clear?"

"That include what Archie said, er, I thought he said?"

"Respond to the questions, Mr. Baker. Short, concise answers.

"And ?"

"Don't volunteer anything."

"Excellent. I know there's some concern in the community about how others' actions might have influenced the outcome, but this hearing is not about that. It's strictly about the events leading up to Mr. Medders' death. The Abilene pathologist said it was suspicious circumstances, and that's how we must deal with it. It's the law. Any other questions?"

"What happens if somebody in the room speaks up?"

"If they're not a witness being questioned, they're escorted out. It's a public meeting, not a public forum."

"Good. That's a relief."

"Mr. Baker, I think we're through here. You'll hear a lot of this repeated by the judge tomorrow. Please be patient. If there's nothing else, I'll let you go."

Dan pushed the receiver button to clear the connection, dialed St. Anthony's Episcopal, exchanged pleasantries with the secretary, waited for Costley.

"Hey."

"How ya doin', padre?"

"Better than I was a few minutes ago. Mazie Medders and her mother are gone. That was about the most emotional session I've ever had preparing for a graveside service."

"Glad I wasn't in your shoes."

"Amen. Best I could tell after they settled down, the body will be available for viewing first thing in the morning."

"Boy, timin' is everything."

"What?"

"Thinking out loud. That's the time for the coroner's inquest tomorrow morning."

"Coroner's inquest?"

"Yeah, the Abilene doctors said the death was suspicious, which triggered all sorts of legal gymnastics. Long story short, Judge Akers will hold the inquest in the morning and call witnesses, includin' me."

"So that's what Mazie's mom meant by 'that damned meetin' tomorrow.' She seemed to think it's going to cover up anything leading to Archie's death. I had no idea it was as formal as it sounds."

Dan went over all the details of the meeting and the possible outcomes.

"I guess this will be worked out by the people over at Logan's, but Mazie said they don't have any money to spend on 'some fancy-assed funeral'—her words. After we talked a little bit, I suggested a graveside service. She seemed to like the idea of its simplicity."

"She and her mother were headed over to the funeral home next, so I hope I'll know before the end of the day when's what. Boy, those are two lost souls—three, if you count the little one they had with them.

"I'm guessing the services will be Saturday morning. I don't think the state allows a body to be out any longer than that."

"Lemme know if I can help."

"I'm always telling people I'll pray for them, Dan. Maybe you can do some of that for me. And I think I can go to your fellow vestrymen and get their approval to pay for Logan's services. I guess you wouldn't have a problem with that. The Catholics picked up the last indigent service. Guess it's our turn.

"After all this is over, who knows? Maybe you'll invite me out to your place for a beer and some decompressing."

"You got it, Reverend Graham. We'll both need some of that. You're a good guy."

Dan put the phone in the cradle and leaned back. Dumbass jumped in his lap, and Dan began to stroke the ancient one-eyed cat while staring at the ceiling. His cell phone buzzed, LaDonna's number on the ID.

"What's goin' on with you?"

"I was going to ask you the same. What's up with the inquest tomorrow? Everybody here at school is asking about it."

"I'm afraid it's gonna be a mess." The cat stirred, looked up, expecting more petting, then jumped from Dan's lap to the desktop and bedded down. "I'm glad it ain't my deal. From the chat with the county attorney a few minutes ago, it sounds like all I've got to do is talk about what happened when I found Archie in the pickup on the south place."

"I hope you don't get all snarled up in this. What about the sheriff, and what's his name coming for the pickup?"

"Oh. You mean Freddy? I guess I'll keep it under my hat until the sheriff says otherwise. I've got some uneasy feelings about the way the Sheriff and Freddy keep showin' up together. First, it was that little show they put on for me at the hospital, and then they come for the pickup.

I've got one of those 'tight shirt' feelin's 'bout them." Dan looked up at the wall clock. *Four o'clock.*

"So, are you done? Heading home?"

"No, I'm sponsoring the cheerleaders again. We have a meeting at four-thirty. No point in driving out there and then back. You want to meet somewhere for early dinner?"

JerriSue walked up to Dan's office door and pointed over her shoulder toward the showroom. She put her hands on her hips and stared at Dan.

"Somebody waitin' on me. Look, let's go to Thrasher's. I'll see you there 'bout five-thirty."

"Thrasher's? Yuk. I guess it's that or Big Jimmy's. Okay. See you there. I love you."

"I love you too, always." Dan hung up and turned palms up at JerriSue. "What?" She pointed over her right shoulder. Dan looked past her and saw Ronny Joyce pretending to read a tire display.

"Hey, Ronny. What's goin' on? Here, sit down." He pointed toward a wooden armchair on the other side of his desk.

Ronny twisted around in the chair, tugged at his handlebar mustache, and jerked his head up to look at Dan. "Uh." he rubbed his eyes with the back of his right hand.

Dan leaned forward and looked into Ronny's eyes. He was concentrating on not raising his voice. "What, Ronny? This about Drake?"

Ronny looked toward Dan's office door.

Dan stood, walked to the open door. "No calls, nothin', JerriSue. Okay?"

She waved without looking back. With the toe of his boot, Dan nudged aside the small ceramic frog doorstop. He picked it up, turned it over in his hand. Janelle, almost fifteen years ago. He put it on his desk, looked at Ronny, who was moving side to side in his chair.

He started to speak but managed only a hiss. He swallowed, licked his lips, sat up straighter. "Dan, I, I talked to Drake about this. He said I should tell you."

"Tell me . . .?"

"I asked Drake about your place, an, an, an, well . . ."

"Go on, say it. We're big boys here."

"He said, he said . . . well," He looked right and left, licked his lips. "He said you could kiss his ass." His eyes begged forgiveness for the insult. "If you want to know when we'll get to you, then you'll have to talk to him. I'm sorry, Dan. This ain't me talkin'. We're friends. You and me have been friends a long time."

Dan kept his voice calm. "Don't worry, Ronny. You're deliverin' a message. All you had to do is call me. I appreciate you coming here in person. It shows a lot of class."

Ronny's smile was fleeting. He grabbed the chair's arms as if he was about to get up, then settled. "Dan, all I ever wanted was to fly.

That's all I want to do now. I don't want to get in anybody's messes.

That's got nothing to do with flyin'. You know what I mean?"

Dan and Ronny stood. Dan extended his hand. "You got nothin' to worry 'bout from me, Ronny. You're all right. We're square." Dan put his hand on Ronny's shoulder and led him back to the showroom.

"Keep on, keepin' on. Okay?" Dan pushed back at the anger rising inside.

As Ronny walked out of the store, Dan slammed his office door.

"Goddamnit. You sonofabitch. You're gonna call my hand, aren't you?" He kicked his wastebasket against the wall and felt heavy as he sat in his office chair. A slight rapping came at the door. JerriSue was looking through the door's window. Dan motioned her in.

"Looks like your gonna need a new trash can. I'm goin' to the post office and the Dollar Store. Guess I'll get you one." She looked around the corner at the crumpled wastebasket. "Don't blame you. That Drake guy is gonna be a lot of trouble."

Surprised by her rare display of friendliness and a smile, he started to ask how she knew but decided he didn't want to know how much she knew or how she knew it.

"Uh, thanks, JerriSue." He took his sweat stained Hillson Elevator baseball cap from the hat tree and headed for the door. "I'm gone. I probably won't be in tomorrow mornin'. And, by the way—new coffee maker."

Because of interruptions, it took Dan and LaDonna an hour to eat at Thrasher's. It seemed they could take only two or three bites before someone they knew came in. Everybody wanted to talk about the inquest.

Dan, between heaping forks of brisket and Cole Slaw, said, "Yeah, it's gonna be interestin'."

"No, I got no idea what killed him. No, I don't think the Mexican mafia is involved. Probably doesn't have anything to do with illegal immigrants. Don't know what I'm gonna say. Depends on what they ask me. Ernie, could I have some more tea? Yeah, unsweet. I have no idea who they'll find guilty. It's not a trial. Could we have a to-go box? Food's gettin' cold."

One more greeting, a questioner in the parking lot. "Hey, good to see you. Huh? No idea. I gotta go. Got heifers to feed."

LaDonna opened the door behind her driver's seat and put the togo box on the floor. "We don't have heifers."

"Had to come unstuck some way. I do have to go back to the store.
I've gotta make sure JerriSue sent that check to Toyo Tires. We get
a big break for paying early. She didn't say anything about sendin' it."

LaDonna got in her car and lowered the window. "I'm going ahead.
I've gotta grade some papers and call Janelle." LaDonna waved as she
drove out of the gravel parking lot in her Blazer. Dan went in the
opposite direction.

He spent a short time at the store looking for the invoice. He located
a registered mail receipt on JerriSue's desk, addressed to Toyo Tires,
Abilene. As he left the store, he glanced up and saw the light in

Jimmy Akers's office on the second floor of the courthouse a block
away. Sheriff Mose Britten's big SUV was parked at the rear at the one-
story Criminal Justice Center across the parking lot. There was a light in
his office, too. "Wish I was a mouse in that room right now." He glanced
at his watch. *Seven o'clock. Time to call it a day.*

Dan drove west out of town as the sun went behind a broad band of
clouds on the western horizon, stretching from north to south. He
thumbed the radio volume down as *All My Exes Live in Texas* began.
"Shit. It rains very much, we're gonna have big problems if that damned
cotton lays down 'cause of wet leaves and stalks. Damnit."

As he turned into the lane to the house, he saw parking lights on the
road about a mile to the west, looking near the Starkey place. Then
headlights. There was a bright blue beam from a hand-held flashlight,
swinging back and forth, left to right. It looked like a signal for help. His
first reaction was to drive toward the flashlight. His neighbor Ray might
be having trouble. But then, the searchlight went out, and the car lights
got brighter, moving closer. Ray wouldn't be doing that. Dan slowed,
then decided to go on toward the house. "Probably some kids makin'

out. But what was the deal with the searchlight?"

As Dan turned down the lane to his house, he could hear the oncoming car accelerating. But, as he stopped beside his house, Dan heard the muffled blut-blut-blut of a high-performance engine slowing. As he turned around in his seat, he could see it slowed almost to walking speed as it approached the turnoff. Dan got out of the Suburban and turned to watch the distant car move past the turnoff. Red brake lights. Then, the searchlight again, sweeping from left to right and then pausing as it appeared to follow the road to Dan's house. Then, off again.

He could almost make out the color and shape of the car, not a pickup. The sound of the revved-up engine echoed across Dan's shop and the seed barn. And then, the squeal of tires and the guttural tone of a turbocharger gasping for air. As he watched, the car swerved back and forth as it disappeared to the east, picking up speed until the sound blended into the cooling dusk.

"Silly-assed kid showin' off the car daddy bought him." But the voice of a slight burning sensation inside whispered, *It was a warning, a threat, and you know its name.*

He felt the knife-edged grit of the desert sand against his boots as he adjusted his binoculars. Lights were moving on the horizon. The intel briefer had told the platoon leaders the lights were Iraqi decoys to draw attention from their scout vehicles, which would come from another direction. As he put the binoculars down, there were the whines of incoming mortar fire and screams of two of his men caught in the open. Dan walked up to the berm and carefully looked over the edge.

"What are you looking at?"

Dan jumped when he heard LaDonna. She was standing at the porch railing outside the kitchen, tying her robe.

He swallowed hard, sweating despite the coolness of the November night. "Oh, somebody's got himself a new four-wheeled dick extension. I'm watchin' him gettin' ready to buy some new tires." He looked again toward the road and to the east and rubbed the top of his head.

The automatic blue floodlight was at his back, his face in shadow.

LaDonna could hear the worrying huskiness in his voice. "Danny, come on. It's time to come inside." He turned and watched as she gathered her robe against the chill and went back into the kitchen.

Dan parked the Suburban, locked up, "shook hands" with Sniff, walked up the four steps to the kitchen.

He opened the refrigerator, took on a small bottle of Real Orange, opened it, swallowed it in three quick gulps, his hand still shaking. "I wonder what's gonna happen tomorrow." He opened the trash bin, threw the empty in as LaDonna wrapped her arms around his chest. He leaned back against her. "I can't get it off my mind."

He turned to face her. Her bathrobe had somehow come untied. A familiar signal. He took her in a bear hug. "I thought you were gonna call Janelle."

"You might say I have a different calling right now." She took his hand and led him upstairs to the second floor.

12

D an reached over to pat LaDonna at dawn, but she was already out of bed and in the shower. Six fifteen. He stretched, pulled the covers up, rolled away from the sound of her singing in the bathroom.

A few minutes later, he felt her sit on the edge of the bed. "Better get up." She was buttoning her blouse.

"Oh, shit. What time?" Six-thirty. He leaned up on one elbow. "Teacher, can I get an excused absence today?"

LaDonna leaned over and kissed him on the forehead. "Hmmm. No fever. I'm afraid not. You want breakfast?"

Dan grabbed for her, but she dodged as she stood. "How about breakfast in bed, like last night?"

"Sorry. You'll muss me up. What do you really want for breakfast—from downstairs?"

"Don't think I can eat. I'm gonna get dressed and go to the store before the inquest. I'll take a rain check."

Dressed and downstairs before seven, he followed his wife out the door and down to the driveway. She unlocked her Blazer and turned to him.

"Don't worry about today. You've got nothing to hide. Everybody knows you. Everybody respects you. All you've got to do is say what you know. Nothing more." She smiled, tugged at his lapel, gave him a quick kiss. "Don't forget to say bye to your dog." Sniff was sitting a few feet away, paw ready.

While LaDonna was pulling onto the path next to the house, Dan leaned down and took the dog's paw. "I really envy you, boy. This is your only worry. Keep a good lookout today." He scratched the mutt's drooping ears and climbed into his Suburban. Sniff watched him pull away, then went to his igloo doghouse under the steps and settled in.

When Dan got to the shop, the Monarch Tires truck was parked at the overhead doors at the side of the store. Dan walked up to the cab and slapped the door. The sleeping driver's head popped up and turned to look at Dan.

"How long you been here?"

"Dunno. Maybe thirty minutes. I drove in from the warehouse in Fort Worth. You're my first stop."

Dan and the driver unloaded the six-foot tires and rolled them into the shop. They had been ordered by one of the corporate farms north of town, so they wouldn't be in his way long.

An hour later, Dan walked up the courthouse steps and saw Cora Whittle, Jimmy Aker's secretary, waving at him. She pointed to the sheet on her clipboard. "You sign in here. Witness list."

"So far, only five, huh? I don't see Drake Kilborn's name here."

"You're right, honey, you don't. You won't." Cora took the clipboard and gestured toward the door with *Jurors* on the frosted glass insert. "Wait in there. All of you will be sworn in any time now, and then the judge will ask those not testifying to wait in the room. The judge wants the witnesses to not discuss anything about the inquest until they're called. After you're through, you're welcome to leave the courthouse. You must have some pull with him. You're first up. Say hi to my sweet cuz, will ya?"

Dan acknowledged the others around the long oak table and sat at one end. The EMTs to his right were staring straight ahead. The taller of the two was reading *Field and Stream*, dog-eared by successive occupants of the stuffy, windowless room. His partner was fiddling with his cell phone, chirps and beeps coming from an electronic game, and glancing sideways at the man at the other end of the table. Behind him, a solid wood door that led into the courtroom. Next to it, a sign said *No Cell Phones In This Room.*

Dr. Fernand Acharya, Taylor County pathologist and medical examiner, sat ramrod erect at the other end of the table. Almost motionless, except for his long bony fingers, typing in rapid bursts on a small notebook computer. His Sikh turban apparently had a profound impact on Deputy Marvin Harter.

Harter was standing against the wall, the back of a chair tucked into his crotch. He shifted from foot to foot, eyeing the exotic doctor, then looking at the others as if gauging their potential support if a battle broke out.

Dr. Randall Chin sat near Acharya but at a respectful distance. Colleagues not equals. He was fidgeting with his key ring, turning it around his thumb. The contrast between the tall Sikh and the small, thin-boned Chin was profound. Acharya in Brooks Brothers, Chin in a too-large blue blazer, off-white shirt, and charcoal pants.

He had looked up as Dan entered the room, smiled in recognition, and focused on his key ring. Dan toyed with the notion of yelling "Boo" to see the impact on the gathering. Maybe Harter would spring into action and extract his pistol from beneath his overhanging belly and shoot himself in the foot.

Holden County Justice of Peace Jimmy Akers, wearing his judicial robes because his wife insisted, mounted the two steps to his elevated bench, sat, banged his gavel.

The courtroom wasn't designed to hold more than thirty people, including the five county commissioners who met there once a week. Cora had told Akers there were twenty, maybe twenty-five in the room, some standing. She'd warned him that a few "look downright disagreeable."

Akers spotted the "disagreeables" immediately. One was on the front bench, beside the disheveled Mazie Medders and her mother, the other four on the bench behind them. They would be suspicious in any rural town because of their hairstyles, ranging from bald with a miniature ponytail, bald, no eyebrows, and as best as he could tell, no eyelashes. In the courtroom, they had given rise to a muttering chorus of whispers.

At the end of the curving front pew was the infant H.D., shrouded in a tattered, brown-tinged blanket, sound asleep on his back, not bothered by the occasional wheezy sobs of Mazie and her mother.

There was a distinctive smell of marijuana.

A scattering of ordinary people filled out the room—Jack Knowles from the newspaper, Jim Logan from the funeral home, Ella Parker from the hospital. At the end of the back bench, not far from Ella, the St. Anthony's Episcopal priest Wyman Costley. And at the doors to the courtroom, on one side, Sheriff Mose Britten.

As Akers was about to call the court to order, Drake Kilborn walked in with his attorney Jeff Stangle. Zeke Kilborn followed them, waited a moment at the entrance. He shrugged his shoulders, made his way to the end of the back pew and almost fell while lowering himself in place next to Ella Parker.

Akers picked up the gavel Geraldine had given him at the beginning of his first term fifteen years before and brought it down on a drink coaster.

"All right, ladies and gentlemen, let's get started. This is a formal coroner's inquest into the death of Arthur Harold Medders. He was declared dead on arrival at Hedrick Medical Center in Abilene, Taylor County, at or about eleven A.M., November twelfth last.

Mazie, who had been resting her head on the curved top of the pew, made a feral noise. The male hulk next to her, almost smothered her. It appeared he had meant to put his arm around the general vicinity of her shoulders, instead clamped down on her head.

Akers then explained the reason for the autopsy and how the inquest ended up in Holden County. There was another cry from Mazie, then her mother.

"Ladies, I understand your grief . . ."

"You don' unerstan' shit." Alice Faye was on her feet, waving her arms. Her outburst caused a fresh keening from Mazie and woke H.D., who added his wail. "My son-in-law is dead, over there 'cross the street being prettied up for a funeral we can't afford, an . . ."

"Mrs. Ferris, as I said, I understand your grief, but if there more outbursts, I'll have no choice but to have you removed. You understand that?"

One of the giants sitting near her leaped to his feet. "Whut yew don' unerstan', yer honerrrr, is that we're pissed 'bout this whole deal, and we want some answers. Mazie, her momma, and that there little 'un wants some answers."

Mose Britten touched the cover on his mace holster and started down the aisle to the front. A bead of sweat ran down Akers' side, causing him to shift in the oversized robes.

He stood, held up his right hand, causing the sheriff to stop.

"Everybody, we're gonna have a ten-minute recess right now. While this inquest is in recess, I want the courtroom cleared except for Mrs. Medders and Mrs. Ferris and the people with them. Anybody got a problem with that?" Several people in the audience bobbed their heads. The sheriff turned and retraced his steps.

Drake made no move to help his father. Ella and Costley got that job. The last one to the door was the sheriff. He looked at Akers, waiting.

"It's fine, sheriff. We're not gonna have any problems, are we?" He scanned the faces of the Medders' entourage. Reluctant nods in agreement. "Good. Check back in with me in about ten minutes, okay?"

Akers left his desk and walked down to the railing. He leaned in and made a special effort to lower his voice.

"Now folks, I know this hurts like hell . . ."

Murmurs. "You're goddamned right." "Fuckin'-a." "No shit." ". . . but we gotta get through this. There may be deep suspicions 'bout Archie's death, but we gotta do this the right way. I've got my job to do. I want to hear testimony. I want the county attorney to be able to do his part, so we can move on. I want to do that—an' I think you want to do that—to honor your lost husband, friend, and son-in- law. Am I right?" Nods.

"My biggest responsibility is to have this hearing end as quick as possible, so I can look you in the eyes and tell you without flinching that you have the court's permission to go ahead with your plans to celebrate Archie's life and commit him to the earth. If you think this is going to be too much for you to bear, you could go now, and I'll meet with you afterward to tell you what I've decided – I certainly wouldn't blame you."

Mazie leaned forward as far as her bulk would allow, pulling at her bleach-blond hair, which had taken on the appearance of a ragged dust mop. One of the men stood up behind her, rubbing her back. She settled, looked up, wiped her nose on a dishtowel that she pulled out from somewhere within her tank top, and looked up at the judge.

"So, help me do my job," he said. "Please try to keep outbursts to a minimum while we get through this. You've indicated you want to stay and see justice begin to work here, but don't complicate it. Anybody got questions? No? Good. Let's you and me do this to honor Archie, okay?" Nods again.

Akers stood, buttoned his robes. The sheriff stuck his head in the door at the back. Akers held up a hand, telling him to wait. "Anybody need a bathroom break? No? Sheriff, let'em back in."

The witnesses entered the courtroom and stood at the judge's bench to take their oath. Dan was first in, so he got to watch the crowd's reaction when Dr. Acharya appeared. There were audible gasps, and several in the group moved closer together. After the oath, the witnesses went back to the jury room.

"One little housekeeping announcement, folks, no cell phones. Right now is the time for you to turn them off, mute them, whatever

"One little housekeeping announcement, folks, no cell phones. Right now is the time for you to turn them off, mute them, whatever you want to do. If I hear a cell phone ringing or see somebody talkin' or textin' during these proceedings. I'll stop everything and, please, believe me, I will call the offender before this bench and charge him or her with contempt of these proceedings and confiscate the device. So, everybody, check your phones." There was a rustle in the room as phones were taken from purses, out of pockets.

"Thank you. At this point, ladies and gentlemen, I'm gonna turn this procedure over to the Holden County Attorney Russ Jennings.

He'll tell you what happens next."

Jennings stood from his place at the lawyers' table in front of the bench. "This inquest is established under the law for one purpose, to hear the testimony of everyone who has relevant information in the matter of Arthur Harold Medders being hospitalized here in Jerrod and eventually transferred to Abilene, where he was declared dead on arrival. Specifically, this inquest will determine how the justice system should respond to the medical examiners' ruling of 'death due to suspicious circumstances."

"When we finish here today, Judge Akers should know enough to make one of three recommendations to the district attorney: take no action, turn it over to the authorities for further investigation, or refer it to a grand jury."

Jennings took his black-rimmed glasses from his nose, looked at them, then put them back on. "This isn't anything like a trial. I'm going to ask all the questions here. There will be no cross-examination. We're not looking for guilty people or innocent people. Nobody in the spectator area has a part in this process, so I'd ask your indulgence as you watch one of the small gears of our justice system turn."

He walked to the judge's bench, straightened his tie, buttoned his jacket. "Your honor, I'm ready for the first witness." Akers looked at his list and nodded to Cora, who went in the side door. After a moment, she came back, followed by Dan Baker.

Dan scanned the courtroom and noticed some subtle changes. The sheriff and Freddy were standing next to the double doors at the back of the room. On the other side, Drake and Jeff Stangle. And, a pleasant surprise, the space between Wyman Costley and Ella Parker on the back pew had narrowed. For the last time that morning, Dan smiled.

Jennings led Dan through the sequence of events on the previous Friday, his discovery of the ailing Archie, the 9-1-1 call, the open container in the back of Archie's pickup. He was surprised the acne-scarred, square-faced Jennings with the glasses didn't ask him what Archie said to him as he was being loaded into the ambulance. But ". . . short answers. Don't volunteer anything" buzzed in his memory.

Jennings thanked Dan, reminding him to not discuss the case with anyone until the judge's decisions were made public. He left the witness stand, walked through the gate in the rail, up the outside aisle, and stopped behind Zeke Kilborn, sitting at the end of the pew with a shawl covering his legs. He squeezed Zeke's shoulders. Zeke reached up and patted Dan's hand.

Dan winked at Ella, turned, walked toward the double doors, passing Drake and Jeff Stangle. He glanced at Drake as he pushed through the doors. *He avoided looking at me*, Dan thought.

13

F reddy's cell phone ID showed *Tomas Ascencio.* "This is Freddy. Can you hang on a minute?" He stored the tools he had used to install the new nozzles on the second spray plane. "Hey, Tomas. *¿Que pasa mi amigo?* How are things at the cement plant?"

"*El mismo,* you know. Noisy. Dirty. Noisy. Dirty. Hey, I'm on lunch break. Remember you asked me to keep a watch on Archie's trailer?"

"Yeah."

"I woke up about six and looked out the bathroom window and seen that Drake guy."

Freddy started walking toward the front of the hangar. "And?"

"It was still kinda dark, so I couldn't see him real clear until he turned on his flashlight. It was one of them high-powered dudes, puts out enough light to set the weeds on fire.

"Anyway, he's walkin' round 'n round Archie's pickup. He picked up a stick and poked at something in the bed, threw it away, and bent down, lookin' under the pickup."

"About what time was this by now?" Freddy took his small notebook from his back pocket, put the phone on *speaker*, leaned against his car.

"You still there?"

"Yeah, sorry, brother, *adelante*."

"I first thought he was gonna drive it off, but that didn't make sense. His big ole Mustang was sittin' there behind the pickup. Why would he want that pickup pile of junk? He got down on all-fours and stuck his arm under. He fished around a little and then—well, this is what I think I saw. You an' me still okay with all this?"

"Absolutely. *El bono*."

"He brought out something that looked like a big black glob. He stood up, leaned on the pickup, started unwrappin' it. It was done up pretty well, several layers of that heavy-duty black plastic. Anyway, he finally got it open, and there it was, a gun."

"A gun?"

"*Si. Un gran arma.* Big sonofabitch. I bet it was a .38, something like that.

"He was lookin' it over, you know, checkin' it out. Then the porch light on Archie's trailer comes on. Well, he shoves the gun in his belt, high-tails it for his car. He pulls out, spinnin' his tires big time. Not wantin' anybody to see him, I bet."

"Yeah, probably not." Freddy put his notebook back in his pocket. "*Mi amigo*, thanks for the call. This really helps."

"Wait. One more thing."

"Sure, *que*?"

"Got a call from *mi hermana* 'bout thirty minutes ago. You know, she teaches at the grade school?"

"You mean Mariel? She your sister?"

"Yeah. Little sister. Anyway, she's real worried. About eight last night, she's in her apartment, gradin' papers. She got up to pull the curtains on her front window and sees this car sittin' in the back of the parking lot downstairs from her apartment. Keep in mind, it's dark already. She can't make out who's behind the wheel. Its parking lights were on.

"So, she pulls the curtains, goes back to gradin' papers. Few minutes later, she turns off the livin' room light then looks out the little window in the door. The car had pulled up under a street light. Sure 'nuf, it was that Drake guy. He sat there for a minute, guns his engine real big burns a lot of rubber and high-tails it."

"Tomas, did she call the cops about this?"

"Naw, that's why she called me. She's a high-powered teacher an' all, but, well, we don't exactly trust cops. She wanted to take out a protective order on him after that time in Abilene. I've been giving her some self-defense pointers on how to handle rough *hombres* since then."

"Protective order?"

Tomas recounted the confrontation between Mariel and Drake in Abilene. "She called the cops then. She was there with a bunch of teachers from Jerrod. I think maybe it was in early October. You could ask any of those teachers."

Freddy made more notes. "Look, Tomas, I really want to thank you for all this. I'm tryin' to decide whether I want to work for that sonofabitch anymore."

Sounds of Tomas breathing, then, "Freddy, you're a cop, *¿sinceramente?*"

"Uh . . . Tomas, *Nuestra palabra es nuestra hermandad.*"

"*Si.* Our brotherhood. I gotta go too."

"*Gracias*, Tomas." Freddy closed his notebook. His cell phone rang before he could pocket it—Drake on the ID.

"Freddy."

"We need to go to storage. What are you doin' right now?"

"Just replaced some nozzles on Number Two."

"You heard anything from Drake this mornin'?"

"Nope. You?"

"Nothing. By the way, what were you doing standing next to the Sheriff at the inquest? What was he talking about?"

"That was where I ended up 'cause it was so crowded. I got there first. He stopped and started talking about Archie's pickup. Wonderin' if I'd seen it. I told him I thought Dan Baker had driven it to his farm for safekeepin' until he could turn it over to Mazie or somebody in her family. I don't know anything after that."

"Call that a family? I've seen wild pigs with better family life. Baker, huh?" Five counts of silence. "Okay. Meet me at storage, thirty minutes, tops."

In high school, when things went wrong in football practice or Dan argued with LaDonna, he would drive north of town about three miles and park beside the Jerrod Creek bridge, where he was now.

It was a favorite nighttime make-out spot in high school. It had special significance for him, LaDonna, and Ella Parker.

Dan and Ladonna had dated all the way through high school, and everybody assumed they'd get married. But, they had a major argument at the beginning of their senior year, and it looked like a lost cause.

A group of seniors had gathered at the creek one hot April night.

Ella and Dan, who'd gotten there with other people, ended up sitting together on the bank.

That night, on impulse, Dan had leaned over and started to kiss Ella. She got up, stood in front of him, hands on hips. He'd never forget her direct scolding tone, "Dan, don't even try it. I don't want this; you don't want this. You want LaDonna, and I want you to be with her. I want us to be friends for the rest of our lives. We've got to have good memories of each other. It stops here, okay?" And so it did. Dan and LaDonna went on the mend, graduated, Ella went to nursing school, and it was all right.

He made his way down the caliche bank and into the streambed. Cliff swallows were darting in and out the bridge's underside carrying tiny dabs of mud in their beaks.

A slight, tentative breeze made its way down the creek bed, nudged at the quiet willows, settled. A small frog jumped toward the tiny water flow, floundered a moment, then made its way up the opposite bank.

"Yep, I got no choice, Mr. Frog. I gotta clear the air with Zeke. I owe it to him. I owe it to me. Mr. Frog, you got it easy." Dan dusted the back of his jeans and headed back to the Suburban. "Ella," he said to one of the swallows. "Call Ella. She'll know about Zeke."

He got back to the SUV, leaned against the fender, and took out his cell phone. Better not call. She might still be in the courtroom. He punched in her number and texted, *still in the court?*

no Akers thinking I guess

how's Zeke?

ok got him to his car he went home not feel well

thx

no prob

Dan put in Zeke's number. "Hey, Zeke, it's Dan."

Zeke's voice was raspy. Dan had hoped he'd sound well. "Yeah, saw you on caller ID. You heard anything from Akers?"

"He's still going over everything, I guess."

There was the sound of coughing and heavy breathing, then Zeke's voice cleared. "I'm worried about what's goin' on in my boy's head.

Last night, he showed up about midnight, and I thought he was drunk 'cause it sounded like he was talkin' to himself. I know better than to confront him, so I let it go. I woke up about two to go to the bathroom – damned diuretics – and I could hear him still talkin'. Talkin' and cryin'. So, I go down the hall thinkin' I'll knock on his bedroom door.

"When I got to his door, I could tell he was havin' a conversation with somebody. I thought, well, he'd brought a girl home, so I'd let it be. But I kinda eavesdropped and" – distant cough – "Dan, it was like he was talkin' to Bertie. He'd laugh a little, cry a little, make little noises like he did when he was a boy. It was like she was there in the room with him.

"And then, I see this bright light comin' under his bedroom door. I mean, it was like he had a spotlight of some kind in there with him. It went back and forth under the door." *That light* . . .

"Dan? You there?"

"Damn, Zeke. I'm sorry to hear all this. You rather I call back?"

"No, Dan, please. I gotta get this off my chest."

Dan stood and started to walk across the bridge. "Zeke, he caused a problem 'bout Janelle's boyfriend she'd invited from college for the weekend." Dan's footsteps echoed on the bridge. He explained the confrontation between Rob and Drake as he walked back toward his vehicle.

"I hadn't heard anything about that, Dan. Drake damned sure hasn't said anything to me about it."

Dan could hear Zeke turning away from his phone and coughing several times. His voice came back even quieter. "Dan, he went to

Abilene a couple of months ago – said he was going to meet his girlfriend there – and came back with a damned handgun. I've seen him playin' with it in the house, cleanin' it, pointin' it around. He even shot at stray cats in the backyard a couple of weeks ago. I told him then I didn't want to see that thing in our house again, and there was no reason to have it out at the hangar. I don't know why he's got it, but it worries me."

Dan got in the Suburban. "Zeke, let's let this go and hope it works out for Drake. I liked the kid, but I can't say much for the man. Maybe he'll get his act together."

"Sure, Dan. I appreciate it. Now, let's get your defoliation job handled. I'll call Ronny right now and tell him to set it up with you."

"Zeke, don't worry about it. Take care of yourself. Do what you can. If it doesn't work out, then I can figure somethin' else out."

"Gimme 'til at least tomorrow mornin', okay Dan? You'll hear from Ronny by then. I swear you will. That work for you?"

"Sure. I'm sorry to bother you 'bout this, Zeke. I owe you a beer."

"Okay. Hey. You heard anything about funeral arrangements for Archie?"

"Nope, nothin'. I'm gonna check on that now."

"Will you let me know?"

"Zeke, I talked to the preacher yesterday, and he said it's All Saints Episcopal's turn. It'll be graveside, so there won't be any expenses at the church, but there's still all Logan's has to do and the casket, hearse, limousine, *et cetera*. I think we'll have to pass the hat."

"You can count me in on that. Archie was a little goofy but a good employee. We owe him a decent burial."

"You're right. Archie was good when he worked for me, too. You know, he was something like twenty-two years old. I don't understand how a man can get to be that age and leave such shallow footprints.

"I had noticed over the last year or, that he was getting slower and slower fixin' flats, making deliveries, stuff like that. I'd have to repeat the simplest instructions two or three times. Then, he'd be his old self. It was tough to see him go downhill like that. He didn't seem too concerned 'bout his health, so I let it go."

They talked for a few more minutes, then Dan said, "Take care of yourself, buddy. We'll get through this."

Zeke drew a shallow breath. "And with nobody else gettin' hurt."

Hope you're right. "We'll talk. See ya."

———

As Dan drove through Jerrod, he waved at several people. He remembered how disorienting his homecoming from Iraq was.

LaDonna and Janelle, his mom, dad had met him at the Abilene airport. On the way back to Jerrod, the seeming nonchalance of the drivers they passed on the way to the farm confused him.

They waved, he waved back, but there was nothing in their faces that said they understood he had been shot at, injured only ninety days before. That swarthy little man with the ridiculous mustache had

They waved, he waved back, but there was nothing in their faces that said they understood he had been shot at, injured only ninety days before. That swarthy little man with the ridiculous mustache had intended to kill him. Yet, they didn't seem to care—business as usual.

He was surprised his high school buddies still living in Jerrod seemed distant. He found a star high school football player – five years younger than him – had been killed in action. He was buried in the Jerrod Cemetery as Dan was completing his convalescence in Germany.

The death of the promising athlete had so stunned the whole town, as his father Big Dan put it, "that there's no room in their hearts to welcome anybody home right now."

Dan noticed the vague barriers begin to disappear as days turned into weeks. "I felt the same way when I got back from Vietnam," his father had told him. "One day, I knew I was really back when I started dropping the g's on the ends of my words; started soundin' like Jerrod again, not like my buddy from Maine who I'd got to know so well." *God, I miss you so much, mom and dad. I really could use your help,* Dan thought.

He blinked and realized he was parked in front of the store, his forehead resting on the side window; for how long, he had no idea. JerriSue was standing at the front window, hands on her bony hips. She probably knew how long.

He walked in, avoiding eye contact, so she stepped beside him and handed him a clump of Post It notes. He took them, walked into his office, and sank into his chair. Tired. Feeling very tired, no. No, weary, very weary.

He propped his feet on his desk and peeled through the yellow squares, making a note to call, write or ignore. Last in the stack, Wyman Costley. Dan dialed his number.

"Wyman. What's goin' on?" Dan skipped the usual good-natured honorific for the preacher.

"What was your opinion of the proceedings this morning? You left early."

"On purpose. I knew everybody's story. Couldn't see any reason to hang on."

"Out of curiosity, I decided to stick it out. The testimony from the Sikh doctor was riveting. He laid out all the procedures he used during the autopsy. As he talked about weighing the organs, Mazie collapsed.

"Bless Jimmy Akers' heart, he was sensitive enough to call another recess so Mazie's friends and her mother could help her out of the courtroom. The place was packed, but there was no talking. We followed her out."

"We?"

"Me and Ella Parker, you know, the nurse?"

"Yeah, I know Ella. I hear she likes the steaks at the Embers in Breckenridge."

Brief silence on Costley's end. "Steak? Breckenridge? Don't know what that means."

"Sure. So anyway, what was the crowd's reaction to the good doctor?"

"It's fair to say they were dumbstruck. Several put their hands up like they wanted to ask questions, but the Judge reminded them of the rules. The doctor said his last about three o'clock."

Dan looked at the wall clock. "Damn. He's been at it over two hours."

"If you hear anything, will you give me a call?"

"Sure, you do the same. By the way, what about the graveside service?"

"Looks like ten o'clock Saturday morning. I got a call from Logan Funeral Home. Jim Logan was very professional, but he needs to be paid for his services and everything that goes with it. I understand that."

"Me too. You made any calls for money?"

"Several. Most everybody is willing to chip in, and some of them have bent my ear about their dealings with Drake. Doesn't sound like that young man has many friends in the community."

JerriSue tapped at Dan's office window, holding a thumb to her ear and forefinger to her mouth. "Hey, Wyman. I've gotta go. You wanna go to lunch or somethin' tomorrow?"

"That'll work. Tomorrow, Dan." Dan motioned JerriSue into his office. "What? Couldn't it wait?"

"Don't think so. It's Her." *There it is again, my wife of thirty years with no name.*

"Sounded kind of peevish."

Dan sighed. Did she mean "peeved?" He waved for JerriSue to shut the door before dialing LaDonna. "Hey, what's goin' on with you?"

"It's not me. Janelle called. She's really shaken up. Drake called her."

"Drake called her? That asshole." He dropped his feet from the desk, startling Dumbass, who leaped to the floor and ran underneath the desk. "How'd he get her number?"

"She said she vaguely remembered giving it to him two—maybe more—years ago. She hadn't thought to block him."

"What exactly did he say?"

"It was really disjointed, apologies, threats, pleading, crying, how much he misses her, the whole range. What shocked her most was about his mother. Dan, he talked about Bertie as if she is still alive, how they had been having long conversations, and she is helping him decide what to do with the business and where to put Zeke. It was a jumble of words and sentences, his voice going up and down."

"Put Zeke?" Dan stood, then grabbed the phone set before it fell from the desk.

"Janelle said Drake talked about Zeke as if his father wasn't able to take care of himself, that he needed to be in some sort of extended care."

"Convalescent home?"

"I guess that's what he means."

Dan sat for a moment, then got up again. He could feel the ache growing in his leg. "What else did he say?" He could hear road noise and a radio in the background from LaDonna's phone. She was driving and talking. Unusual.

"Dan . . ."

"What? What else did he say?"

"He said he was going to pay you back. Now, Dan . . ."

"Pay me back?" He felt his rage growing, sending hot spikes down his arms, across his back, through his shoulders. "That sonofabitch, that Godamned asshole. We'll see who's gonna pay whose ass back." He slapped the desk as his voice rose, causing Dumbass to run from underneath, face-first into the closed door, and cower under a nearby chair.

"Dan?"

"I'm gonna find that sonofabitch. We'll see about payback."

"Danny? Danny, don't you go anywhere. I'm on the way right now. You wait right there."

He slammed the phone, ran out the front door.

Dan climbed in the Suburban. As he turned the key, the backup camera showed LaDonna pulling behind him and stopping, her Blazer crossways blocking him. She got out, walked up, and slapped his window several times.

"Danny. Wait. Danny, you put this window down right now."

He lowered the window and looked past her at some invisible point in the distance. "I've got to go." His grip on the steering wheel distended his knuckles.

LaDonna reached in and grabbed his shirt collar. "No, you don't. You most assuredly do not have to go. You'll have to drag me with you to do it. You want that? You're not going anywhere right now."

Blank stare unbroken. Gravelly half-whisper. "I've got to do somethin'. You don't understand."

She bunched his collar in her fist, reached in, took his chin in her other hand. "You don't understand, Daniel Fenton Baker. You don't understand? It's about us, all of us."

He couldn't remember the last time she'd used his real name. Their wedding? Or, the morning after when he woke to see her standing naked before the full-length mirror on the motel room door and, with a giggle, say "Good morning, Mrs. Daniel Fenton Baker." The memories brought her face into focus, inches away.

"Listen, don't be a donkey's butt," she whispered. "Don't go hanging your balls out with a bullshit macho stunt we'll all be sorry for. I want you to follow me home right now. You hear me?" His breathing settled, the pains in his arms subsiding. He relaxed his grip on the steering wheel.

She stroked his cheek and released his collar, smoothing it against his windbreaker. "Now, I'm going to get in my car, turn that corner, and I'm going to drive to our house. And you're going to follow me. Yes?" She fixed her eyes on his, teacher to balky student.

Dan exhaled. "Okay. But we've gotta do somethin' 'bout this. We've gotta."

"We've got to go home now. Right?"

She drove halfway down the block and stopped. It was clear she was waiting for him. He backed out and moved in behind her, feeling like an errant child but very, very grateful.

While waiting for cross traffic at the highway, he slid his cell phone into the holder on the dashboard and scrolled to the National Weather Service. There it was, freeze tonight. He punched in the

Kilborn Flying Service number. He turned right, following LaDonna.

"Ron Joyce."

"Ronny. Dan. I know you're gonna call me in the mornin', but I'm a little nervous 'bout the weather. Saw it's supposed to freeze tonight.

What about sprayin'? Have you heard from Zeke?"

"Just got off the phone. He said he'd talked to Drake, and we're on for Sunday."

"Good. Supposed'ta have a week of rain startin' Monday afternoon or Tuesday. I don't want leaves on that cotton any later than Sunday. You understand how critical this is?"

"I know. I'm on it."

"Whose gonna fly it?"

"Not sure."

"Ronny, I want it to be you. Do I need to tell Zeke?"

"No, I'll make it happen. I'm sorry 'bout all this."

"You didn't do it, but thanks anyway."

1 4

Freddy was waiting as Drake pulled up to Stangle's Self Storage. "That damned Dan Baker has been pushing at my old man. We got to get him sprayed Sunday so I can move on," Drake said.

He watched as Freddy worked the rusty padlock and shoved the door up. It was one of twenty overhead doors in two long metal buildings facing a gravel driveway. There were smaller units on each end of the two buildings. Inside the Kilborn Aviation space was a collection of car parts, a busted propeller, a jumble of tools, and four large square plastic containers, called totes, in the back corner.

Drake began clearing away piles of rope and oil-soaked canvas from one of the containers. It looked like a giant collapsible water bottle in a frame of steel rods. He took a stubby black flashlight from his pocket and scanned the top of one of them as Freddy unloaded the forklift from the truck and rolled it in. The flashlight was almost too bright. Freddy had remembered it from the time Drake had spilled about a gallon of what looked and smelled like *Adios* defoliant on Archie during a mixing session. Freddy had gone back to the hangar after that and drew a sample from the tote. It was in the right people's hands.

"This one." Drake slapped the top of the tote. "Load it and get to the hangar. I gotta go. I'll see you out there tomorrow morning, so we can mix this shit." He pulled out of the gravel path between the buildings, spraying small stones that reminded Freddy of machine-gun fire as they struck the sides.

Freddy was relieved. He would not have to load the tote on the truck and take it to the airport. With Drake gone, it would be a matter of moving the container to another space at the end of the storage building, then switching labels.

Freddy took his cell phone out and dialed the Sheriff's private number. "This is Espinoza. He wants to mix this stuff tomorrow morning. He's gonna spray Baker's cotton Sunday."

"Have you loaded it in the truck yet?"

"Nope. I've got the lift right here. Kilborn left. He said he'd see me in the morning, so we're okay. I watched where he handled the totes, so we'll have a good set of prints. I'm wearing gloves loading and reloading."

"Good. We don't want to risk anything. Can you move those to the other unit without being spotted?"

"I'm there with the forklift. I'm going back for the truck and will make the transfer. There doesn't seem to be anybody around."

"Then if it works for you, go ahead and do it. How did the labels come out?"

"I'm pretty sure they'll be okay. I'm gonna make the transfer when I get those out of the other unit."

"What else can I do for you?"

"Nothing right now, sheriff. I appreciate your help."

Freddy walked back to the first unit, pulled the overhead door down, reset the padlock, and drove to the end unit. Above the two padlocks on the door was a sign, Holden County Sheriff's Office.

One tote, identical to the two Freddy had on the forklift, sat at the unit's front. A large handwritten card was temporarily taped to the top, **Texas Depart of Agriculture – JERROD**.

Freddy drove the forklift into the unit, removed the card, and replaced it with a copy of the tote's label, smoothed the blue and white label on the side. He rubbed the wrinkled corner with his thumb and stepped back. "Can't tell the difference," he said.

He moved the forklift under the replacement pallet, picked it up, lifted it to the truck bed. He raised the forks to fit in the slots in the bed, raised the forklift, chained it to the truck.

He drove to the airport hangar, raised the door, backed the truck in. By the time he'd finished, it was dark.

––––––––––

Dan was sitting with LaDonna at breakfast the next morning. He'd had a restless night, waking several times, uneasy, worrisome fear nudging him awake then following him back to sleep. He put his cell phone down after looking at the weather maps.

"It's Sunday. It's gotta be that way. We've got to get that defoliate on, so it'll knock those leaves off before the harvesters show up Monday. It worries me we're supposed to have these weather fronts with a lot of rain come through startin' late Monday.

LaDonna poured him another cup of coffee. "I talked to Janelle."

"Did she change her phone number?"

"No, Rob showed her how to block Drake's calls."

"Good. How's school?"

"She did well on her quarterlies. They have almost a whole week off beginning next Tuesday."

"They?"

"This was cute. Rob actually got on the phone. He said he hoped he hadn't done any damage because of his set-to with Drake."

Dan spread grape jelly on the second piece of toast. "He doesn't have anything to apologize for as far as I'm concerned."

"I told him that. But he insisted. He said he hoped we'd invite him back sometime. I told him he's welcome for Thanksgiving if he doesn't have any plans. He said thank you over and over and over. It was good to hear Janelle laughing in the background.

"When she got back on the phone, she whispered, 'can we use the Grandma House again?' I said yes to that, too. It's kind of romantic."

She got up to take the dishes to the sink. Dan slapped her backside as she passed.

LaDonna smiled and pointed at him. "Now, that's not romantic."

Dan's cell phone vibrated. *Jerrod Citizen* on the ID. "Hey Jack, how ya doin'?" He listened as he stood and poured the last cup from the coffee maker. "I guess that's not surprisin'. What's a criminal referral exactly?"

"Knowles said Russ Jenkins sent a letter to the Breckenridge district attorney asking that Archie's death be considered a criminal matter. That was because the medical examiner had found the death was due to suspicious circumstances."

"What happens now?" Dan asked. "When will we know who's named in the letter?" *Bet I can guess.*

The newspaper editor said he understood that it would be up to the DA, who would conduct her investigation and then refer it to Mose Britten for action.

"How long's this gonna take?"

Knowles said he had no idea but was chasing some squirrels. He asked Dan to let him know if he found out anything before the coming Tuesday when the paper went to bed again.

———————

Dan stopped by the post office and then drove to the store. JerriSue was already in.

"Guess you heard?" She handed him the *Jerrod Citizen* as he walked by.

"Heard? Oh yeah. Don't know much about it, though."

"I know somebody . . ."

It hit him that off-handed suggestion irritated him. He jammed his fists in his denim pockets. "Damnit, JerriSue, exactly what does that mean? It sounds like one of those gangster shows on television, where somebody is hired to 'rub somebody out.' That's not what you mean, is it?"

JerriSue looked up and grinned crookedly. Dan had forgotten about her solid gold incisor. "Oh, hell no, boss. I meant I know somebody who knows stuff. You need to chill."

Dan felt the moisture return to his mouth. He sat on the stool next to JerriSue's desk. "Who? Who knows what?"

"I can't help you with that, but this might be a clue." She opened her middle drawer, raised the pencil holder, took out an envelope with the county attorney's return address top left. SENSITIVE, OFFICIAL USE ONLY was rubber-stamped in the middle. Dan turned the envelope over. It had been opened and taped closed.

"Enjoy." She turned, moved her mouse around until a spreadsheet appeared on the monitor. Her signal the conversation was over.

There it was in turgid legal prose, two paragraphs dripping with legalese. It appeared to be a request from the 113th District Attorney to

Sheriff Mose Britten for information that might lead to filing criminal charges in Archie's death.

The verbiage thicket and ended with ". . . our entreaty that this request for assistance from the Office of the Sheriff of Holden County be executed with all deliberate alacrity as relevant authorities and precedents and the criminal code of the Sovereign State of Texas allow." In other words, get on it.

He was trying to decide what to do with the sheaf of papers when his cell phone buzzed.

Spray Sunday. Call

Dan called Ronny's number. "Hey, Ronny. I figured it was gonna work this way. What time?"

"I checked with the Abilene weather site. Looks like we're gonna be calm all the way through noon. I want to get on it first thing Sunday, say seven-thirty? Looks like we're gonna have a slight dew after four A.M. Should be clear after then."

"How long's it gonna take?"

"Lemme see," Dan heard sounds of papers being shuffled. "Yeah, here it is, a quarter section on your South Place. Last time I figured a hundred-seventy-five gallons.

"Lemme see," Dan heard sounds of papers being shuffled. "Yeah, here it is, a quarter section on your South Place. Last time I figured 175 gallons. I'd say forty-five minutes to an hour flyin' time tops."

Dan hadn't crossed his fingers in a long time, until now. "You're flyin' this, right? Tell me you're flyin' this. Ronny? Yes? You are, right?"

"Hang on." The sound of the phone being rubbed on cloth. Muted voices. "Yeah, I'm doin' it. Zeke called me while ago."

"That's a relief. Am I interruptin' somethin'?"

"No, no, I was talkin' to Freddy. Yeah, I could see how it would be a relief to *you*. I gotta watch out for Drake, though. He went stormin' out of the office and drove off a while ago after Zeke spoke to him. I heard them arguing about a gun Drake had been carrying around. It was spooky, Dan. Drake said he was gonna talk it over with his mother. I felt sorry for Zeke standin' there looking at the shut door."

Dan let the silence settle in. He wanted to change the subject. "So, I'll be out at the south place Sunday mornin'. Will that work?"

"Yeah," Dan said, "that will be okay. Freddy will meet you out there. He'll set up the perimeter flags and have a two-way with him and will check my pattern. I think I can make clean passes if I stay right on the deck."

"OK, Ronny. Thanks for callin' and settin' this up. I know it ain't easy for you out there."

"Lot simpler up there," Ronny chuckled. "See ya Sunday."

Dan looked at the legal document on the desk, pushed it with his index finger. He was about to pick it up and throw it in the metal trash can when his cell phone buzzed again.

On the caller ID, *Holden County*. "Hey, Jimmy."

"What's on your mind, young man?"

"Legal shit."

"What can I tell you?"

"What happens next with Archie's case? How long will it take the DA to do something?"

"How'd you find out? Never mind. This place leaks like a two-day-old diaper. Jennings, the county attorney, told me he'd talked to the 113th District DA, and she decided to deputize him so he can proceed with the case locally."

"When does all this start to happen?"

"When Jennings says it does. I suspect he's going to take his time. You're welcome to contact him, Dan, but I promise you he won't discuss the case with you. He may come off a little disheveled and unkempt, but he has a first-class legal mind and will do this by the book."

"That works for me. Thanks, Your Honor."

"' Your Honor.' my ass. You outta run for this office, then I'll call and give you a ration of shit."

"No, it's too much fun the other way 'round. Glad you got to talk to me."

"Oh, sure. Hanging up now."

15

D rake arrived at the airport about nine the next morning. He pulled the company truck out of the hangar, drove it under the overhead horizontal tank beside the long metal building.

Drake put on a full-face respirator with a long tube connected to a battery-powered blower on the back of his belt. He climbed up on the truck bed, unscrewed the cap on the horizontal tank, and put a long hose in.

Ronny Joyce pulled up beside the hangar and got out of his car. From the look on his face, he seemed surprised to see Drake handling the mixing equipment. He gave Drake a small wave.

Drake nodded, picked up the respirator, attached the hose to the back, put it on. He reached around and flipped the switch on the blower.

Freddy knew all he could do was watch. He'd been briefed on proper procedure for mixing the full-strength defoliant with water, and Drake wasn't following it. But Freddy had moved about twenty feet away in case of a spill. He continued to watch Drake's every move as

Ronny walked up beside him.

"What the fuck is he doing?" Ronny asked. Freddy shrugged.

Drake hooked the hose to a small pump, then opened the cap on the tote and shoved in the hose leading from the pump. He paused, bent down to read the label. Freddy held his breath a moment as Drake ran his finger across the label, paused at the corner Freddy had fixed. Drake rubbed the corner down, turned to look at Freddy, expecting Drake to pull the respirator off and ask embarrassing questions. Instead, he turned on the pump.

It took him several minutes to move the concentrate up into the tank. Drake reached up to the cutoff valve on the tank and then jumped to the ground. "Okay, you can unhook. I want to take Number One up. Is it topped off?"

"It's topped off, but the dispenser tank is dry. What are you gonna spray?" Freddy eavesdropped any time Zeke and Drake were at the airport at the same time. More than once, he'd heard violent arguments between the two about Drake's excessive joyriding. It never seemed to make any difference.

Ronny said, "Drake, wait a minute. What are you doing? Do we have a job I don't know about?"

"Nothin', a check ride." He walked over to the grey and white Agwagon with a large number 1 on the fuselage, pulled the blue tarp off the cockpit, lifted the plane's tail, and walked it onto the taxiway. Still ignoring Ronny and Freddy, he did a preflight check and climbed into the cockpit. He ran the engine up, taxied out onto the runway, took off.

As he pulled up and away, Freddy said, "Strange duck."

Ronny smirked. "Yep, drakes are known to be hostile."

"Loners, too. 'Specially if they're not getting any."

Dan pushed the half-empty bowl of stew to the center of the table. "Okay, pastor, I've got one of those heavy theological questions for you."

"All ears." Wyman pushed his stew away and sipped at his coffee.

"Callin' on my considerable skills as a psychoanalyst, I'd say Drake Kilborn is goin' bat-shit crazy."

"Hmm. Thoughtful analysis, Dr. Freud. 'Bat-shit crazy.' Is that in the textbooks anywhere?"

"Should be—no kiddin'. Drake was a highly motivated young man with a future until his mother's death. Then, almost overnight, this demon shows up in his clothes, drivin' his car, flyin' his airplanes. Best I can tell, he fits the day-to-day definition of evil."

Wyman cleared away the cornbread debris and stabbed at the cold brown beans. "*Evil* is a tough call. Anything we don't understand, 'specially if it runs counter to our faith or our perception of a 'good' life, is in and of itself evil. The Old Testament had said pigs were evil . . ."

Dan formed a pistol with the thumb and forefinger of his right hand and pointed it at a smoke-stained landscape on the opposite wall.

"Yep, they're sure evil enough 'round here."

Wyman continued. "So, Jesus and his boys put demonic spirits in them and shooed them over a cliff. Jews flunked the evilness test during the Inquisition. They were set on fire for their refusal to get in step with Torquemada."

"But, if there's no explanation for the kind of behavior that keeps on regardless of its bad impact on others, isn't that evil?" Dan drained the last of his weak tea.

Wyman ran his finger down his glass then pushed it aside. "You know, I think I've got a handle on good versus evil, then that idiot murders seventeen innocent kids. I have to ask myself, what in the hell —

and I use that word advisedly — are we supposed to believe? Don't tell me that guy wasn't evil. If he wasn't, what does it take to hang that tag on someone who willy-nilly kills all those young people?

"We don't know what has gone through a head like that until after the fact. There is evil. It is in not knowing the danger we face as a civilization, whether it's the psychotic shooter or a rogue politician.

And know what, my friend? Not a damned thing we can do about it."

Wyman looked toward the door. "You gotta tell me if I'm shouting. This really mashes all my buttons." He leaned forward in his chair, lowering his voice. "It's that we backward-collar types get nervous when people start asking us how a good God and an evil spray plane pilot or mass murderer can co-exist in the world. We don't like the idea of a God who's not in charge of everything. Kinda makes it seem He created evil and allows it to prosper."

"Tough call in a Sunday mornin' sermon.

"I hope to tell you."

"Makes it tough for you to put a happy face on that graveside service comin' up tomorrow."

Wyman smiled. "Let me tell you a little inside-the-pulpit secret. All the ministers I know, regardless of the color of their suede shoes, hate funeral services. They are expected to put a belt and suspenders on the same tired clichés you've heard forever. Everything happens for a reason. God works in mysterious ways. She-slash-he is at peace now. It is God's will. Blah, blah, blah."

Wyman threw his napkin in his empty bowl. "My best friend from seminary preached my wife's funeral. I made him promise beforehand to lay off the clichés and talk about Margaret and her faith, family, and friends. He did it and got a bunch of complaints that he wasn't caring enough, that he didn't comfort the family enough.

"You know, Dan? This was one of those times I was glad we didn't have kids. I couldn't imagine trying to explain why the Holy Spirit decided it was time for a good, unselfish, always happy woman to succumb after such pronounced pain."

Dan leaned his chair back. "Okay then. Now I know what'll be goin' through your skull tomorrow."

"Assuming anything is. You know, it's really kind of stressful, trying to say and do something positive for the family, not knowing if you're hitting the mark or not. I hate to say it, but I kinda put myself on cruise for these things. They have a rhythm of their own. It starts with prayer, then Bible reading, words about the deceased, words about his faith—whether or not he had any—words about his family, prayer, amen."

Dan rubbed his forehead. "And now, on a lighter note, what you got planned for tomorrow night?"

"Nothing much. Hospital visit, review sermon, drink a couple of beers, force myself to stop at three pieces of pepperoni pizza with mushrooms and black olives. You know, like that. Got a better idea?"

"I hope so. How 'bout steak and baked potatoes at our place? You bring the beer and – wait for it – a guest if you have anybody in mind. Hint, hint."

"You're gonna force me to say *who,* aren't you?"

"Naw, don't have to force you. I think it's pretty clear by now."

"What makes you think she would be free?" "Easy enough to find out. Call her."

"Call who?" Wyman's grin was extra broad.

"Call Ella, for God's sake. You two are gonna have to work on sneakiness."

"One more thing." Wyman looked around and lowered his voice.

"Do you have a vacancy for two in your Grandma House?"

Dan almost tipped his chair over as he laughed. "Whoa. Speakin' of evil. Guess it's better than the Ridge Motel in Breckenridge."

Wyman blushed. "Now come on. How'd you know?"

"Guessed."

Wyman gripped Dan's hand. "Thanks for being my confessor, Dan. I'd get you some extra indulgences if that was in my job description."

16

D an helped Charlie Weathers load new tractor tires in the Galaxy Farms truck. As he was climbing back into the cab, he asked,

"Dan, you're friends with Zeke Kilborn. Know his kid?"

"Why?"

"We've had them spray for bindweed, defoliation, and such several times. Always got good service outta them, but . . ."

"But what, Charlie?" *I don't want to hear any more Drake stories, please.*

"I got out to the farm 'bout ten this mornin', piddling around, not doing much of anything. I'm sitting there in my pickup beside one of those wind generators when all of a sudden, I thought the tower was fallin'. Then, the noise passed, and I realized it was comin' from overhead.

"I looked up, and sure enough, one of Kilborn's spray planes was about a hundred feet overhead, banked hard before it would'a hit the wind tower.

"It finally leveled off at, I'd say a thousand feet, and then the strangest thing, it started circlin', big lazy circles. It did that for maybe five minutes, then turned and flew north, toward town, I guess."

Dan stood and brushed his hands together. "Yeah, I know. They got problems."

Charlie started the truck. "I know it wasn't Zeke. He told me he wasn't flyin' any more. I know it wasn't Ronny 'cause I had coffee with him before I went out there. It could only be . . ."

"Drake."

"That his name? I couldn't remember."

"Yep. It was him. Hard to figure that out."

"Hope he doesn't kill somebody. Damned near hit that tower. Coulda hit me."

"Yeah, I hope not too." Dan realized it was the first time anyone had said anything about Drake killing anyone. He realized it was only Charlie talking, but the possibility nagged at him.

Charlie slipped the truck into reverse and began to inch backward. "I better go. We're supposed to have a 'conference call' – Charlie made air quotes – "with all the Galaxy managers in 'bout an hour. Those idiots love to hear themselves talk and want to make sure us peons love to listen." Charlie adjusted his outside mirror.

"Livin' the dream, Charlie. Just livin' the dream." Dan waved as Charlie backed out of the driveway.

———————

Mazie Medders had to get away from the noisy drunks and shouting mother and needed a cigarette in the worst way. She bundled sleepy H.D. into the baby carrier, drove to the Zip Stop Mart. It was where she and Archie had gone for subsistence groceries, snacks, beer, and lottery tickets. The clerk was their casual Somali acquaintance Osman Ali, thin as a telephone pole, black as asphalt.

"Ah, Mazie girl. I am so regretfully saddened that I know of your sweet man's death. It is a sad time for all we persons. The Archie man was a good strong fella, full of love and happy laughter."

Mazie put H.D.'s carrier on the floor, stood on tiptoes to see her favorite brand of cigarettes in the bottom of the rack behind the counter. "Thanks, Alley. We're missin' him too. Gonna put him to rest Saturday mornin'. Hope you can come to the service at the cemetery." Osman put two packs on the counter.

Mazie pushed one back. "No, Alley, I only got 'nuf for one."

"It is not a severe problem at all, Mazie. That is memory present from me. For the good Archie."

Mazie sniffed back a tear, left H.D. in his carrier, and stepped to the nearby cooler for a half-gallon of milk and a dozen eggs. She put them on the counter and began to dig in her purse.

Ali waved an elongated hand, his fingers shaking like windblown reeds. "No, Miss Mazie, this is memory, too."

The door chime signaled another customer. Ali looked up from sacking Mazie's groceries. "A moment, sir, if you will. I am being with you quickly."

Drake Kilborn walked past the beef jerky display, pushed the door on the popcorn machine shut. He stepped up behind Mazie, eyeing the sleeping H.D. "Goddamn if that ain't the ugliest baby I've ever seen.

I'm gonna have to tell momma 'bout this. I gotta check my watch to see if that bundle of fat slowed it down." He leaned over, about to poke his finger in the gurgling infant's chest.

Mazie turned, palms forward, and shuffled toward him like a windup toy. "What did you say? You talkin' 'bout my baby?" She moved forward, matching Drake's retreat step for step. Having backed him to the chips-and-dips display, she bent over as if retrieving something from the grease-slick floor, brought her pudgy fist full force up under his chin, buckling his knees.

He made a soft puffing noise and waved his arms in half circles as his eyes rolled back, scattering sacks of Spicy and Crunchy Cheetos, Flamin' Hot Doritos, and small cans of bean dip. His eyes fluttered and closed. He rested on his back, mouth agape, spittle mixed with blood oozing from one corner.

Ali was stock still, a life-sized smiling cardboard display, his eyes moving from Mazie to Drake and back.

Mazie leaned over, thumbed one of Drake's eyelids open, and wiped her hands on his flowered western shirt. "Alley, if you don't mind, I'm gonna get one more thing." She massaged the reddening knuckles of her right hand.

Wide-eyed, Ali continued to smile, audibly swallowing.

She walked over to the beverage dispenser, filled a thirty-two ounce cup to the brim with sugary pink liquid, went to Drake's twitching form, and emptied it on his face.

He shook his head like a dog climbing out of a pond, showering everything near his resting place with a sticky coat of lemonade-zero real juice. He looked up at Mazie and raised his hands defensively.

She leaned over her short bulbous nose a foot from his face. "Archie always said you was an asshole, and now I see why, you miserable piece of shit. Don't you get up outta yer little nest there 'til I get out that door." She walked back to the counter and grabbed the two sacks Ali was holding at arm's length. She hefted the carrier with the still sleeping H.D. and started toward the door.

She called over her shoulder as she reached the grease-stained glass door covered with cigarette ads and promises of wealth from the Texas

Lottery, "We square, Alley?"

He looked up from scooping the scattered bags together, avoiding Drake, who appeared to be trying to make sense of the water stains on the ceiling tiles. "Oh, yes and certainly, Miss Mazie. My absolute condolences of sorrow on all of you."

Turning to make sure she was gone, Drake regained his footing after skidding on two bags of pretzels. He rubbed his swelling jaw and fumbled in his sticky shirt pocket for his lemonade-stained dark glasses. He left the store without looking back at Ali, whose smile remained fixed.

Drake slid into his car after failing to dry himself with a handful of paper towels from above the window-washing fluid tank between two of the gas pumps. He shut the door and rubbed his jaw. "Momma, they're gonna be sorry for this. I'm right, aren't I?"

17

————

A s Drake sped away, Freddy fell in at an anonymous distance. He'd gotten a call from the Holden Sheriff's Office because Drake had been seen prowling the area near the apartment house but had driven away when he spotted the cruiser. The deputy saw him again walking into the Zip In. It was on Freddy's way to Tomas Ascencio's trailer, so he decided to spot up.

He followed for several blocks until Drake pulled into Zeke's driveway. Freddy selected a contact on his phone and texted *down for the night*

He was going to eat with Tomas and his wife. He was happy to see Tomas' sister Mariel had been invited.

Pozole, sopa de enchiladas, carnitas, and *maíz dulce* were on the menu. He knew pozole and the enchilada soup from his Valley upbringing, but the fried sweet corn with butter and spices blew him away. He went on and on about the corn, telling Tomas's blushing wife he had to have the recipe. She looked at Tomas, snickered, pointed to Mariel.

After eating, they moved into the living room area at the end of the trailer. The conversation drifted from politics to football and back to politics. Over the hour, Mariel made a point of getting up to get Freddy another *Osa Negra*. When she handed it to him and sat next to him on the love seat, Tomas winked at his wife.

The Ascencio's daughter Bea came in to say good night and stared at Freddy from under her father's arm. She whispered in his ear while pointing at Freddy.

"She wants to know if you're spending the night. No, Bea, he's a friend of Mariel's. Go shake hands with him."

The little girl walked over to Freddy and held out her tiny hand.

"My name is Beatriz Mariel Ascencio, and I'm almost five years old. Most everybody calls me Bea." Freddy took her tiny hand and moved it up and down carefully. She looked back to Tomas for approval.

"Bea, I'm happy to meet you. My name is Federic Alberto Paz Espinoza."

"That's a very long name for Freddy."

Freddy looked into the smiling child's eyes, glanced at Mariel. "Sometimes I use my whole name for pretty girls like you and *tu tia*." Freddy glanced at Mariel, her head tilted to one side, eyebrows up.

The child hugged Mariel, who kissed her forehead. *"Buena noches, mi preciosa."* The little girl stole one more glance at Freddy before scampering down the hall. He waved at her with three fingers.

About nine o'clock, Freddy's phone vibrated. It was Mose Britten.

He stepped out onto the deck. "You set up for in the morning?"

"Yeah, I switched them over yesterday. The evidence is in storage. Drake mixed and loaded the good ones this morning."

"What time?"

"I'll be out there 'bout six. I want to make sure Ronny is going to be in the cockpit."

"You expect any problems out of young Mr. Kilborn?"

"Don't think so. From what Ronny Joyce tells me, Drake's father laid down the law. He made sure Drake understood Ronny was going to do the spraying."

"Guess there's no way to keep him from showin' up at the airport, trying to mess things up?"

"No . . ."

Mariel opened the trailer house door a crack.

"Yeah, thanks a lot, ma'am. It's good to talk to you too. I hope it all works out for you, too."

"Oh. Understood," Britten said. "We'll talk tomorrow."

"Good idea." Freddy put the phone in his pocket and reached for the door. Mariel was standing inside. She had put her coat on and was searching her purse for keys, indicating she wasn't going back into the trailer.

While she was looking in her purse, in a whisper and without looking up, "You want that recipe?"

"What . . . Oh y-y-y-yeah," he stuttered, "I'd really like to get it from you. I'll call you in a couple of days." He assumed she was leaving as she stepped by him out onto the deck. *Did she brush against me?*

She took her keys out of her purse and held them up to the porch light as if making sure she had the right one, then lowered her head, so she appeared to be looking at him from under her eyebrows. "I don't see anything wrong with you following me to my apartment right now, so I can, uh, give it to you. That is if you don't have anything else to do."

Freddy hoped she couldn't see the blush coming on his light brown skin. "Ah, yeah. I could, I mean, I will do that. Definitely do that."

He stuck his head in the trailer door as Mariel walked down the two steps to her car. "Hey, thanks for everything, Tomas, and I mean everything. Guess I'm going."

"Yeah, looks like you are. *Buena suerte,*" Tomas' wife tittered. "Enjoy the *maiz.*" She and Tomas were laughing as Freddy closed the door and headed toward his car.

At the Prairie Vista Apartments, he followed Mariel up the stairs. She stepped inside and made a fast scan up and down the block. She shut the door, closed the curtain, switched the porch light off, and hung her coat in a small closet next to the door.

She turned to him, smiling like a six-year-old who'd learned a secret. "You're a cop, right? Federico Alberto Paz *Espinoza*? Really?"

"What? Uh, did Tomas tell you?"

"Nope. Our uncle is police in Uvalde. I know how they talk, somewhere between interrogating and interviewing, not a lot different from getting the truth out of a sixth-grader."

"That obvious, huh?"

"A hunch based on the conversation during dinner. And using your real name . . . now, about that recipe." She kicked off her Nikes and moved close to him. "What kind of police are you?"

"The busy kind." He held her by her shoulders a moment. "You're a teacher, right? What are the neighborhood gossips gonna say?"

"All us gossips in this neighborhood, upstairs and downstairs, are single teachers. You might say we have an unspoken apartment agreement. What happens in the Prairie Vista Apartments . . ."

". . . stays in the Prairie Vista Apartments," Freddy observed.

"Right." She moved close to him. "Now about that recipe?"

He lifted her chin and kissed her with the passion borne of months of loneliness and charade.

Their time in her *Tabu*-scented bed seemed to last only minutes. Over the two hours, they paused their love-making two or three times to assure each other of the rightness of what they were doing. Before they had begun undressing each other, she had opened the bathroom door, reached in, and turned on a soft blue nightlight.

Now, as they lay in the bed, her head on his arm, came intimacy made awkward by silence.

"How was the recipe?" She got up on one elbow and traced her finger down his nose.

He closed his eyes and smiled. "Going through my checklist here. Humm. Let's see." He looked over at her. "That's unusual."

"Unusual?"

"I generally don't like trying new—you know—recipes."

"I hope you found it to your liking."

"No stomachache so far."

"I certainly hope not." She kissed him once more, rolled out of bed, and walked toward the bathroom.

Her blue-rimmed silhouette in the doorway was remarkable. That was the only word he could think of. No deep-culture *palabras de amor*, no timeworn high school Tex-Mex cliché, instead, an old Gringo standby. He laid back onto the silken sheets redolent of her, them, and the Tabu. Remarkable. It was re-fucking-markable.

As she closed the bathroom door, he glanced at the digital clock.

Twelve fifteen. What was that saying about time flying when you're having fun? Fun? It was clear in his mind that *fun* was a small part of what had happened.

He sat on the bedside and waited for her to come out of the bathroom before getting dressed. He stood and embraced her.

"Look. I don't want to go."

"But you have to."

"I do. If tomorrow, er, today, wasn't so important in my job, believe me, I'd stay and stay and stay some more."

"I know. I believe you. You'll have to come back. I've got a large recipe collection, some newer than others."

He laughed as he pulled on his pants, shirt, and boots. "I can imagine." He stood and kissed her once more, then led her to the living room. "Okay. I'm going. Look, do me a favor, turn off this overhead light, and don't stand in the door when I open it."

"Cop stuff, huh?"

"Something like that. I'll call. Maybe for Saturday night?"

She smiled and made an exaggerated shrug. "Never can tell. Tomas knows a lot of single *hombres*."

"Maybe *chicos solteros*."

"*Si*, I have to admit you're right," she said, tapping the button on his jacket pocket.

Freddy let his hand move down from her wrist, savoring the life pulsing beneath. "Hey, I got a question. We met once at church, then I said hello when I was putting that A-V equipment in your classroom. I've seen you a couple of times around town, but how did you know I was, like, okay to get involved with?"

"Several things. For one, there's *church*. I've seen you there more than once. That tells me you're worth knowing. You believe in something besides yourself. Even if we bent the rules about no sex before marriage here tonight, and who knows, might again, the church is important to me. It has a strong place in my life."

"And?"

"And I watched you with little Bea tonight. There was a genuine appreciation for her in your eyes. That's big for me.

"Now, we got to go to bed – separate beds." She stood on her toes and kissed him again.

He went down the long stairway two steps at a time to the parking lot. He felt good about the night with Mariel. And, he felt like his work was almost finished in Jerrod.

The sound of a growling engine made Freddy turn around. It was Drake's Mustang, sitting in a faint halo of exhaust vapor, parking lights only. Freddy could see him in the instrument panel glow. He walked to the driver's side of the car and bent down. Drake was staring straight ahead.

Freddy tapped on the window. Drake turned his head as if it were mounted on windup clockwork. *There are those dark glasses again*. That sent a chill down Freddy's back.

Drake lowered the driver's window halfway. "What?" Then, blinding light. It was the piercing blue he'd first seen when they loaded the totes from Mexico into the King Air 200 on the dirt landing strip fifty miles north of Del Rio.

That night, Drake had used the Shadowhawk flashlight to signal a pickup truck carrying four nervous *trabajadores*. They'd worked with drug shipments from Mexico before, but none of the *gringos* had been stupid enough to flash a light back and forth. The men grumbled in Spanish that the gringo's piercing blue light could be seen for miles in the desert night.

They had grunted and sweated over the two heavy plastic tanks in rod cages for twenty minutes. Drake persuaded the overloaded King Air, a Vietnam veteran, into the air at sunrise, Freddy in the right seat. When they made a refueling stop at Lampasas, Freddy made a phone call that ran interference for the rest of the trip, but those days were over.

Freddy covered his eyes with his left forearm. "Turn that fucking thing off, dammit. What the hell are you thinking?"

Drake turned the light off and threw the unit into the passenger seat.

Freddy leaned toward the driver's window and scanned down, looking for a weapon. He looked at Drake. "What the hell are you doing here?"

"Visitin'."

Freddy leaned into the window slamming his open hands on the door, causing Drake to jerk back. "*Visitin'* who? Don't bullshit me, Drake. She doesn't want anything to do with you."

"Who doesn't want anything to do with me?"

Freddy looked at his watch and then turned it so Drake could see the digital display. "You got two minutes."

"Or what? I outta fire you."

"Yeah, go ahead. Fire my ass. See who'll fix those wrecks of yours then." Freddy stood, zipped his jacket up, and stared at Drake. He had spotted the scanner mounted under the dash and thought he'd seen a pistol grip on the floor at the end of the passenger seat.

Drake faced the steering wheel and sat, hands at ten and two. He stared into the distance, willing Freddy to walk away. Without looking at Freddy or bothering to raise the window, he crept forward. "What do you think he's doin' here, mom? He's trouble."

Freddy watched the Mustang leave the parking lot, turn right, and then left at the next street. *The way to Zeke's house?* Freddy hoped so. He reported his encounter with Drake to the dispatcher and asked him to send a patrol during the night shift. He reminded the dispatcher of the protective, described the Mustang, gave the plate number.

18

E arly the next morning, the Ag-wagon was parked under the overhead tank. Drake ran a hose from it to the plane's cargo tank and drained the liquid into it.

They walked the plane onto the taxiway. Freddy could feel Drake's eyes on his back. He breathed in, relaxed his shoulders, and walked over to his car. "Ronny, I'm goin' out to the Baker's field. I got the twoway right here." He took the small radio with a stubby antenna off his dashboard.

"Com check." Ronny leaned over into the cockpit and brought out the throat mike. He reached back in and threw a switch.

"How copy?

"Good. How me?"

"Good." His voice on the radio registered down to a whisper. "You headed out now?"

"Roger."

"I've got to go through my pre-flight. Should be wheels-up in about twenty minutes. I'll check in when I get leveled off."

"Roger. Be safe today. Out."

Ronny jumped from the wing and began his walk-around. He stopped behind the rudder and nodded toward the hangar.

Freddy put his radio on standby and looked at the open door. Drake was standing inside it. He was waving a small flashlight back and forth, the beam playing around the interior. Then, he stopped, aimed the beam under his chin, smiled, flashed it at Freddy, turned it off, and walked to the back of the hangar.

After placing boundary flags at each end of the field, Freddy stopped his car behind Dan's Suburban on the edge of the cotton field.

Dan got out and walked to Freddy's car. "You gonna be spottin' for Ronny? It is Ronny, right?"

Freddy pointed to the radio. "Yep, he'll let me know when he's inbound. Should be any time now. Guess you're ready to get this done."

Dan looked toward the field. "You can't imagine."

"*Bet I can*," Freddy thought. As he was getting out of his car, his two-way squawked.

"Kilborn Two inbound."

"Ten-four. We're parked on the north side." Freddy shaded his eyes with his right hand. The low buzzing of the spray plane was barely at hearing range. Then, a speck came up above the eastern horizon.

Dan retrieved his binoculars off his dashboard and looked east. "I can see him." He pointed to the east.

Freddy keyed the two-way. "We gotcha."

"Roger. I'm gonna make a dry pass. Let me know if I need to correct."

"Will do. Flags are out."

The two-way squawked. "I see them. Comin' around."

The plane banked to the north in a shallow climb, then turned around and leveled off.

"Here goes."

The plane cleared the electrical line on the border of the cotton field. It rose what seemed to be two or three feet, cleared the line, and dropped to ten feet above the ground.

It followed the edge of the field until almost disappearing in the south before it rose, banked sharply, and headed toward them. Ronny's voice blended with the motor noise. "Okay. I got it. Gettin' ready for the pass. No wind, so I'm gonna fly it on from the north."

Freddy got in his car and headed toward Dan. "We're movin'."

There was a moment of static. "Okay. I'm clear. On the way."

The plane flew two miles north, climbed, turned back south, and dropped close to the earth. As it topped the electrical line, a shower of blue liquid began cascading out of the piping below the wing's trailing edge. The plane paralleled the fence line southward, almost out of sight before climbing and lining up for the next pass. This time, two wingspans away from the fence.

Ronny finished the pass, made his climbing turn to the north, leveled off. Freddy's radio squawked.

"What the hell?"

Freddy looked at Dan. They both strained to hear Ronny over the engine noise. "Say again, Ronny."

"Look ninety degrees. It's Number One."

Dan raised his binoculars. There was a growing speck on the same track Ronny had used earlier. He looked at Freddy. "Another plane?" Freddy shielded his eyes. There it was, growing in the east. No mistake. It was the other Kilborn spray plane. Freddy keyed the radio.

"Ronny, what's goin' on?"

"Damned if I know."

Ronny had decided not to make another pass but started making a long figure eight about 500 feet up, two miles away. "I'll go to the other frequency. See what the hell's goin' on. Stand by."

After about ten seconds, "He's not respondin' on 128.5. See if you can raise him."

"Roger." Freddy changed the radio's digital display. "Kilborn One, this is Paz. Over."

There were two clicks, signaling *I hear you but not responding.* Number One was visible to the east in a steep climb. It spiraled upward until it was no bigger than a thumb. Then, it was over Baker's cotton field flying downward in a slow, lazy circle. Freddy switched to the original frequency.

Even through the electronic haze, there was an edge to Ronny's voice. "Freddy? What did he say?"

"Nothin'. Two clicks."

"Crap. I don't know what to do. I didn't top off before I left."

"Stand by."

"Not for long."

"Gotcha." Freddy changed the frequency again. "Kilborn One, do you want to declare an emergency?" He took his thumb off the transmit button and looked at Dan. "I hope that'll wake him up."

Dan lifted his binoculars and followed Kilborn One as it leveled off.

Freddy could see the tension in Dan's jaw muscles. Freddy spoke into the radio, summoning a matter-of-fact tone. "Drake? What are you doin'? Do you need help?"

"Me and Mommy are on a merry-go-round. Havin' fun."

Freddy's voice rose. "Drake, you know this ain't right."

"Fun."

Freddy turned to Dan. "What do we do?"

Dan tracked the circling plane and then glanced at Ronny's plane, making figure eights in the distance.

"Dan?"

He realized Freddy was trying to get his attention. He shifted his focus. "Sorry. Now, what?" He dropped his binoculars.

"Can you video on your cell phone?"

"I think." Dan dug it out of the top pocket of his coveralls and looked at the screen. "Yep, there it is." He aimed the phone at Drake's plane.

Freddy pressed *send*. "Drake, you're a safety hazard right now. You keep this up, and I gotta call the FAA. You know that."

"Oh, okay. Have it your way, you meanie. We're goin' back. Mommy's tired, anyway," followed by loud, cackling laughter. Number One made one circle, leveled off, and turned east. "Bye, everybody."

Freddy swiveled his head, trying to ease the tension in his neck. He changed frequency on the two-way. "Ronny?"

"Yep?"

"You hear all that? He's leavin'."

"I heard. I've only got enough fuel now for one pass."

Dan pocketed his cell phone and was watching Drake's disappearing plane.

"Good. Uh, Ronny, when you go back, give him time to land and to get the hell away. Hard to tell what he'll do if you confront him."

"Yeah, all right. Hope nobody's monitorin' this frequency. Starting now."

Ronny made the circuit and disappeared to the east. Freddy and Dan leaned against the Suburban.

"Did you get all that?"

Dan looked at his phone. "I think so. Lemme check." He pulled the phone from his pocket and watched the video. He showed his phone to Freddy.

There it was, the moving image of the plane in a tight bank above the cotton field, Kilborn Aviation and Number One visible. "What do you want to do with this?"

Freddy scratched his chin with his forefinger. "Nothin' right now. We need to have it in case . . ."

"In case of what?"

Freddy turned and looked out over the cotton field. "In case."

19

When Drake landed Number One, he left it on the runway as soon as he could stop. He cut the engine, climbed off the wing, and left the plane sitting on the asphalt, halfway down the 2000-foot strip.

Almost to the hangar, looked behind him. "Mommy, did you like the ride? We showed 'em, didn't we? Did you like the merry-go-round?" A slight breeze arose, and he spun around. "Mommy, where are you now? Are you hiding?"

Drake landed ten minutes ahead of Ronny and parked his plane across the runway. He broke into sneering laughter as he watched Ronny abort the landing and fly over Number One.

Drake slapped the Mustang's fender. "Wonder how you're gonna like landin' on the grass?" Drake started his car as Ronny repeated his original landing pattern. He had to put his plane down on the narrow grass strip between the runway and the border fence. Drake spun the car around and cleared the ground as he sped over the railroad crossing.

After refueling, Ronny's bright yellow Ag-Wagon made a dozen passes and then headed back to the east. The engine didn't mask the anger in his voice. "You guys are never gonna believe what just happened to me."

Freddy watched as Ronny headed for the eastern horizon. "What?"

"Not now. Out."

Dan climbed into his Suburban. Freddy walked up to the open driver's window.

"I guess I need to go see Zeke about this. He's gotta know." Dan closed his eyes tight and rubbed them with his thumb and forefinger.

Freddy could almost feel the fatigue in Dan's gesture. "Before somethin' worse happens."

Dan started his engine. "I'm damn sure it will. God, I feel sorry for Zeke."

"Yeah, and Archie, too."

"Absolutely." Dan started his engine. "Guess I'll see you guys at Logan's tomorrow morning. First time I've been a pallbearer in a while. Hope the weather holds." He pointed toward the northern horizon.

"Nothin' 'til Tuesday. Big rain comin', they say. Guess we got this done in time. The Brady brothers are supposed to strip this field Monday. Looks like everything will be all right for the service. See you tomorrow."

Freddy followed Dan toward Jerrod but turned to cross the tracks at the airport. Ronny was waiting at the front of the hangar, between the two spray planes parked inside.

Freddy got out of his car. "So, what happened?"

Ronny told him about having to land on the narrow grass border because Number One was parked across the runway. He parked his plane then used the stripped-down utility Jeep to tow Number One to the hangar.

"What are we goin' to do? Aren't we supposed to report this kinda thing to the FAA?"

Ronny took his gloves off and threw them onto the wing of Number Two. "Yeah, I could probably lose my license for not, but if I file a report, there'll be hell to pay around here." It was clear Ronny had memorized the regulations: "At least two charges, operating an aircraft in an unsafe manner to endanger the life of another pilot operating in the same area, and – this is as bad – purposefully interfering with the operation of a public airport by illegally denying access to a clearly marked, active, documented runway."

Freddy looked to the north and then to Ronny. "What would the Feds do when they get the report?"

"Shut this place down. It'll be crawlin' alive with FAA shirts and maybe Texas Rangers."

Freddy put on a look of mild shock. "Rangers?"

"Yep. Wouldn't be surprised."

Why? Let's see what you really know, thought Freddy.

"A hunch. They get involved in whatever they want to."

"Don't know much about that." Freddy shrugged. *Just wait,* he thought. "So, you gonna call the Feds?"

"No, I like Zeke. He's always been good to me. He hired me when I couldn't get anybody to talk to me. I owe him for that. I imagine he'll be callin' me, but I'd bet Dan Baker is already fillin' him in. They're buddies. He deserves a chance to help Zeke work this out."

"So, no cops in on this?"

"Nope. Let's see what happens. I've cleaned up the mess, so there's no evidence of any wrong doin'."

"What about Dan's video?" Freddy asked.

"What video?" Ronny stood and took a step toward Freddy. "What are you talkin' about?"

"He took the video on his cell phone. I'd guess he picked up the chatter on the two-way as well."

"Why'd he do that?"

"I suggested it. Wanted to make sure there was proof of what Drake did. Just in case."

"In case of what?" Ronny looked back at Number One.

"In case Drake wants to go pooping around in the sky before this is all sorted out. And, I figure wires missing off the key switches in those planes will cramp his style." Freddy climbed onto Number Two's wing, took off the cockpit cover, climbed in. He leaned toward the firewall.

He went over to Number One and repeated the procedure.

Freddy chuckled. "That oughta hold the Drakester off for a while."

"Probably piss him off, too."

"Don't give a shit."

Freddy remembered the words of the instructor in the academy's undercover operations class. "If three people find out your true identity, regardless if they're your bed buddy, second cousin, or the guy next door, you can assume your cover is blown. Statistically, that's the way it works out."

Everything seemed to be falling in place, ready for next week when he and the sheriff could agree on where and when to arrest Drake on suspicion of complicity in Archie's death. "Memo to self," he said to the windshield. "You're outed to Tomas and Mariel. That's two. Don't screw up now."

Zeke was talking to JerriSue when Dan walked in the store. She handed him four Post It notes. He sorted through them.

"See what the Goodyear supplier wants. The others can wait. No calls."

He motioned Zeke to his office and shut the door. He felt sorry for his old friend.

It was clear Zeke was uncomfortable with the tentative process of sitting in the wooden chair. He stared at the ceiling, then reached for Dan's nameplate and moved it a quarter of an inch, and the brief silence held. He looked up. "Get the field sprayed?"

"Yep, Ronny did a good job—"

"But?"

"Zeke, I don't know how to tell you this, so I'll show you." Dan leaned forward, swiped across his cell phone screen, turned it so Zeke could see it, and tapped the screen. The conversation between Freddy and Ronny was distorted by background noise but understandable.

It was apparent Zeke had seen enough. He slumped in the chair and covered his face with his hands. Dan was afraid his friend would burst into tears. Instead, there was resignation. He moved his hands. "I guess Ronny's not goin' to contact the FAA?"

Dan pursed his lips, frowned, and moved his head sideways.

"That's one thing. Least I'll have business after—I don't want to say it, Dan."

Dan pocketed his cell phone. "What can *I* do?"

Zeke looked to the left and closed his eyes. Another silence. Then, "Ahhhh, shit. Bertie, why did you . . ." He looked frightened when he opened his eyes. He raised his hands from his lap and held them palms up, stared wide-eyed at Dan. "Listen to me. Will you listen to me? I'm followin' Drake right over the edge. I guess I need to have Ronny disable both planes, so we don't get in real trouble."

"Ronny hinted he'd done that."

"You know what, Dan? Right now is the lowest I've felt since Bertie passed. It's got to where I don't even look in the mirror anymore. I've stopped shavin'. No point." He stood and brushed the front of his shirt.

Dan remembered the reflex from when Zeke smoked two packs of Pall Malls a day, right down to his lower lip. He stood and moved around the desk to Zeke's side.

For the first time in thirty minutes, Zeke offered a weak smile. "Old habits hang around, like crippled dogs, don't they?"

"Kinda like old friends." Dan saw a tear make its way down Zeke's weathered face and through the salt and pepper stubble on his chin. He stood and held out his hand. Zeke took it as Dan squeezed and then drew back.

"You know what, Dan? All this bullshit with Drake's behavior is about as bad for business as you can get. I worked all my adult life to get a good reputation. It can be torn apart overnight by all this." Zeke's voice took on a pleading, almost mourning quality. "Spray plane pilots have always had a reputation of being airborne throttle jockeys playin' out a death wish at the end of each pass. Hell, if this don't make it true in some people's minds." He turned his head and stared at the ceiling

"You wanna walk out the back way? There's nobody in the shop." Dan wanted to hug him but knew it would be too awkward for them. *Too bad, too bad*, he thought. We both need that right now.

Zeke smudged the tear. "Yeah, thanks. I need to find my son and see what I've got to do for or probably *to* him. You'll be at the graveside tomorrow?"

"Yeah. Pallbearer. See you there."

20

M ornin', pastor." Saturday morning, Dan saw Wyman Costley's name on his caller ID.

"Hope I interrupted your breakfast."

"Yup. What's goin' on?"

"Who are the Sentinels? What do they do at funerals?"

"The Sentinels. Yeah. It's a dying tradition from the late eighteen-hundreds with the Jerrod homestead. A lot of the cowboys and early residents didn't have a pot to piss in or a window to throw it out of when they died, so old man Jerrod would have two of his cowboys stand with the casket at the graveside service and take donations.

"They'll take off their hats and hold them upside down for people to put donations in. After they take their places, they won't talk to anyone or make eye contact. After it's all over, it's traditional for them to hand the donations to the officiating pastor, who'll get the money to the widow."

"Well, good. We'll be ready for them. One more thing, We still on for tonight?"

"Who's this 'we'?"

"The Lord doesn't always like a smart ass, Dan."

"Yeah, we'll have everything ready by seven-thirty. It's still warm enough to eat on the porch. I suppose you're coming alone."

"Yeah, we decided it's better to take separate cars, little towns being what they are. I'll be there by seven-fifteen. She'll be ten minutes later."

"Stealthy."

"Ridiculous."

"What are you gonna do 'bout the graveside in the mornin'?"

"Called a buddy of mine at Perkins Theological Seminary in Fort Worth. He found me an eager-beaver preacher pup. He'll help me with prayers this morning and run the show Sunday. The kid's laced pretty tight. He's called me six times since Wednesday."

"So, you and what's-her-name can sleep in tomorrow mornin'?"

"That's the plan."

"I want you to know we feel guilty about helpin' you live in sin."

"Goodbye, Judas."

LaDonna would meet Dan at the graveside service so he wouldn't have to ride the limo both ways. He imagined the allure of stale marijuana smoke mixed with sweaty cycle leathers and unwashed bodies on his way into town.

After loading the casket, three of Archie's biker friends with road worn, vikingesque costumes, accessorized with chain and chicken bones, piled in the pallbearers' limo. Then, Dan, Ronny, and Freddy got in the limo. They, coats and ties. The bikers made low grumbling noises while lighting up an enormous reefer and passing it around, without a glance toward Dan and the others, who tried not to inhale.

Before the cortege could get underway, Mazie had to be coaxed off the hearse's rear door by one of Jim Logan's assistants. A counterpoint to her piercing wail was offered up by H.D. with a recitative of wracking liquid sobs and staccato profanities from Alice Faye Ferris.

The hearse and limos were joined en route to the cemetery by a hodge-podge of pickups with dung-encrusted stock racks, a sedan of indeterminate age and vintage stalled with each change in direction, an ATV, and seven motorcycles. Even from inside the limo, the procession sounded like a parade of threshing machines and bulldozers.

They went west from town, north over the tracks, between the Windy Acres Trailer Park and the concrete plant and up a slight rise to the cemetery. It had been part of the old Jerrod Ranch, chosen for the broad creek valley's panoramic view to the north.

As they pulled into the parking area, Dan was pleased to see a crowd of at least twenty. He and his fellow pallbearers unloaded the casket and delivered it to the chrome framework over the vault.

At each end of the casket stood weather-beaten cowboys with their hats brim-up in their gnarled hands. Their dirt-brown tans joined stark white skin at their hat lines. They were the real thing. Dan was glad they were there. He had known Amos all his life and smiled at him.

Amos blinked, eyes fixed on the horizon.

The pallbearers maneuvered the casket to the frame over the freshly dug grave and followed Dan to the rear of the tent. A flash of red caught his eye. Drake was waiting at the Mustang's front as Zeke appeared to struggle with the passenger side door. He got out and shut the door. Drake walked toward the burial site with Zeke shuffling behind.

Dan turned and willed a rebuke at Drake. *He's your father, you miserable little roach—all you've got. At least help him up that foot trail.*

Drake stopped, glanced at Dan, turned toward Zeke. *Had I said that out loud? The thought that powerful? Maybe.*

Drake walked the few steps back to Zeke, took his elbow, and moved with him to stand with the pallbearers. Zeke was next to Dan, who gave him a gentle nudge. Zeke half-smiled. Drake, behind his dark glasses, looked ahead, rubbed his jaw, and moved his head back and forth as if trying to relieve a sore neck. He stopped and then began a gentle sway—a whiskeyed sapling teased by a rising breeze.

Dan felt LaDonna's fingers mesh with his as she joined him in the line. Again, the gladness of her. She glanced sideways, wrinkled her nose, sniffed. Dan realized the abundance of marijuana smoke in the pallbearer's limo was still with him. He leaned forward and nodded to Ella and Mariel, standing next to LaDonna.

The service lasted about forty-five minutes and would have been shorter but for intermittent outbursts from Archie's widow, son, and mother-in-law. Each time, the young seminarian helping Wyman shuffled nervously and stared hard at the *Book of Common Prayer* in his mentor's hands. By the last prayer and despite the cool November breeze from the north, he had obviously sweated through his cassock and collar.

Archie's heirs and friends were calm at the end. Mazie stood from her front-row seat and placed a single wilted rose on the coffin. Alice Faye, while attempting to restrain the squirming H.D., followed suit.

Then, to everybody's surprise, Mazie turned, stared through the crowd, made eye contact with Drake, slowly raised her right hand, wrapped in a soiled Ace Bandage. Then she turned and plopped on the padded chair, took the infant from Alice Faye, and began to rock him gently.

Mazie's silent confrontation with Drake spread a momentary shallow silence over the crowd. The bikers filed past the casket, the men and women leaving bandannas, right-hand gloves, and one a brass knuckle on the lid. After the seminarian's benediction, the rustle of leave-taking began. A few women and fewer men token-hugged Mazie.

Dan and LaDonna were the last of that group.

"You know how much I liked Archie, Mazie." Dan had flipped through his mental condolences, finding mostly tiresome clichés. "He was a damn good worker and told me over and over how much he loved you and little Harold Dean," LaDonna mumbled agreement.

Mazie smirked and wiped one eye with the edge of Harold Dean's blanket. "You at least gave it a try. Better'n I can say for that prick there." Mazie looked toward Drake, who was escorting his father down the path.

Dan shook her hand. "Let me know what we can do for you, Mazie. We'll help all we can."

"You betcha." Mazie looked Dan up and down. She tugged at her mother's flowery drool-stained tent dress, motioning her toward the waiting limo. "Guess we'll at least have a high-class ride back down that road to the trailer. Sure as hell beats the trip Archie's takin'.'"

A few other mourners stopped Mazie and Alice Faye on the walk to the limo. On their way to their parking place, Dan and LaDonna walked up to Amos McLaren, one of the Sentinels.

"We, 'preciate you and Ernie bein' here. It means a lot. Looks like it meant a lot to the others too." Judging from the bills and checks in the crown of Amos's upturned hat, Dan was confident Mazie would get several hundred dollars from Wyman Costley.

Ella was speaking to the other cowboy, her great uncle Ernie. She patted his shoulder, then walked toward Wyman. She glanced at Dan and LaDonna, mouthing, "see you later."

Freddy and Mariel walked ahead, down the gradual incline to the parking area. The four stopped as they had encountered an invisible wall.

Drake was halfway into his car when he paused and stood between the door and the driver's seat. Though the dark glasses hid his eyes, there was no doubt he was staring at Freddy and Mariel.

Freddy leaned as if to take a step toward Drake. "No," Mariel whispered as she tightened her grip on his hand. "*Simplemente no.*" Drake leaned over to get in his Mustang.

Then, a razor-edged keening wail rose on the slight north breeze fixing the group where they stood. Dan felt the skin crawl and hairs stand on the back of his neck. In the distance, out on the rolling prairie, sitting atop a slight knoll, was a solitary animal – a dog, Dan was sure.

Its primal cry rose to just above silence and ended with three mournful yelps. The creature stood, stretched, and disappeared down the rise.

21

———————

That afternoon, Freddy, Sheriff Mose Britten, and county attorney Russ Jennings entered the courthouse by separate doors. The courthouse square was deserted, but none of them wanted to feed the gossip grazers. It was imperative that Freddy not be seen with any of them. It would be too hard to explain why a private citizen was in the huddle. He was the last one to enter the conference room.

Jennings was surprised when Freddy walked in. He remembered seeing the man he knew as Paz with Sheriff Britten at the inquest but had dismissed it as part of Britten's outreach to Jerrod's growing Hispanic community. Now, here he was, and with the sheriff's blessing. For a moment, Jennings thought Paz was a material witness the sheriff decided to invite to their meeting.

Paz stood behind the chair across from Britten, who was already sitting. He motioned Freddy to sit.

"Mr. Jennings, I believe you've met Mr. Paz before."

Jennings looked over his thick-rimmed glasses at Freddy. "Seems like we said hello at the Holy Saints fiesta, and I think I saw you at the inquest." Jennings leaned back in the heavy chair, eyeing Freddy.

"Mr. Jennings, it's time you understand more about our friend here." Britten turned to Freddy and nodded.

"Mr. Jennings, my actual name is Federico Alberto Paz Espinoza. I'm a Texas Ranger detailed to the Texas Department of Agriculture."

He pulled the badge holder from his pants pocket, opened it to the Rangers star and ID, and slid it across the table to Jennings.

Jennings studied the laminated ID, put it back in the holder, slid it back to Freddy. He let his chair drop with a resounding thud. "How long's this been in play, Sheriff?"

"Ranger Espinoza contacted me when the subject—Mr. Drake Kilborn—moved here to help his father, Mr. Zeke Kilborn. He gave me the courtesy of informing me about his undercover work in the county.

He was not obligated to do so under the law."

"He's correct, Mr. Jennings," Freddy added. "This is all legal. I hope it doesn't inconvenience you in any way. In any case, we're about to the end of my work here." Freddy put on his best gringo smile, lots of teeth, head back, eyebrows raised.

Jennings looked to the sheriff, back to Freddy again. "Guess it doesn't make any difference now." He flipped through his notes and pulled out a copy of the report from the coroner's inquest.

"Department of Agriculture? All right, Sheriff, what the hell's goin' on? What's he got to do with Archie Medders' death?" He leaned in toward the sheriff, who held his large hand up and motioned toward Freddy.

"Mr. Jennings," Freddy began.

"Russ. It's Russ. I have a feelin' we are about to get to know each other very well."

"*Bueno*, Russ, I've been working undercover with the Ag

Department since January of last year. They had a dozen or more complaints about a suspicious herbicide that is normally used on weeds being illegally used to defoliate cotton."

Jennings was writing in his leather-bound notebook. He looked up.

"Suspicious? How do you mean *suspicious*?"

"Acting on complaints from immigrant field hands' families, the Ag Department confiscated several large empty chemical containers – totes – and had them analyzed. They showed significant traces of Agent Orange."

"Agent Orange? Like the stuff used in Vietnam?"

"Yeah, like that."

"I thought that shit was illegal."

"Yeah, it was outlawed domestically in the late '80s. Some Vietnam vets who came in contact with it died from liver cancer directly attributable to it. I got involved undercover to try to chase the stuff down, but we were too late to get any information out of the field workers who might have died from it. Their families had taken them back to Mexico and didn't return."

"So, where did the stuff come from?"

"The Ag Department got a line on that from Homeland Security. Seems like they had found out Agent Orange—technically 2-4-5-T— was being manufactured in a chemical plant across the border from Del Rio and shipped under the brand name *Adios* to large corporate farms in central and south America."

Jennings looked at his notes, at Britten, then to Paz. "But, you think it was being smuggled into the U.S.?"

"I don't know a lot about how this all went down. But other investigations made it pretty clear it was being smuggled across the border, stashed at desert landing strips, and picked up by domestic air haulers. Unscrupulous applicators can save a lot of money using it instead of the real *Adios* or something like it."

Jennings took off his glasses, wiped them with the back of his tie, held them up to the ceiling fan light, put them back on, and leaned toward Freddy. "Air haulers? Like companies who move equipment and supplies with small cargo planes? Like oilfield companies?"

"Specifically, those companies who ship drill bits and well parts one way but make the return trip empty-handed, that is, unless they find something to pay for the flight back." "Something like Agent Orange?"

"Exactly. This is where I got involved. Because of my background as an A and P mechanic . . ."

"A and P?"

"Airframe and power plant. That was my military occupational specialty in Afghanistan."

"Oh. Makes my JAG work over there sound kind of lame."

"We all had our job to do. Anyway, that was what got me in this UC work," Freddy said.

"Let me interrupt here a minute, Mr. Jennings." Britten stood, walked over the conference room door, rattled the knob, and returned to the table. "Mr. Paz—er, Ranger Espinoza, here—is skipping over some critical details out of a sense of modesty

"He graduated *magna cum laude* from UT-Permian Basin with a. criminal justice degree. Had such an outstanding record with the Department of Public Safety, he was accepted by the Rangers after only eight years on the job, almost unheard of. His law enforcement background and his work as a military aviation mechanic made this one of those rare perfect fits."

Jennings, scribbling furiously, looked up at Freddy. "Perfect fit?" "About the time the Ag undercover job came up, the Rangers were working with the DEA to catch air haulers smuggling drugs from Mexico. They had started looking at Case Aviation in Abilene. They seemed to be more and more successful despite the ups and downs in the oil market.

"So, I managed to get an A&P job with them and got to be pretty good friends with . . ."

Jennings dropped his pencil. "Don't tell me. Let me guess. Would it be someone called Drake Kilborn?"

"It would."

"Kiss my ass. Pardon me, gentlemen. We busted him for DWI right after moving back here from Abilene to help his father out after his mother died. I remember him telling me about working air transport in Abilene. So, how about that? You happened to move with him. Well, isn't that cute?"

"That's the way it worked out." Freddy smiled.

"And you saw Kilborn flying this counterfeit *Adios*, this Agent Orange in here, first hand?"

"In fact, we have his last two shipments stored. We substituted legal defoliant. Far as I can tell, he doesn't have a clue. We used it last week on small farms in the area, and Drake didn't blink an eye."

"What's this got to do with Medders' death? You're not going to tell me you knowingly let Kilborn expose Medders to toxic levels of this stuff, right?" Jennings looked down at his notes.

Freddy paused. "No, that's been goin' on a long time. When I this stuff, right?" Jennings looked down at his notes.

Freddy paused. "No, that's been goin' on a long time. When I worked with Archie, he told me some hairy stories about having the defoliant spilled on him or getting caught in the mist when the nozzles were cleared on the planes. I worked with him two years and could see him gradually goin' downhill—bad cough, congestion, blotches on his skin." Freddy stared at the ceiling for a moment, then continued.

"Archie told me was he had handled a half-full tote and spilled some of the concentrate on himself as he was mixed. Drake had been spraying bindweed on the Galaxy Farms operation north of town."

Jennings interrupted. "Wait. What? Did you say 'when Archie was mixing it'?"

"Yeah, that's what he told me."

"Drake got a permit from the Ag Department to do the mixing. He's the only one who should have been handling it. He was required to file a copy of his permit with me." Jennings wrote a couple of lines then circled them.

"Didn't always happen that way, according to Archie."

"Did you ever see Drake tell another employee to do the mixing?"

"Not while I've been with him."

Sheriff Britten held up both hands, signaling a stop to the conversation. "I think we're running into the bar ditch here, gentlemen. Mr. Jennings, you're the one with the report from the Coroner's Inquest. Don't you think we can move forward with a warrant for Mr. Drake Kilborn?"

Jennings flipped through several of his legal pad pages. He ran over several lines with his finger, closed his eyes momentarily, then put the pad down. "I guess so, but I'm worried what a good lawyer will do with these ambiguities."

Britten turned in his seat to face Jennings head-on. "We gotta get this off dead center. I think young Mr. Kilborn senses something is about to happen. I don't want him to 'rabbit' on me. We—Ranger Espinoza and me—have done too much work to let this fall through the cracks."

"All right then." Jennings looked at his watch. "The district attorney over in Breckenridge authorized me to act on her behalf, so I'll get the judge to sign a bench warrant. Let me call him, see if he's available. Hang on a minute." He got up and walked out the door. He came back in a few minutes.

"We're out of luck."

Freddy's stomach tightened. "What's going on?"

"He's gone hunting. Won't be back 'til Saturday late."

"What about his cell phone?"

"I was talking to his wife. She said he's real picky about not being bothered on his hunting trips. Evidently, all his buddies feel the same way."

"We're going to have to hope Mr. Drake Kilborn doesn't kill somebody – or himself – before Saturday morning. Sounds like we've got no choice." The sheriff stood, retrieved his hat from the chair next to him.

"Got to hope for the best. Maybe a good rain Monday evening or Tuesday will keep him from moving around too much."

Freddy suppressed a laugh. "I've worked around him for two years. Nothing like a little rainstorm is gonna hold him down. At least he won't be flying." He and Jennings walked toward the door.

Britten stopped and turned toward Freddy. "What do you mean he won't be flying?"

"Won't be flying. Take my word for it." Freddy held the door open as the other two men walked out.

22

————

At sundown, Wyman pulled into the parking area in front of the Grandma House. He held up two bottles of wine. Dan was on the phone with his shop mechanic, Dup. He gave a thumbs-up to Wyman.

"Yeah, the Bradys are gonna strip the south place startin' about ten tomorrow mornin', so I'm not gonna be in town. Probably will be out of pocket Monday, too. What kinda shape's the wrecker in?"

Dub said he had the transfer case fixed and felt like everything was all right with the wrecker.

"Good. I betcha we're gonna have a lotta people to pull out of bar ditches come Monday afternoon and night, rest of the week. It's supposta come a turd-floater. I'm gonna be outta pocket Monday, and we're goin' to Abilene Tuesday, so you and JerriSue will have'ta handle it. Make sure the sheriff's dispatcher knows you're on call. Let me know if you need anything."

Dan tucked his phone in his pocket as Ella drove up. She motioned him over to her car and handed a large casserole dish out the window.

"Cherry cobbler. Heard you liked it."

"Liked? That's puttin' it lightly. Get yerself outta that car. What'shis-name is waitin' up there."

She acknowledged Sniff before going up, stopped, and pecked Wyman on the cheek, went into the kitchen.

Dan walked over to the railing and looked west. The sun had disappeared, but the afterglow silhouetted a long low band of grey clouds lying a pencil width above the horizon. "Only one day. Please."

LaDonna took the cobbler. "Worried about the rain?"

"We could've had this done by now, except for that business with Archie and that . . ."

"Don't say it. Let's enjoy our friends."

As they ate, the conversation ranged from national politics to the coming year's county primary elections to the possibility of the school system being downgraded to Division One.

"That really worries me. Six-man football. What a wimpy damned excuse for a football team. Football's been played in this town for ninety years, always with eleven players on the field." Dan speared a chunk of meat, turned to the left, and flipped it over the rail, passed the steps. They heard Sniff unfold himself from his shelter, run onto the parking lot in search of the morsel.

Ladonna touched Dan's hand as he turned around. "Let's concentrate on this year. The Strikers will be playing Jeff City next Friday here. They win, they'll be in the semi-finals next week."

They all lifted their wine glasses. In unison, "The Strikers."

"Yeah, all eleven of them." Dan raised his glass and smiled at Wyman and Ella, who had moved closer together when the cobbler was served. "Isn't it about bedtime for you kiddoes?"

Ella didn't smile. "Dan, I saw Zeke today."

"Where was he?"

"At home."

"And?"

"I called him after the funeral to see if he wanted to go to lunch. He said he did, so I went to the café and ordered hamburgers, but he never showed up. I ate mine then called him. He said he wasn't feelin' so hot, so I decided to take him the hamburger and some chips.

"I knocked several times, and finally, he yelled for me to come in, to come upstairs.

"Dan, I had to shove that door open - clothes were scattered everywhere. When I got in, it was obvious something really bad had happened. Bertie's books were on the floor, broken plates on the coffee table, their big-screen TV face-down. I was almost frightened to go up the stairs." Ella paused, looked down at the table then continued.

"They were littered with clothes – I think Drake's – all the way down. And here was the disgusting part: Bertie's wedding dress was lying spread out on the landing like it was ready to put on.

"Damnit. That dress was so precious to Bertie. It was our grandmother's. She wore it when she married Zeke. We spent three months mending the split seams and replacing missing clasps. We had to look in dozens of catalogs to match the lace overlaid on the bodice and down each arm. When we finished, she was so pleased that someday, if Drake had a daughter, it would be worn by her." Wyman scooted his chair closer. She pulled a handkerchief out of her pocket and wiped a solitary tear away. "Zeke was in his room. That was a mess too, but I could tell he had been trying to clean it up."

She talked about Zeke's growing fear of Drake, of the threats to put him in New Horizons Convalescent Home. Zeke said Drake was angry at not flying either plane, livid when he figured out what had happened. He shouted about wanting to take one of the planes for a check ride after the funeral, then got real quiet."

Ella wiped away another tear and took a deep breath. "He said he'd gone to check on Drake—saw him carefully lay the dress out on the stair landing.

"When he realized Zeke saw him, Drake ran into his room and came out, arms full of clothing. He ran down the stairs, scattering clothes, stormed into the kitchen, and threw dishes, pots, and pans into the dining room, cussing Zeke and cryin' for his momma. He pushed the TV off its stand, hurled books out of two shelves, ran out the door, and took off in his car."

Ella leaned on Wyman's shoulder. "Zeke was still stunned as he talked the whole thing through. He was sittin' there on the side of his bed, shaking. I finally got him calmed down and talked him into goin' on a drive in the country, so he could eat his hamburger in peace.

"On the way down the stairs, I picked up the dress and started to hand it to Zeke. He told me he couldn't guarantee it would be safe under his roof and for me to take it." Ella picked up her wine glass, swished the liquid, then put it down again.

"Now, where was I? Oh yeah, as we were driving off – we were two blocks away and turning a corner –I saw Drake pull up. I didn't say anything to Zeke. We drove around almost two hours – nearly to Breckenridge. We talked a lot about Zeke and Bertie, us growing up together, how fortunate we are to have you as friends. You know, it was as if he and I were reminiscing after Bertie's funeral. It was almost a a re-run. Spooky. And the whole time, I worried about what Drake was doing at the house."

She wiped her eyes, put the handkerchief back in her pocket, fiddled with the top button of her blouse, and pushed an errant strand of hair behind her ear. "You'll never believe what we saw when we got back. It was spotless. During the little time we were away, Drake had found the Garcia sisters, and they'd gone through the place like a whirlwind. They'd even picked up the TV and put all the books back in place in the living room. Drake was gone, and the sisters' mini-van was leaving as we pulled in the driveway."

LaDonna looked at her fingernails then up at Ella. "That means he had his little tantrum, had second thoughts about it, decided to get things fixed up. It probably didn't dawn on him 'til he got back that Zeke was with you. You know, in his mental state, he probably didn't even think about the impact on Zeke."

"He never thought about the way he affected others, no time in his life," Ella said. "Every time he got his butt in a crack, whether it was sassin' a teacher or wrecking a car, Bertie was there to pull his feet out of the fire. She was my sister, and I loved her, but I think she loved Drake too much if that's possible." She took another sip from her wine glass.

"His behavior didn't change after Bertie died. It was the same or worse. The difference is that she's no longer here to help him. Zeke gave up trying to discipline him, make a responsible adult out of him a long time ago. There had been a kind of unspoken truce between him and Bertie where Drake was concerned. I guess for Zeke, it was better than having to go head-to-head with both of them all the time." Ella stood, rubbed her eyes, and sighed. "Look, I'm sorry to be such a wet blanket. Thanks for lettin' me vent." She squeezed Wyman's shoulder. "Give me a minute, okay?" She went in the kitchen door, headed for the downstairs bathroom. She was back in five minutes.

Dan and LaDonna had cleared the dishes and were leaning side by side against the porch rail. Wyman moved to put his arm around Ella.

She smiled up at him and looked from side to side, blushing like a nervous teenager on a first date.

LaDonna and Dan moved toward the kitchen door. "Okay, you guys, you got the place to yourselves. I've got cotton to be stripped tomorrow, so I'll be outta here pretty early. 'Donna's gonna be here when you're ready for breakfast. If you get bored, there's a closet by the stove with all sorts of board games in it."

Wyman wrinkled his forehead, smiled, and extended his hand.

"Board games? Really? You think of everything, buddy."

"Don't want you two to be bored. By the way, I won't be at church tomorrow mornin'."

"Us neither," Wyman said over his shoulder as he and Ella walked down the steps.

———————

Dan and LaDonna sat at the kitchen table for half an hour talking about Thanksgiving weekend. "We need to call Nelly and find out when they'll be here Wednesday, probably about four o'clock or so."

Dan could feel a list coming. The old saying rang true, "If momma ain't happy, ain't nobody happy." For his safety, he had learned to back off when a list – spoken or written – was in the works.

His exit line had always been "whatever you think's right." With that, he left her at the kitchen table, furiously scribbling on the ubiquitous blue legal pad. "Goin' to bed."

In bed after his shower, Dan had his own list to manage. Hope for a successful cotton harvest beginning in less than twelve hours was foremost as he stared up into the dark. The grey band he'd seen on the northern horizon at sunset pushed its way forward in his mind. And, there was a growing threat to his best friend, Zeke. From what Ella had told them, it was apparent Zeke was in danger from Drake. That washed over the other thoughts, but he managed to push them into one corner of his mind and sleep.

Toward morning, he rose to heed the call of nature and parted the curtains. Behind his image, there was the insistent wind-born scratching of a bare live oak limb next to the window, a reminder of weather change coming.

23

When LaDonna came downstairs, Dan was finishing his waffles about to take one final swig of coffee. She poured herself a cup and sat beside him. "You all ready?"

Dan looked at the clock over the stove. "Yeah, looks like we're gonna do it. Marsh Brady said he'd call me by now if somethin' changed. Guess it hasn't." He didn't realize he was tapping his coffee cup with his fork.

LaDonna put her hand on his and took the fork. Over the years, she knew this was a signal that his mind had left the room. "You better go on now. And don't do anything silly to wake our guests. You know, with that damned fog horn on your Suburban?"

Dan stood, kissed the top of her head. "I'm a little offended you'd even suggest such a thing." He put his plate in the sink and took his cap and Carhart jacket from the peg beside the door. "Would be kinda fun, though."

She smiled and wagged her finger, admonishing his inner teenager. "Okay. I'll let you know when we're through. Towards dark, I suspect."

"You want food?"

"No, somebody will bring burgers after a gin run. I have a feelin' we won't start 'til about ten. Probably a lot of moisture in the air." He went down to his Suburban. Before he got in, he looked east, relieved to see the sun breaking free of a cloudless horizon.

As he turned off the lane to the highway, he called up the latest weather radar display on his cell phone. A massive blue and purple blob covered the horizon's sweep, almost due east around the north, west, and to the southwest. The weather advisory for Abilene said rain should start there midafternoon. "I hope late afternoon for us." The gritty weariness in his voice surprised him.

Twenty minutes later, he drove onto the edge of the cotton field on the South Place. The long rows of cotton plants looked like small bare trees without their leaves. The large bolls clung to the gnarled twigs, ready for plucking. The defoliant had done its work. The ground below the plants was littered with shriveling leaves.

The Brady twins were unloading their hulking John Deere stripper. Marsh Brady was easing the machine down the steel ramps, Matt signaling from the back. In half an hour, the harvest crew gathered, and the large open-topped rectangular metal box, the module-maker, was on the ground, ready for the first bales of the day.

Dan and Marsh conferred for a few minutes, agreeing on a test run. Marsh climbed up to the stripper cab, moved the machine down the fence line, turned into the cotton, lowered the cutter head, and started down the field. He was back in ten minutes.

Dan walked up to the header and took several bolls out. He pulled long filaments out of one, mashed them together, and rolled them between his palms. He waved to Marsh and stepped aside. The harvest that had worried him so much had begun.

Within an hour, the module-maker operated by Matt produced the first thirty-foot module. It resembled a gigantic loaf of bread. Each module load was fifteen bales of cotton. Dan estimated this was from the first seven acres—three hundred-thirteen to go. He smiled with satisfaction. He didn't compute what the cash value would be. His father always said it might jinx it. But it would be nice, very nice.

He could feel Big Dan's presence among the growing rows of modules. After each was put on the ground, Dan shook a can of red paint, took off the cap, sprayed *DBII* on both sides and ends. "Yep, Dad, the boys at the gin will know we're back again," he said as he capped the can.

By eleven, the first of Brady's module trucks drove up to take the long white loaves into the trailer and head for the gin. Thirty minutes later, the fourth load was gone.

Dan checked his watch. Noon. He saw more gray on the western and northern horizons, folding eastward. Cold-edged wind was freshening out of the north. He started to check the radar on his cell phone again. It buzzed, *LaDonna* on the caller ID.

"Hey. How's it going?"

"Great. Looks like we're 'bout halfway done." He could hear the dishwasher humming and clanking in the background.

"What about the yield?"

"We'll probably be able to get a new dishwasher."

"That good, huh?"

"Yep. At least. What's the weather there?"

"About clouded over. It's moving slowly."

"Good. Slow is good. What about our guests?"

"That was really cute. Ella came in first, Wyman about ten minutes later. I reminded them they didn't have to time their entrances out here. When they were eating, they kept stealing glances at each other, blushing and giggling, even holding hands under the table."

"Ah, young love."

"More like midlife lust. When will you be done?"

"Probably 'bout dark, long as it don't rain. Fingers crossed. Marsh just pulled up. Gotta go."

Marsh Brady had turned over operation of the stripper to one of his workers, followed one of the modules to the gin, came back to the field with hamburgers and good news. The first round of modules had been ginned. According to the run slips Marsh showed him, the yield was a little less than two bales to the acre.

Marsh handed Dan a small paper sack that held a double burger and fries from Big Jimmy's. "Damned glad I follered him in. That ole truck broke down in the gin yard. Had to tow it to the scales. Our equipment is 'bout tuckered out. We need to go to round bales next year, but I don't know if we got the bidness or not."

Dan picked up a cotton boll and teased the seeds from the strands. "You know you always got my business. We go way back to grade school Marsh, me, you, and your brother. I can't imagine this harvest without the Bradys."

"Danny, same goes for us, but I'm afraid there may be some folks movin' inta this county who don't operate on a handshake."

"Like who?"

"We heard Galaxy Farms is gonna buy two of them high-techy pickers, the ones that make the big round bales covered with plastic."

Dan dropped the empty husk and flicked the seeds away. "Yeah, I saw some of those last year when I was visitin' my cousin up in the Panhandle. Looks like they're a lot easier to handle."

Marsh dug a shallow furrow in the ground with his boot heel. "Lots easier. You can move the same cotton in 'bout half the time. We can't compete with that, Danny."

"Why would Galaxy buy those only for its operations? Bet those things are half a million each."

"Oh, I doubt they'd shut 'em down after they've stripped their stuff. I bet they can undercut our prices whenever they're good'n ready. We've got all this equipment," He gestured past the module-maker and three waiting trucks, "An' it breaks down all tha time. Should be in a museum."

"Damn, Marsh, hope it don't work out that way."

Marsh pulled off his sweat-stained D. Baker Tires cap, smoothed his grey hair back. He held his hands waist level, palms up. "You can hold a fresh cow patty in one han' an' *hope* in the other and see which fills up faster. I gotta get these 'burgers around." He drove into the stripped part of the field and headed for the harvester.

Dan leaned against the Suburban and unwrapped his hamburger. "Marsh, I'm afraid you're right. You guys are about to get swallowed up, and it's only a matter of time before it happens to a little store like mine. Shit. People can order tires – order anything – and get it next day outta Amazon." The sound of his voice always surprised him. *When did I start talking to myself?*

At sunset, the last module was hauled out. Dan waited until the crew had trailered the module-maker and drove out of the gate. He pulled through, got out, dragged the barbed wire gate closed, put the double loop of wire over the top, and stood for a moment, looking out over the barren cotton plants. *It's done again, Dad.*

He followed the last module truck as they headed for the gin. He felt the tension leaving. He and LaDonna would do some shopping in

Abilene Tuesday. The kids would be in Wednesday afternoon. They'd have a feast and zone out Thursday and then that big game Friday. He turned up the heater enough to knock the sunset chill back, put the Suburban on cruise. There was a light mist, cleared by the wipers.

He crested a hill and saw flashing red and blue lights ahead. It was his wrecker. As he got closer, he recognized Drake Kilborn's car. He turned on the company two-way and took the microphone from the clip under the dash.

"Baker Two, this is Baker One. Got your ears on?"

"Hey, Baker One. What do you know?"

"I'm behind you."

"Oh, roger. Didn't see ya. Got ourselves an impound."

"Why impound?"

"DWI, I think."

"Who called you in?"

"Sheriff dispatcher, 'bout an hour ago. Marv Harter's got him."

The rain was getting heavier. Dan sped up the wipers. The pounding on the roof was beginning to mask road noise. "Okay, take it to the shop and lock it up where the boat and trailer are parked. Where's the deputy?"

"Shouldn't be very far behind. Can we talk?"

It was Dub's signal to change to cell phones. "Sure. You hands-free in there?" Dan forgot his company two-way was easy to monitor for anyone with a scanner. "Callin' now. Stand by." He put the mic back on the clip.

Dan pushed the cell phone button on his steering wheel to call Dub. "Okay. So, what happened?"

"Marv told me Kilborn pulled over and stopped right after he lit him up. He said the guy was weavin' from side ta side, even did a donut.

Didn't give him any trouble at all. He got Kilborn out of the car, had him stand in front of the cruiser, and started to give him a breathalyzer test when the kid slumps to the pavement and begins to cry like a baby. Marv picked him up, cleared his pockets, and put him in his cruiser. He said it was real spooky, the guy cryin', beggin' for his momma."

Dan realized the impact this would have on Zeke. Zeke with the pacemaker. Zeke mourning his wife. Zeke watching as his son rushed toward a cliff.

"Hey Dub. Don't forget to chalk the left rear tire's sidewall and extend the line about a foot out on the blacktop. We don't want anybody claimin' we hot-rodded that car. And, I don't care if the law says you gotta have your overheads on when you get close to Jerrod, will you turn'em off? It's gonna be bad enough when word gets out. We don't need a light show when you're puttin' the car in storage. Put the key fob in the night slot. And if you've got a tarp, cover the car, will ya?"

"Sure, Dan, I understand. You be in tomorrow?"

"Hadn't planned on it, but the rain'll keep me from workin' outside. I'll be in sometime in the mornin'."

Dan hung up the phone as he was driving onto the gin parking lot. The rain had slowed to a light shower, but the blue spiked strobes of lightning to the west said it was only a pause. He spent a few minutes in the gin office, collecting run tickets and chatting with the manager. Luckily, most of his modules had been put through the gin and turned into bales for shipping. The few still waiting in the storage area had been covered with large tarps.

He scanned the bale count on the run tickets. *Two bales per acre, 320 acres. Five hundred pounds per bale, $1.10 per pound.* Even after settling with the Bradys, this would be good Christmas money all the way into next year.

As Dan pulled out of the gin and drove toward Jerrod, he called LaDonna and filled her in on how the harvest had gone and broke the news about Drake's arrest.

He told her someone should be with Zeke when he got the news from the sheriff's office. He asked her to call Ella and said he would call Wyman Costley. They'd both need to stick close to Zeke. Dan said having Ella was essential in case Zeke had a heart problem the pacemaker couldn't handle.

Dan then spoke Wyman's name to his hands-free phone.

"You've called to increase your tithe?"

"How you figger that, reverend?"

"Been checking my portfolio. Took a peek at commodities. A little calculating tells me your half section did pretty well by you today."

"Let's put it this way. It'll take the edge off hunger. Hey, got some bad news."

"Listenin'."

"Sheriff's office busted Drake Kilborn for drunk drivin'."

"Uh, oh. When?"

"Thirty minutes ago. Yeah. Look, Donna is callin' Ella. I'm worried 'bout how Zeke's gonna take this. I imagine Ella will be payin' him a visit."

"I'll call her right now."

"Thanks. Your check is in the mail."

"I know. I promise to respect you afterwards."

Dan let himself smile again. "You should know after that episode of the Datin' Game last night."

"Good to hear from you, Deacon Baker. Please call back anytime."

The rain and wind grew more insistent, buffeting Dan's Suburban. He could make out the streetlights of Jerrod when he realized he was behind the Holden County Sheriff's Office SUV. He could see Drake silhouetted in the back seat, rocking back and forth, his head lolling from side to side.

Dan slowed as he went by the city limits sign. He almost turned off the highway to head for his store. "No, that's gonna happen tomorrow. Don't go looking for bad things. They'll find you."

He punched the hands-free button and spoke his home number. LaDonna answered.

"You comin' home?"

"Absolutely. I'm, I'm . . ."

"Worn out?"

"Yeah, that'd be it."

"I can always hear it in your voice."

"I feel like I need to talk to Zeke."

"He'll call you when the time comes."

"I've got his son's car locked up."

"Come home."

White-hot brambles of lightning fused in the sky, followed by a dozen rising thunderclaps folding over each other. "You hear that?" The rain changed with a lightning flash from mist to pounding torrent. Dan rolled his wiper selector to maximum. "Yep, felt it, too."

"How's the road to the house? I'm glad I got that gravel put down. We underwater?" Dan sat up straighter, clicked off cruise control.

He could barely hear LaDonna, but he felt the words. "Danny, come home. I need you. I want you."

24

Dan had decided to sleep away the previous day's strains, but the phone rang at eight o'clock. Wyman Costley's number. "Hope you've got good news or money."

"Afraid not either this time. Zeke Kilborn had a heart attack about eleven last night. Ella was with him, thank God."

"Uh, oh. Drake's D-W-I?" Dan sat up on the side of the bed.

"Yep. Zeke was overnighted at the Jerrod hospital, thinking they could stabilize him with his pacemaker, but that evidently didn't work very well. Ella said Doctor Chin decided Zeke better be taken to Abilene. I got a call from her. She rode the ambulance with him. She said he was awake and lucid, so there may be some hope."

"Wow. Drake has finally done it. Bet he feels special right about now."

"I don't know anything about what he's doing or feeling. All I know he's in jail. I thought you might be able to find out something through your source."

Dan tried to focus on the bedside clock. "My source?"

"JerriSue?"

"Oh, yeah. I'll get back to you. Thanks for bein' with Ella last night."

"I wouldn't have wanted it any other way. And, thanks again for Saturday night."

Dan went to the store an hour later. JerriSue looked up from her computer monitor. "He'll be able to make bond sometime after seven tonight."

"What? How'd you?—oh, never mind. Zeke's in the hospital in Abilene. Who's gonna post his bond?"

"Jeff Stangle, probably."

"How's he get out this easy? I figured with two DWI's, they'd hold him longer."

"He can only be held until he sobers up. He didn't kill nobody or damage property, so he won't be arraigned on the DWI charge until the blood tests come back from Fort Worth. That'll probably be Monday, earliest."

"I ask you again, how you know 'bout this kinda stuff?"

"I know people." She half-smiled and handed Dan a stack of mail, turned back to the monitor, and knocked the ash off her Pall Mall.

"I guess I'm dismissed," Dan muttered and sat at his desk. He went through the mail, called two tire wholesalers, and decided to look at Drake's car.

He got the key fob from JerriSue and unlocked the storage area gate, and was about to pull the tarp back.

"Mr. Baker?"

Dan turned to see Freddy Paz, hunched against the cold drizzle

"Hey Freddy. What's up?"

Freddy turned, looked up and down the street, waited for the thunder to die down. "Can we talk? You know, out of the rain?" Dan pointed to the open shop door.

Freddy looked around again as they walked into the shop. He sat at one of the two counter stools Dan pointed to. "You think we'll be interrupted?"

Dan narrowed his eyes and studied Freddy. *Why would an airplane mechanic worry about being interrupted?*

Freddy reached in his back pocket and handed his badge-holder to Dan. When he thought about the conversation later, Dan was pretty sure he looked like one of those toy birds that dipped his beak in a glass of water, looked up, dipped his beak again, and so on.

"Well, bite my butt Fre . . ., er, Ranger, uh, Espinoza? You're damned good at this, aren't you?" He handed the badge-holder back.

"I have two favors to ask of you, Mr. Baker." Freddy looked around the shop, pointed at the door to the front. "But first, can that door to your showroom be secured?"

Dan walked over, pushed the deadbolt, and walked back to his stool. "There. Favors?"

"First, I'm taking a real risk talking with you about this, but I don't want to have to get a search warrant, all that. I would like to put a device on Drake Kilborn's car, so we can monitor driving habits over the next few days."

"Before you lower the boom on him for the defoliant?"

Freddy looked down at his hands and back up. "So we can monitor his driving habits over the next few days. Would that be possible?"

"Sure, I guess. Where do you put it?" *Don't want to talk about Archie, huh?*

"It'll be in a secure place not connected to the electrical system in any way."

Dan realized his palms were dry, as they had been during Army intelligence debriefings. "And what else?" He stood and walked toward the open overhead door, held out his hands, caught water dripping from the metal roof, and rubbed them together.

"I had to reveal my identity to you to place the device," Freddy said. "I could have done it with a search warrant, but the judge doesn't get back . . ."

". . .you want me to say nothin' about you to nobody. Is that it?"

"That's it. The sheriff and I debated this a lot before I called my superiors. You've got a good reputation in the community, you're ex military, so you understand security issues."

"You need to know I don't keep anything from my wife, okay?" Freddy smiled. "I understand."

"Okay, do your stuff." Dan glanced at the grey overcast. The mist had stopped falling. Thunder was moving to the outskirts of town.

"Looks like as good a time as any. You need me hangin' round?"

"No thanks, I'll only be a few minutes. The less you see of this, the better. And, if you need to talk to me – about anything – call this." He handed Dan a laminated business card with *FAE* and a phone number below.

Dan took the card, put it in his shirt pocket, unbolted the door to the front, and walked back to his office. *You're damned right, Ranger Espinoza. The less the whole town sees of this mess, the better.*

His cell phone buzzed. LaDonna's ID. "Did you get my text?"

Dan unbolted the shop door and walked toward his office. "Yeah, that's so sad. Have you heard anything else from Ella?"

"Nothing. What about Drake?"

"Looks like he'll make bail at seven this evenin'. I'll have to be here to turn the car over to him." He pulled Freddy's card out of his pocket and put it in his billfold.

"That'll be awkward."

"Yeah, probably. We'll see." Dan sat and turned on his computer.

"I have to sponsor the science fair, so I won't be home until about eight, anyway."

Dan glanced up at the wall clock. "Did you get a sub for tomorrow?"

"Yeah, that's set. We can go by Hedrick to see Zeke when we're in Abilene."

"Yeah, we need to."

The class change bell rang in the background. "Gotta go. Love you." Then the sound of her cupping the phone to her mouth. "Don't know what you were up to last night, but I'm pretty sore today."

"It's what you get for showin' up at the back door with no clothes on."

"Worth it. Bye."

Dan spent the rest of the day puttering around the store. He rearranged the tire display in the showroom, added two new tires and a couple of advertising displays, went for barbeque at Thrashers. For the first time in months, he cleaned off his desk, filled two trash cans with magazines, catalogs, receipts, clumps of cat hair, church bulletins, and faded Post It notes.

He walked to the front window several times, staring at the courthouse a block away, trying to imagine what the day had been like for Drake, for Zeke.

Late in the afternoon, Ella called to say Zeke was resting, and the doctors thought his heart rate was low but strong. They wanted to keep him through Thursday if something had to be done with the pacemaker, which seemed to be running about ninety percent of the time. She said she'd been a nurse long enough to know that things were not going to get any better for Zeke.

"Dan, tonight I'll stay with one of my friends who works at the hospital, but would you mind if I rode back with you and LaDonna tomorrow after you see Zeke? I need to get back to work there."

"No problem whatsoever, Ella. You bet. I don't know what time we'll get there, but we'll call when we get into Abilene."

After Ella hung up, Dan texted LaDonna, who responded with a simple *okay.*

JerriSue had left for the day when the phone rang.

"Dan Baker."

"Mr. Baker, this is Jeff Stangle. I represent Mr. Drake Kilborn. I believe you have his vehicle impounded."

"Right, a red Mustang."

"Mr. Kilborn has other business and has asked me to take possession of his vehicle on his behalf at seven o'clock this evening." *What 'other business'? Doesn't want to face me. Never mind.* "That's fine by me. I'll need a release order from the sheriff, a witnessed affidavit from"—he couldn't make himself say Drake's name— "the *owner* designatin' you his representative. I also want a cashier's check or cash for the impound fee. It's seventy-eight dollars."

"Fine. I'll see you there at your store a little before seven."

Three hours later, Dan was waiting in his Suburban when Stangle tapped on his window. Dan hadn't seen a car, so he assumed the lawyer had walked from his office across from the courthouse three blocks away. *Drake is waiting in Stangle's office*, Dan thought.

"Do you have the key fob?"

"Hang on. Lemme see the affidavit and release order."

Stangle handed the papers and a cashier's check through the window.

Dan scanned and folded them, leaned over to put them in his glove compartment. He removed a small envelope.

"That the key fob?"

"Here it is. There's a receipt in there, too." He handed the envelope to Stangle. "The car's over there." He jerked his thumb toward the unlocked gate. "I can't drive it out of the impound area. It's the law."

Stangle looked over his horn-rimmed glasses. "I know about the law, believe me."

"Bet you do." *I believe you're an asshole among assholes. If LaDonna was here, she'd whisper, "stop it."* He watched the lawyer pull the tarp away, unlock the Mustang, get in, turn on the lights, and drive it out.

Dan began to relax as he left town, looking forward to getting home. The last slow pulses of sunset showed under the cloud cover to the west. Then he happened to glance to the right at the Kilborn Flying Service sign, the arrow pointing across the railroad tracks.

A deep sadness welled up within him, last felt at his father's death, but not a sadness of what was or what is, but of what would be. He drove the rest of the way to the farm hunched over his steering wheel.

25

Sheriff Mose Britten's first call Tuesday morning was from county judge Jimmy Akers. It was not the call he'd been waiting for. Akers and his wife were leaving town and staying with his brother in Lubbock the rest of the week. No, he didn't want to authorize an arrest warrant for Drake Kilborn. He made it clear he wanted to talk to the county attorney first.

Britten managed a terse "Have a good Thanksgiving" and hung up. Well, he thought, *If he's not going to be in town, I'm not either*. He called Marv Harter and told him he was in charge until Saturday and "not mess anything up." The thought of leaving Harter in charge caused a slight shudder. Still, he figured goose hunting in western Oklahoma would make it bearable.

His next call was from Jeff Stangle. "Sheriff, I don't know if you heard, but my client's father, Zeke Kilborn, had to be taken to Hedrick Memorial in Abilene early yesterday morning."

"Mr. Stangle, you can assume I heard. I dispatch the ambulance."

"Oh, sure. I have an unusual request associated with the elder

Kilborn's medical status."

"And that is?"

"I'm aware the conditions of my client's bond constrain him from leaving the county, but I'm wondering if there might be some leeway possible?"

"Such as?"

"Granting a forty-eight-hour compassionate waiver in case of family emergency."

"Don't think I've ever heard of such a thing."

"It's in the criminal code. Would you like a copy?"

"No, let me do some checking. I'll get back to you in an hour or so."

"Is there any way, Sheriff, it could be expedited?

"I'll get back to you as soon as I can."

"I hope so. I know you've got to talk to Russ Jennings. I've already spoken to him. We discussed the section of the code I told you about. He said he saw no problems with it."

Mose Britten sat up straighter and lowered his voice. "Then I have to ask myself, what was is the call about, *Mister* Stangle?"

"Look, Sheriff, I don't want there to be bad feelings between us, but you understand I must represent my client in the most efficient way possible. Now if we could . . ."

Britten cut Stangle short. "I'll be getting back to you." He called the county attorney's number.

"Morning, Sheriff. Let me guess who you were talking to."

"Stangle said he'd spoken with you."

"Yeah, about twenty minutes ago. Great way to start the day."

"Did you tell him it was okay with you for this 'compassionate waiver'?"

"Sorta, except I told him you'd have the final word."

"Little early in the day to be passing the buck, isn't it, Mr. Jennings?" He was making an effort to hold his anger and sarcasm in check.

Jennings cleared his throat. "Look, he read me the section from the Code about compassionate waivers. I looked it up. It can be done. It is legal. And, I don't want to get in a nose-to-nose with Stangle over a minor issue like this. It's going to be enough of a hassle as it is." Britten was breathing through his nose into the phone. "Sheriff?"

"Okay, Mr. Jennings. I guess I'll give him the go-ahead for two days, but I assure you I am going to note my objections in my com log, and I'll send you and Mr. Stangle a memo doing the same."

Without bothering to say goodbye, Britten hung up. He called Stangle and told him he agreed under protest.

After the call was over, intuition told him Drake Kilborn had headed for Abilene right about sunrise. His lawyer was covering his client's tracks. "We'll see what Ranger Espinoza's little toy tells us about his trip." He pushed his glasses back and rubbed his eyes with his thumb and index finger.

LaDonna had tried to talk Dan out of his funk at breakfast, but he remained quiet, almost removed, during the three-hour trip to Abilene. "I hope you can perk up a little before we get to the hospital. Zeke's got it bad enough."

"I know. You're right," Dan said. "All this stuff is crowdin' in on me, on us. I've got an uneasy feelin' 'bout what Drake might be up to, now he's out on bond. I'll perk up. Don't worry 'bout it."

On the way to Hedrick Memorial, LaDonna called Ella. Dan could tell by his wife's expressions the news wasn't good. They talked until they pulled into the hospital parking building.

"What's up?"

"He's in the cardiac intensive care unit. The doctors said the pacemaker wasn't regulating Zeke's heartbeat right, so they would do catheterization to look for new blockages. We can only be there a few minutes."

"So, should we be botherin' him?"

"Yeah, Ella said he asked for you specifically. Drake was in the room at the time. And, she said he yelled at Zeke for wanting you to mess in their business. I'm sure that upset Zeke and the monitors started beeping. Ella said the nurse in charge threatened to have Drake physically removed."

Dan rolled both hands forward and back on the steering wheel as if trying to twist it apart. LaDonna leaned over and took his right hand.

"Danny, I know this is going to be tough, but we've got to visit Zeke."

"Is, is, *he* still there?"

"No," Ella said. Drake left, stormed out without saying anything else, not even a goodbye to Zeke." A few minutes later, the courtesy shuttle took them to the hospital's front entrance.

As they got off the shuttle, Drake was walking out of the sliding doors toward them. Dan and LaDonna paused as if expecting Drake to say something, but he put on his sunglasses as he walked by, close enough to almost brush Dan's sleeve. Dan turned as Drake walked away. As he was about to speak, LaDonna put her hand on his arm, squeezed, and said, "Stop it."

As Drake was getting on the shuttle, he turned and pointed at Dan, then LaDonna, then back to Dan. LaDonna took Dan's arm, nudged him to turn around.

Ella was waiting outside Zeke's cubicle in the cardiac ICU. She said he had been taken for the heart catheterization and would be gone about an hour. She and LaDonna took seats in one corner of the waiting room.

Dan paced, moving from chair to couch to chair, not finding comfort anywhere. He orbited the room several times, stopping to pull a tattered *Popular Mechanics* from the magazine rack, riffle the pages.

He signaled LaDonna he was going for a walk. She waved and pointed to the elevators.

Thirty minutes passed, his cell phone vibrated.

"Danny, he's out and back in the ICU. He can have one visitor for about ten minutes. Where are you?"

"I'm walking back in right now. Be there in a minute."

LaDonna and Ella were waiting outside the ICU. The doctor had found two new blocked arteries near Zeke's heart and was going to try clot-dissolving medication first but didn't rule out more stents or surgery. The cardiac charge nurse said Zeke's appearance would be a shock, then walked through the ICU door with him, stopping at the nurse's station to introduce him.

The nurse, stationed to watch two cubicles at once, pointed at Zeke. He was lying flat, staring at the ceiling, his mouth barely moving as if he was whispering to someone only he could see.

Dan touched his hand. "How you doin', buddy?" He swallowed hard when Zeke turned to face him, trying hard to hide the shock. Zeke's eyes were two off-white marbles with black centers. Dan couldn't tell if he was focusing on him. There was several days' growth of stark white stubble covering his jaw and down his neck.

Zeke moved his mouth, straining to speak. Then he focused on Dan. "Did you see my boy, Danny? He said he'd be right back. He was in a big hurry to get us one of them foot-long hot dogs from Dairy Queen. He's full of surprises. His mom wants one, too." He turned to look toward the foot of his bed and lifted his emaciated hand, and pointed a knobby finger. "Kiddo, Danny is here. Did you say hello?"

Dan squeezed Zeke's other hand. It felt cool, gray as wind-blown dust. Dan didn't know what to do next. The decision came with an insistent beeping, rising in volume. He backed out of the cubicle as the nurse rushed in. He watched as she adjusted the oxygen flow, quieting the alarm. He turned and went through the double doors into the waiting area.

"I saw him." He looked to Ella, then LaDonna, then to the gray-haired volunteer at the information desk, back to LaDonna. "I don't know. Can we go?" Without waiting for an answer, he started down the hall.

"Danny?" LaDonna, Ella at her side, caught up with him at the elevator doors. "Here." She handed him his baseball cap. He started to put it on, then rolled it up and out again. LaDonna took his arm.

"Zeke's in good hands. You're all right. Let's go home."

After collecting Ella's bag at her friend's apartment and getting coffee at the Alsup's on the edge of Abilene, they settled in for the three-hour trip. An hour passed, the sun set, and conversation ebbed.

The silence of miles was barely interrupted by Dan, Ella, or LaDonna. Regardless of how each tried to start a conversation or offer The silence of miles was barely interrupted by Dan, Ella, or LaDonna. Regardless of how each tried to start a conversation or offer an observation, the others had no discussion, only head shakes, hunched shoulders, and noncommittal mumbles. Communication settled to occasional eye contact between Ella and Dan in the rearview mirror, glances at LaDonna's reflection as she stared out her window.

Dan shifted from side to side in his seat, grunting as he tried to take the strain off his left leg. He pushed the radio's scan button. The numbers advanced stopped for ten seconds, then searched again. He found a station that said there was rain forecasted, beginning overnight and continuing through late Friday. "Perfect for that game," he mumbled, "goddamned perfect."

Ella's phone chimed as the lights of Jerrod came into view. "Hey. Yeah, we're almost there. Another ten minutes or so, I guess. You are? Oh, I'm so glad. Please wait. No, I don't care who sees you in my driveway. Good. That nonsense is over. Okay. We're on our way. I really need to see you. Good. Bye."

She leaned forward, the first smile of the trip in her voice. "That was Wyman."

Dan's mood lightened. "Now, that's a surprise. Good for you. Good for Wyman. Good for all of us."

Wyman was standing beside his car in Ella's driveway. He retrieved her suitcase from the back seat and stopped at Dan's open window.

"Got a bandanna here if you need a mask." Dan smiled as he poked his finger at Wyman.

"I can will myself invisible. It's a priestly power."

"Look forward to seeing that in church Sunday."

"Never can tell what a little extra in the collection plate will do. Hey, thanks for getting her home. I guess your daughter and her fella are coming tomorrow?"

"Yeah, we're really lookin' forward." He paused a moment and looked at LaDonna, then back to Wyman. "Hey, what are you guys doin' Thanksgivin'?"

Wyman looked at Ella. "I don't know. We haven't even discussed it."

"Why don't we do City Café? They put on a good feed. One o'clock?"

Wyman looked at Ella. "You know, that sounds good. Okay with you?"

"Sure. I guess we're ready for the busybodies to gasp and cover their mouths when we show up together – in one car."

LaDonna was pleased to see her husband relax and smile for the first time that day.

They talked a few more minutes, then Dan raised his window and pulled out of the driveway onto the street, turned left, headed for the highway by the high school. As they were about to pass Zeke's house, Dan slowed and stopped underneath the corner streetlight.

"What are you doing?" LaDonna drew back as Dan lowered her window.

"Lookin'"

"At what?"

"See Drake's car? It doesn't look like it's been driven anywhere. The chalk mark's still on the tire from when we put it in storage." Dan took his flashlight out of the center console.

"So how did he get to Abilene?"

"Look's like he drove Zeke's Ranger." Dan aimed his light at the rear wheel well on the driver's side of the pickup. "What do you

"It's muddy on the back fender."

"Zeke sure hasn't driven it since the rain. How could it get muddy? There wasn't any mud on the road to Abilene." Dan raised LaDonna's window, put the flashlight back, and headed for the road home.

Neither of them saw Drake watching them from the blacked-out second-story bedroom.

All the way home, Dan felt the dread building. He tried several times to put a voice on it but didn't want to worry LaDonna. It came to the surface as they turned and headed down the gravel road to the house.

A vehicle had veered on and off the road several times, sometime in the last few hours. The pasture was still muddy from the previous days' rains. Dan sat up straighter in his seat and slowed to a crawl as they passed the fresh ruts. They looked like they'd been made by a truck or SUV. They were very deep in several places, suggesting the driver had almost been stuck several times, only to scatter mud as it got traction again.

LaDonna heard Dan's breathing becoming more forced and distinct as he slowed and then stopped beside their house. Both hands were gripping the wheel, back and forth twisting.

"Aren't you going to pull into the back?"

Dan put his hand over his eyes and pulled it down below his nose. "Huh? Oh yeah. Was thinkin'."

"Thinking what?"

"Never mind." He slowed, pulled ahead, and stopped in front of the shop under the yard light's iridescent blue cast. "I'll get the stuff out of the back. You want most of it in the barn, right?"

"I'm gonna unlock." She got out and walked around the Suburban as he raised the hatch. "Dan, Sniff isn't here."

In his ten years, he'd never failed to unfold himself from this shelter under the step and come running to LaDonna's feet, where he would sit and extend his paw. Not tonight.

LaDonna walked around the steps and looked in the shelter. She looked over at Dan, who'd picked up more boxes, walked through the open barn door.

When LaDonna screamed, Dan dropped the boxes, turned, and ran around the Suburban toward the house. She was standing on the porch, holding her stomach with one hand, covering her mouth with the other. Her shoulders heaved with sobs.

Dan ran up the steps. She moved her hand away from her stomach, turned, pointed to the kitchen door.

Sniff's body was lying half propped against the door. There was blood streaming from an open wound between his eyes, his face distorted as if a giant fist had opened a space between his ears. He had died with one paw extended outward.

A line of blood smears followed the steps down to the gravel where Sniff had greeted someone. His body had been posed against the kitchen door after his death. Dan felt his stomach churn but fought off the urge to vomit.

He put his right arm around LaDonna and led her down the steps and back to the Suburban, opened the passenger door, helped her in, and closed the door. He went around, opened the driver's door, reached in and started the engine, and pressed the heater control on the steering wheel. "Wait right here. I'll be back in a few minutes."

He could hear LaDonna's sobs as he shut the door and walked back to the porch. He moved the dog's body aside, went into the kitchen, found a large garbage bag, and went back to the already rigid form. He slowly pulled the bag over Sniff's body, hefted it, started down the steps. On the bottom tread, a muddy footprint, not his, not LaDonna's.

He stepped away from it and carried Sniff's body behind the Grandma House. He put the bag down, found a spade sticking in the loose soggy dirt of the garden plot, and dug deep enough to assure undisturbed rest.

He was beginning to feel the hot sting of revenge coursing through his body.

LaDonna walked up behind Dan, who was on all fours. He was sweeping the muddy dirt and cottonwood leaves from side to side. He paused, took a deep breath, patted the moist earth.

LaDonna bent over and put her hand in the middle of his back. "Come on. It's done."

Dan stood and brushed the soil from his knees. "Can you wait a minute? There's one other thing . . ."

"No, sweetie, it's all right." She touched his cheek. "I've already cleaned up the blood and other stuff. Come on, let's go in." She put her hand under his arm as they walked to the steps. Dan glanced toward the igloo-shaped shelter, expecting Sniff to come out, sit and shake hands.

26

The bursts of light began to fracture Dan's sleep. After each flash, the sound of metal barrels being thrown onto the barn. Another white stroke and the barrels again. Soon, the two came together, bringing him upright.

"What are you doing?"

"What was that noise?" He looked around as LaDonna turned on her reading light.

"It's a storm. Been going about thirty minutes now. It's four A.M."

Then, the rain began to pulse against the balcony French doors. He felt dumb. Why did this particular storm do this to him? He usually slept through. Then, he drew a breath. The footprint. He turned on his reading light, put on his slippers, stood, and hurried out of the bedroom. "Where you going?"

"The footprint," he yelled back as he ran down the stairs, "I've . . ." His voice and thump-thump on the stairs were obscured by insistent peals of thunder and the rising hiss of rain. He shuffled into the kitchen and went to the back door.

The sudden downpour had triggered the spotlights, one shining on the porch, the other slanting down on the steps. He wiped the condensate from the window. The footprint was gone. Blood smears gone. "Why didn't I at least take a picture of that footprint, that blood?

Now, we've got no proof."

"Proof?" LaDonna stood next to him at the door.

"I shoulda covered that print, at least took a picture."

LaDonna walked over to the windows in the door and peered out.

"What good would that have done? What would it prove?"

"It coulda been matched with one of his boots."

"His?" She turned to look at Dan. "You mean Drake?"

She gently turned him and pushed him back toward the stairway. "If we ever had any evidence like that, it's gone." She switched off the kitchen light and followed him up the stairs to their bedroom.

They sat on the side of the bed, Dan looking at his hands resting palm upon his legs. He closed both as if grabbing the steering wheel.

"He can't get away with this. He can't."

She put her hand palm-down on his, causing his hand to relax. "We can think about a report in the morning . . ." She glanced over her shoulder at the clock on the mantle. ". . . this morning. Let's try to get some sleep."

She moved to her side. Dan ran his hand over his head and turned off his light, and pulled up the covers. "He's not going to get away with this."

"I know. Now let's try to sleep."

He stayed beside LaDonna until her breathing slowed. He slipped out of bed and padded down the hallway to the TV room, his favorite late-night haunt. He closed the double-louvered doors to the room full of overstuffed furniture and a wall-sized TV.

He stared at the black screen for several minutes, going over the options. He knew he ought to report Sniff's shooting and the strange tracks to the sheriff's office. Still, He decided there was no point in bothering the night dispatcher based on suspicion. That could wait 'til morning. He didn't look forward to calling the sheriff, but his house, their lives had been violated. If he was powerless, maybe Mose Britten wouldn't be. He willed away thoughts of the terror Sniff must have felt in his final moments.

He woke the TV and clicked through the channels, stopping for part of a *Forged in Fire* episode, watched jewelry being hawked on the *Home Shopping Channel*. He settled on the *Weather Channel,* hoping to get an updated local forecast instead of the Missoula "snowcast." He pulled a bottled water from the small fridge beside his lounger.

Finally, Abilene weather. Perky high-cheek-bones-spike-nails blithely guessed—based on the multicolored blob on the radar—that there would be "quite a bit of rain for those desert folks all the way through Friday evening." No-neck-bad-toupee agreed, then read a fun weather fact, his voice dissolving to a mumble.

———————

"Couldn't sleep. Decided to try TV, huh? What's the deal with the water bottle?"

For a moment, Dan wondered why the weatherman asked something so personal. "What, huh?" He flipped the leg rest handle on the recliner and gave LaDonna a puzzled look. "Oh, hi. I got some sleep. Still rainin'?" He looked at the water bottle in his hand and put it back in the cooler.

"Stopped about five. Get moving - omelets for breakfast."

———————

They finished and cleared the table. Dan stood at the sink, scraping the plates into the trash. "How're you gonna tell Nelly about Sniff?"

Donna took one final sip of her coffee, got up, walked to the sink. "I think the worst we can do is tell her how he died and that we're suspicious of Drake."

"Yeah, I agree. Tyin' Drake to that, even if it's true, would really set her off. And I wouldn't blame her." He dried his hands with a tea towel and sat, stretching his left leg. "What are you thinkin'?"

LaDonna looked out the window over the sink. "I don't think she'll be quite as upset if we blame it on the coyotes. I mean, we've seen a lot of them around here lately. They're known to lure a dog out and gang upon him."

"Yeah, I guess so. Are you gonna call her?"

"Yeah, during my noon break," Ladonna said. "I think their classes are out by then. They should be getting ready to come this way."

Dan slapped his thighs and got up. "Wouldn't work for me to do it. I have a way of blurtin' out the wrong stuff."

"That's why I said *I'd* call her. What are you going to do today?"

"Goin' to the store for a while, probably eat lunch with Wyman. An', I need to talk to Freddy Paz . . ."

She put a hand on each bicep and turned him toward her. "You've got to promise me you're not going to do anything—you know—you're not going to hurt Drake." She took his chin and held it, so their eyes met. "You're *not* going to do anything like that?"

Dan wiped condensate from the small window in the door and parted the curtains. "I, I, don't know what to do."

"What I want you to do is to guarantee you're going to be safe, you're going to be careful, you're going to think about your family all day long today, anytime you feel the anger rising, I want you to think about us, all of us, you included. Okay? Here, look at me."

Dan leaned into her, wrapping her in a gentle bear hug. "Thank you."

For a moment, neither spoke, finding comfort together.

"Of course, sweetie, that's what you and I are all about. Now, one other thing."

Dan was resting his head in the nape of her neck. "Yeah?"

"Can you let me go? I gotta go to work."

Dan put his jacket and boots on and headed out the back door. No sign of the footprint or blood, only a muddy smear,

He looked up and turned to follow the flock of geese passing overhead. As he watched them, he saw LaDonna standing at the window over the sink. He put his open right hand on his chest. She blew another kiss, as she had done many times the last thirty years.

JerriSue had the day off, so when he arrived at the store after checking the mail, he didn't bother turning on the showroom lights. When he walked into his office, Dumbass woke from inside her favorite Styrofoam cooler, hopped out, stretched fore and aft, and rubbed against Dan's leg.

Dan fed the cat and went through the mail, ninety percent catalogs, and once-in-a-lifetime offers. He tossed it all in the trash and leaned back. The late Fifies' central heating clattered and groaned to life, and Dumbass jumped in Dan's lap. He looked up at Dan expectantly, rolled on his back, and began his wheezing purr. "You know, don't you? His scent is on me." The cat righted himself, stretched up to rub his head under Dan's chin, settled back to his lap. "Yep, you know."

An hour later, the front door chime rang, prompting Dumbass to leap down. "Who is it? Come on back." Dan wiped the sleep out of his eyes and cleared his throat. Eleven thirty.

"We going to lunch or not?" Wyman was standing in his office door, pointing to Dan's wall clock.

Dan stood and stretched. "Yeah, sorry, I was supposta to call you. Is it rainin'?"

"Nope, looks like it's going to clear off." Wyman took a seat in the chair opposite Dan's and motioned Dan to sit.

"Hey. What's the problem, pastor?"

Wyman leaned forward. "No problem. I spoke with LaDonna a few minutes ago . . ."

Dan put his hands on the arms of his chair and started to stand.

Wyman motioned him to sit. "No, she's fine. She wanted to make sure you are okay, too." "LaDonna told you about the dog. What happened to him?"

"Yes. She said you were very close to the dog . . ."

"Sniff. The dog's name is, was, Sniff."

"Sniff. She wanted me to look in on you."

"I had me a little nap here, the cat and me. I guess I'm okay."

Wyman scooted his chair a little closer to Dan's desk. "LaDonna told me she worried you'd do something to . . ."

"Not for her calmin' me down, I woulda gone lookin' for his ass first thing this mornin'."

"You probably would not have liked you after you found him."

"You're right." Dan exhaled, stood, extended his hand to Wyman. "Thanks. Say a prayer for all of us, okay?"

"Part of my job description. Now, shall we barbeque?"

27

They went to the small meeting room at the back of Thrasher's long narrow building. Wyman finished his second glass of tea. "Dan, I'm not sure what to do about Zeke Kilborn. Under normal circumstances, I would drive to Abilene and look in on him. Still, my relationship with his sister-in-law may complicate things."

Dan threw the remnants of the paper towel onto his plate. "Complicate? How?"

"Ella told me last night Drake called her when she got back from Abilene with you guys. I stayed about an hour after you left. Ella said she had the uneasy feeling he was somewhere nearby, waiting for me to go. Maybe watching us."

"What did he say?"

"He rambled for maybe thirty minutes – how much he missed his mom, how the hospital was mistreating Zeke; not being able to fly because of the weather. He shifted from his mother's passing to talking about her as if she was still alive. That part really spooked Ella. Oh yeah, she said he didn't appreciate you showing up at the hospital."

"What? Didn't appreciate me? I'll be damned." Dan began to stand, catching his plate before it was about to fall from the table. "Sorry. Gotta hold it down." He sat back on the long wooden bench.

Wyman smiled. "That's okay. Then, he proceeded to launch into her about us, me, and Ella. He said I was out to take her share of her sister's estate and should be run out of town. Dan, I need to go see Zeke, but I'm not sure how to do it without causing a stink with Drake." Dan pushed his plate and tea glass to the middle of the table.

"Shitty. Just plain shitty. I don't know what to say. I don't."

Wyman took off his glasses, wiped them with a paper towel, sighted through them at the wagon wheel chandelier, and put them back on. "I'm not sure I know what to say or do. I'm telling you this by way of heads-up. I think I'll wait 'til Friday morning to go to Abilene, assuming Zeke's still there by then. Ella is pretty sure the doctors are going to hold him past Thursday."

Dan rubbed the rim of his tea glass. "Okay, you want me to go with you?"

"You know, I won't mind that."

"That'll work. I want to be back in time for the football game."

"Me too. By the way, Monday morning, one of the cowboys from the graveside came to the office with a big satchel full of cash for Archie's widow. I asked him to wait while I counted it, so he could have a receipt. He said whatever I did was all right with him.

"My secretary and I counted the bills and loose change and came up with the same amount, $2508.52. I turned the satchel over, and an envelope fell out. I opened it, and there's a check for exactly the same amount from Zeke Kilborn. How'd he know what to write it for, Dan?"

Dan thought a moment, then tapped his forehead. "One of the cowboys is Ella's great uncle. He probably told her, and she told Zeke. I think he planned all along to match whatever was donated at the graveside. Zeke must have written that check Friday afternoon. Probably not long before they had to take him to the hospital."

Wyman stood, put his jacket on. "And there you have it, good and evil sharing blood. You live and learn."

Dan scooted his stool back and put his coat on. Dan stepped in front of Wyman as he was about to pull his billfold from his pants pocket. "Got this one, your grace. Put it on my tithe tab."

Wyman drove out ahead of Dan, who paused at the street entrance to Thrasher's gravel parking lot. He found Freddy's cryptic business card and dialed the number. It rang once. "Espinoza."

"Freddy? Oh, sorry. *Ranger* Espinoza."

"Freddy is fine, Mr. Baker. What can I do for you?"

Dan went over the conversation with Wyman Costley and the hospital encounter with Drake, mud on the Kilborn SUV, tracks in his field, dead dog.

Freddy made noncommittal noises as Dan spoke. "How can I help you, Mr. Baker?"

"That thing that whatyamacallit you put on his car. I guess it's still there?"

"Queried it a few hours ago. It's still active."

"Queried?"

"By cell phone."

"Oh. Look, can you check if it—the car, I mean—moved last night after about seven o'clock?"

"I can, but why?"

"I'd be interested if the asshole stalked Ella Parker, or Father

Costley, or both. I'd really like to know if he was spyin' on Ella." He gave Freddy her address.

"I see. Let me work on that here in a few minutes, then I'll get back to you."

Dan closed his phone, waved, and drove away.

———————

Freddy entered the tracking app password and called up history. At seven o'clock the night before, the pulsing green trace started at the Kilborn house, right after two blocks, left and stopped. The line turned red. The street plot showed Drake parked in an alley. Freddy ran his finger up the screen, advancing the time stamp to eight o'clock, where the line turned green again. He tapped *play,* and the target reversed course, moved back to the start, turned red again.

As Freddy finished texting a summary to Dan's phone, the tracking app chirped. The green line began pulsing at the Kilborn house, turned right, two blocks then left, three blocks, right, west for a few minutes, sharp right turn, forward a fraction, stop, turn red. Drake was at the airport. Freddy knew he had to be there too.

He decided to exit to the Windy Acres Trailer Park, went over the railroad crossing, turned left onto the dirt road beside the tracks, west to the airport. Freddy stopped in the bottom of a shallow gulley about a hundred yards from the airport.

He eased his door shut, crouched and peered through a tall stand of prairie grass on the edge of the gulley. Drake had raised the large hangar door. He was climbing down from the wing of Number 2.

He threw a tool onto the concrete with such force Freddy could hear the clank. Drake's voice turned to a shriek as he walked back and forth in the front of the plane. There was botomless anger in words lost in the muddy field.

Then, Drake turned to one side, threw up his arms, appeared to be talking to someone standing nearby. He walked a few steps, put out his hands as if touching unseen shoulders. Then, in perfect pantomime, relaxed one hand moved the other to about where the invisible neck would be, held it there, and walked toward the rear of the hangar. The distant sound of the metal office door shutting was Freddy's cue to move closer. He drove up to the open hangar, lights out, gently closed his door, and walked toward the office, staying close to the wall. As he moved nearer, Drake's voice was more understandable.

"I know. I know. I know. But I had to do it, Mom." It was the tone of a distraught twelve-year-old, pleading for understanding. "I gave that girl—I gave her that stupid little dog. It was my right to take it back. It didn't want to go. It hid. I had to, well, you know what I had to . . ."

"Baker's dog?" Freddy whispered to himself. Drake was having a conversation with *un espíritu invisible* about killing a dog? Not enough to justify an arrest. They'd warned him at the academy about unguarded utterances made before a suspect was Mirandized. A few feet away, there was a two-wheeled drum dolly leaning against the corrugated metal wall. He stepped over to it, pushed it to the floor with a sharp ringing sound. Adding to the effect, Freddy yelled toward the office door, "Shit. Damn it. Who put that damn dolly there?"

As he slammed the dolly back to the wall, Drake opened the door.

"What the hell you doin' here? We ain't flyin' today."

"Oh, I know. I was drivin' by and saw your car, figured I'd stop and see what's goin' on."

Drake said nothing for a moment, looking at Freddy, then the dolly, back to Freddy, his eyes in slits. "I mailed your check. What do you want?" The fair skin at his temples was taking on a pink hue.

Freddy forced himself to relax, offering a broad, unthreatening smile. "Yeah, I got it. I hadn't heard from you in a couple of days.

Wanted to know how your dad's doin'." He moved a few steps toward Drake and lowered his voice, trying to sound concerned. "Is he still in the hospital?"

Drake seemed to relax. "I saw him the other day. I think he's okay. I think they'll let him come home tomorrow. I'm gonna go to Abilene to get him." Brightening and stepping toward Freddy, he said, "Hey. You could come with me. You could help me get him in the car. We could go to the mall, maybe a couple of bars. It would be fun. What do you say? You could meet my mom. She's stayin' at the hospital with him."

Freddy fixed his smile, put his hands in his pockets. "I'm plannin' on goin' to that Thanksgiving feed at the City Café. I hear it's real good. I guess I better stay in town. Why don't you get Ronny to go with you?"

Drake stepped back as if he was about to go back to the office. "Why should I take Ronny?" His tone cooled. "What's wrong with you goin' with me?" He stepped forward again.

Freddy shifted his weight and moved one foot backward slightly.

He put on his best smile. "I got a date, and she expects me to be there."

Drake's body language warned Freddy it was the wrong thing to say. "Who? Who you got a date with? Who? Really?" He took another.

Drake's body language warned Freddy it was the wrong thing to say. "Who? Who you got a date with? Who? Really?" He took another step forward. "Oh, let me guess. How about *la senorita perfecta*? The schoolteacher?"

Freddy turned and started walking to the front of the hangar. Drake followed, almost on his heels. He reached for Freddy's shoulder, but Freddy sensed the move and stepped aside, causing Drake to lose his balance. He caught himself on the engine cowling of the spray plane.

Freddy turned. "What are you doing, Drake? What's going on?"

"Oh, nothing, *Don senor grande*. You threatened to ruin me if I fired you. I shoulda done it."

Freddy moved his feet shoulder-width and put an edge on his voice. "You firing me?"

Drake narrowed his eyes, sighed, started toward the office. He yelled, "I don't need you out here today. Go away." The textured glass rattled as he slammed the door.

28

This looks familiar." Rob pointed at the lights over the gin yard.

"This is where we turn?" Janelle looked up from her cell phone.

"Yeah, that way."

"Lots brighter than the last time we were here. What are those long white things? They look like loaves of bread."

"Money."

"Money?"

"Each one is thirteen bales of cotton. That times two dollars a pound times seventy-five hundred pounds, and you're talking about real money."

"Some of these your dad's?"

"I doubt it. Mom said he got all his in two weeks ago. I'm sure he's glad all that's over. He had a bad start when he found Archie unconscious."

Rob massaged her shoulder with his right hand. She patted his hand and leaned toward him. He was looking at the long row of town lights in the distance. "That's Jerrod, right?"

"Yep. Almost home." She smiled at Rob and held up her left hand. "I can't wait 'til they see this." The diamond reflected the gin yard lights. She reached out and squeezed his neck.

While Rob was filling up at Zip In, Janelle was on her cell phone. "We're looking forward to seeing you. Huh? I sound that way because I *am* happy. Huh? You'll have to wait and see. No, we burgered in Breckenridge. We're full."

Dan and LaDonna were waiting for them in front of the Grandma House. They walked up to the car as Rob and Janelle got out.

"Hey you two. Welcome back." Dan lifted Janelle off her feet in the traditional bearhug then gripped Rob's hand hard enough to make him wince.

LaDonna hugged Janelle then kissed Rob's cheek. "You guys come on in. It's sooooo good to see you." She started up the kitchen steps, followed by Janelle, Rob, and Dan. Janelle paused on the second step and looked over the railing as the light came on.

"I moved the doghouse, Nelly," Dan said. "I didn't think you'd be comfortable seein' it."

Janelle wiped one of her eyes with a finger. "Thanks, Pop," a slight quaver in her voice, "I'm gonna miss him."

"Me too, kiddo—me too. Hey Rob, throw me your keys, and I'll take your stuff in the Grandma House." Rob gave him a thumbs-up.

A few minutes later, Dan fussed with the coffee maker, and LaDonna pulled a tray of chocolate chip cookies out of the oven. Rob and Janelle were sitting close together at the table. Janelle was holding up her left hand, waiting for them to turn around.

When she saw the ring, LaDonna almost dropped the cookies. She squealed and gathered Janelle in her arms. Dan looked like a toy windup talking bear whose batteries had run down, standing with the full coffee pot, mouth wide open.

Dan put the coffee on the counter, joined in the hug with LaDonna and Janelle, and pulled Rob into the scrum. The celebration gave way to LaDonna's giddy questions about Rob's proposal and when the wedding would be. The chatter ebbed and flowed for half an hour.

"I'm bushed," Rob said, looking at his watch. He stood, watching Janelle's hands. No *stop* signal. She stood, leaned to kiss Dan on the cheek, and put her arm around Rob's waist. "We'll see you in the morning. We're gonna sleep in. *We're* definitely going to sleep in."

They went down the steps, waved at Dan and LaDonna, watching from the door.

————————

LaDonna was at the stove when Janelle walked in the next morning. "Hey. Where's Rob?"

"He's on his computer. I'll go get him when breakfast is ready."

LaDonna handed Janelle a cup of coffee and joined her at the table. "Honey, I'm so glad to see all this happen for you. We think the world of Rob." She glanced down at the ring. "Looks like you do too."

"We've done a lot of soul-searching and truth-telling over the last couple of weeks." Janelle held her left hand up, looking at the ring. "I wanted to talk to you for a minute about Drake and what's going on with him. From what you told me yesterday, he seems to be in a lot of trouble."

LaDonna leaned forward and looked into Janelle's eyes. "Those are *his* problems, Janelle. It will be up to him to work them out or not. They've got nothing to do with us, especially you. You understand? Tell me. Do you understand?"

"Oh, yeah. Oh, please don't get me wrong. That's all over, way over. We're moving on."

LaDonna leaned back and breathed out slowly. "Okay. Good. We're going to the café for Thanksgiving, and I'm hoping he won't be around. He should be going to Abilene to check on Zeke."

"How is Zeke?"

"Not good. It's his heart."

"Is the pacemaker not working?"

"I think his heart is broken. They can't fix that." She got up, walked over to the stove, lifted the lid on the scrambled-egg casserole. "I think we're about ready for breakfast. Go tell Rob." She looked out the window over the sink and held up her hand. "No, hang on."

Dan shut the barn door as Rob was walking out of the Grandma House.

"Mornin' Rob. Did ya'll sleep all right?"

"You bet. That king-sized bed makes room for my snoring and her sleep running."

Dan felt momentary embarrassment hearing about his daughter's sleeping habits but let it go. He moved toward the long wooden bench on the porch of the guest house. "Let's talk a minute."

Dan spared the gruesome details as he told Rob about Drake's behavior over the last two weeks. Rob said little, nodding occasionally. "All I'm askin' is ignore him, walk away, whatever you need to do if he shows up at the cafe. He has gotten very unstable over the last two weeks. As I look back, it's been comin' on a long time, startin' with his mother's death. "Today, I bet he'll go to Abilene to see Zeke. We'll see how that lashes up."

Dan and Rob stood. "I'm proud to be in your family, Dan. And I want you to know I will do everything within my power to make Janelle happy. I do love her so much."

Dan smiled, looked up at the kitchen window. LaDonna was motioning them to come to breakfast.

———————

LaDonna, Janelle, Rob, and Dan got in line at the Jerrod City Café at one o'clock. The line was already out the door and halfway to the curb. LaDonna talked to one of her teacher friends about Janelle's engagement as Wyman and Ella got in line.

"Mornin', guys," Dan said. He leaned toward Wyman and whispered. "Got your disguises ready?"

Wyman smiled and looked at Ella. "We're wearing our hypocrisy costumes."

Dan looked back to the crowd. "Lotsa other folks wearing the same thing here, probably." The line moved slightly. "Ella, go take a look at Janelle's hand."

"What? Are you kidding?" She squeezed past Dan, rushed to Janelle, grabbed her hand to look, and then hugged her. Janelle pointed to Rob, and Ella turned to shake his hand.

"Mr. Baker?" Dan recognized Drake's high-pitched voice immediately and turned to confront him.

"Drake?" He forced himself to whisper. "What are you doin' here?" Dan stepped toward Drake, who moved backward. Dan turned and looked at LaDonna, who was staring back. She started to walk toward him, but Dan held up his hand, signaling her to wait.

He moved two more steps and switched to his inside voice. "What do you want, Drake?" Dan stared at a couple who had stopped a few feet away. They looked away, moved toward the café.

Drake had both hands in front, palms up. "I don't want any trouble. Honest, I don't."

Dan clenched and unclenched his right hand. "You're not gonna talk to anybody in my family, not anybody."

Drake looked down. His posture reminded Dan of Drake standing alone in the parking lot after the parade. Drake looked humbled. Dan glanced toward the café. LaDonna had spread her arms as if to embrace Rob, Janelle, Wyman, and Ella and move them to safety.

Still looking down, Drake said softly. "I'd like to talk to my aunt Ella only for a minute, please."

Dan waited for Drake to look up. "Okay. But I don't want a scene, and I'm sure Ella doesn't either."

Drake stared into Dan's eyes. "Me neither. I need to talk to her a minute."

"Okay. You walk over there to your car and stay there. Don't move. I'll get Ella."

Dan watched him walk away, stepped into the café, and motioned to Ella. She was already seated with the rest of the group. She pointed to herself, questioning. He nodded. LaDonna walked to Dan with her.

"Ella, Drake says he wants to talk to you. To be honest, I can't believe how different he is right now. He's soft-spoken, almost contrite. Humble. That's what I thought of when he was askin' to see you."

Ella looked past Dan through the café windows and saw Drake standing beside his car 100 feet away. "This is kinda spooky. But if I can do anything . . ."

"If you can keep him calm, maybe talk some sense into him, that'd be goin' a long way." LaDonna patted her on the shoulder.

"All right. Something says not to trust him, but he's family, so here I go." She gave a small wave to Wyman, who was pushing his chair back, about to stand. She motioned him to sit again and walked out of the café as Dan and LaDonna joined the others.

Ella nervously rubbed her hands together. "Ducky? What are you doing here? I don't think it's a good idea to go in there and eat, considering all the trouble . . ."

She was so surprised when he reached out to touch her shoulder, she flinched back a step.

"No, Lala, I don't want no trouble either. I'm worried about my daddy. I don't know what to do. I feel like I need to go see him in the hospital. And, and, I feel like I need to apologize to Janelle and her boyfriend."

Ella put her hand on his shoulder and urged him back so that he leaned on the Mustang driver's side door. "Ducky? You know the best thing you can do for Zeke right now? You can go home, stay in your house and wait for me to call you. I've been talking to the nurses where he is, and they've promised to call me . . ."

Drake turned as if to open the car door. "But, don't you think I ought 'ta go to Abilene, be with him? It's Thanksgivin'—Lala, Momma, and Daddy's favorite time. We've always been together at Thanksgivin', Momma and I need to be with Daddy. We need to go see him."

Drake's casual mention of Bertie jolted Ella. She moved beside him and put her arm around his shoulder. Instead of leaning into her when she'd comfort him in the days and weeks after Bertie's funeral, she felt him tense.

"Ducky, things have been kinda strained with you and a lot of people around here. I don't think you're in any state of mind to be drivin' to Abilene. Now admit it, you don't think so either, do you?" She swallowed hard, trying to control the waver in her voice. "Do you think your momma would want you going to Abilene when you've had so much trouble around here?" Drake looked down and shook his head.

"Will you promise me you won't go to Abilene right now? Will you promise?"

Drake looked up then to the side. "I don't know, Lala. I need to see him—we need to see him. I don't know.' He opened his car door, sat, and pulled the door closed. "I'm gonna talk to mom about it." He started the car and backed out.

As he turned onto the street from the courthouse parking lot, Freddy and Mariel rounded the corner. They saw Ella wave at Drake, who stopped in the intersection. He got out of his car, leaving the door open.

Mariel touched Freddy's hand. "What's he doing, Freddy? He looks like he wants to fight."

"Let me see." Freddy got out and walked toward Drake, standing in the middle of the street, legs spread.

Drake pointed at Freddy, who calculated how best to reach for his pistol on the belt at his back. "You need to come to work tomorrow. We got stuff to do." Drake's eyes were like slits in the middle of his face. He reached in his shirt pocket, pulled out his sunglasses, and put them on.

Freddy turned and smiled at Mariel, then turned back to Drake. "Sure. I'll be there. What time?"

Drake got back in his car, shut the door. "Be there by three. I need your help changing the timin' belt out in this car. Now, I gotta go get my daddy." He raised his window and gunned his engine, almost colliding with Freddy.

"Where's he going?"

"To his house, I hope."

"But, he said he was going to get his father."

"Yeah, I heard. He's in his own little world. I don't know what to believe. "What I don't know is what happens next to him. He's obviously movin' toward *loco*, but if I was gonna start arresting people for actin' crazy, we'd need a lot bigger prisons. If the judge had only agreed to sign that warrant before he left town. We coulda taken Drake outta circulation. I'm afraid we're gonna end up reactin' when we oughta be actin'. Right now, I want him out of circulation."

Freddy pocketed his cell phone as he pulled into a parking place. Had he been looking at the tracking app on his phone, he would have seen Drake go to the city limits and head south for Abilene.

29

I t's six right now, Danny. Are you sure you and Wyman are going to be back for the game?" LaDonna looked out the window over the sink. "There are big fluffy clouds out here. Have you checked the weather?"

Dan bit into another slice of bacon and drained his milk glass. "Yeah, before I came down. We might have fog by late afternoon and into the evening. No rain." He took his plate to the sink and ran water into the glass. "I'm supposed to pick Wyman up at seven. We'll be at the hospital in Abilene by ten, spend a couple of hours, be back on the road by noon. What are you doin' today?"

LaDonna was still looking out the sink window. "Rob has to go to the library to work on that med school practice exam. The three of us will have breakfast here in a bit, and then Janelle and I are going into town to do a little shopping, then have lunch with Ella."

Dan kissed her on the cheek and took his jacket off the clothes tree. "See you 'bout three. I'll call when we get there and when we leave."

———

By nine o'clock, Dan and Wyman were south of Breckenridge, about to turn toward Abilene when Wyman's cell phone chimed. "Hey. Good to hear your voice. Yeah? Really? The doctors said what?" Wyman looked at Dan and held up a finger, signaling him to stop. Dan pulled over in a small roadside park.

"Okay. Now, Ella, I'm gonna put you on speaker. I want Dan to hear this. Repeat what you just told me."

"Hi, Dan. I was telling Wyman we got a call from the charge nurse in the cardiac ICU at Hedrick saying Drake had spent the night in the waiting room, waiting for Zeke to be released. She told me Zeke had a rough night, and the chief cardiac surgeon said he didn't expect to release him until some more tests. The nurse said it would be at least

Monday, maybe Tuesday, before he would be able to leave, if then." Dan slammed his fists on the steering wheel, his voice rising. "Wait a minute, Ella. Didn't you tell me Drake said he was going home to wait for you to call him about Zeke? What the hell is he doin' in

Abilene?" Dan paused and rubbed his aching left knee. "Sorry, Ella. Don't mean to shout. It's frustratin'."

"Yeah, I thought he'd calmed down a little and would stay that way, for a while, at least. The Hedrick nurse told me he got there about five yesterday and refused to budge from Zeke's bedside. That means he headed for Abilene right after I talked to him. I'd like to be surprised, but I'm not."

Wyman looked at Dan, who was twisting the steering wheel with both hands. "We're on our way . . ."

"There's no point, guys. The doctor has quarantined Zeke. Evidently, he's worried about infection. That really set Drake off. He stomped around, yelling, demanding to talk to the surgeon. They said he grabbed the bed and wouldn't let go until security showed up."

Wyman looked at the phone. "Where is Drake now?"

Jerrod Memorial's background noise on the phone, and the sound of Ella's hand rubbing on the phone, her muffled voice, then her hand being moved. "Thanks, Lacy. I'm on the way. Wyman, there's no point in you going to Abilene. I don't know about Drake. I gotta go. I'll talk to you later."

Dan turned his SUV around and headed back toward Breckenridge.

"Now, what happens? I'm worried."

"Worried he'll show up at the game and make a scene?"

"Yeah. Despite our little chat yesterday, he's probably still pretty sore at me. Maybe he'll come to his senses if he has any senses left."

After lunch in Breckenridge, Dan spent a few minutes at the John Deere dealership. Before they got back on the road to Jerrod, he called LaDonna. "Can you talk?"

"Janelle met up with one of her high school buddies after we ate lunch with Rob and Ella. She told me about the situation at Hedrick, and she'd talked to y'all. Are you on the way back?"

"Yep. We're ready to come that way. Should be there about two thirty, I'd guess."

"What about Drake? You think he's coming back here?"

"I don't want to think about him or talk about him for the next 48 hours, okay?"

"Gotcha. Hey, we saw Lindy Branch and her fiancé at lunch. She invited Janelle and Rob to go to the game with them. So, it's you and me. Wyman and Ella are going to meet us there. You heard about the weather forecast?"

"No, what about it?"

"Heavy fog, right at game time. I remember it was that way the last game you played here."

"Yeah, I remember. Yep, the fog's coming in. I'll talk to you later."

They could see the creek bed filling with gray fluff as they crossed the two-lane bridge. When they turned at the gin, the fog was obscuring the sky, the tops of telephone poles disappearing.

Dan dropped Wyman at the church and pulled into the Zip Stop for gas. He spotted Freddy's car parked at the end of the building, walked over, and tapped on the window.

Freddy looked up and turned his cell phone face-down on his lap. He held up a finger as he opened his door and got out. "Hello, Mr. Baker, how are you today?"

Dan looked around and said, "Freddy, it's *Dan*, okay? We know each other pretty well by now."

Freddy smiled. "Yeah, you're right, *Dan*."

"Let's cut some bait here. What's goin' on with Drake Kilborn? What happened yesterday at the café?" He smiled. "Answer any question you'd like."

"I was doing a little snooping." Freddy looked down at his cell phone. He turned the phone, so Dan could see the green line snaking across the screen. "Looks like he's on his way back."

Dan filled Freddy in on the phone call about Zeke they'd gotten on the way to Abilene.

Dan could see the part about Drake getting kicked out of the hospital got Freddy's attention.

Freddy pulled out a small notebook from his jacket and made notes. "This is interesting. Look, Dan, I've got to make some calls. Let me get back with you."

As Dan drove away, Freddy called Russ Jennings and told him about

Drake being kicked out of the Abilene hospital. "I don't know what your position is on this, Mr. Jennings, but I'm concerned Drake Kilborn is either gonna go postal, disappear for good, or both. Isn't there any way we could find the judge and get him to move on that warrant?" The tracking app on his phone buzzed. The pulsing green line was on the hill south of the gin.

"The judge is picky about being interrupted on his day off. I'll see if I can talk his secretary into giving me his personal cell number. I'll call him and get back to you as soon as I can," Jennings said.

Freddy looked at this cell phone again. "I think Drake is probably on the way to town. We need to keep him contained until we can get that warrant. I'm supposed to meet him at the airport at about three."

Jennings assured Freddy he'd get back to him in an hour. Freddy checked his watch. That would make it three o'clock.

———————

Larry Britts, the son of Jeff Stangle's secretary, later told a DPS investigator of meeting Drake at Zeke's house about two o'clock. Britts said the Mustang had been driven hard. He remembered popping noises the engine made as it idled. He drove Zeke's pickup to the airport and parked it behind the hangar between an Airstream trailer and the building. Drake drove him back to his car and handed him a twenty-dollar bill. The boy said he tried in vain to start a conversation but would recall Drake did nothing but nod and hum a passage from *The Old Rugged Cross* over and over.

30

F reddy had been waiting in his car at the end of Windy Acres Trailer Park for about fifteen minutes when Russ Jennings called. Jennings had explained Drake's growing erratic behavior and convinced the judge to get his signature scanned and e-mailed to him. "It took forever to explain how that's done, but I guess that's a conversation for another day."

"When will we get the signature?"

"That's the problem. He was out in the middle of nowhere. He asked one of his hunting buddies where he could get something scanned. Looks like it'll have to be at the city hall in a little town about thirty miles from where they are."

Freddy looked at his watch. "He is going to e-mail you the signature?"

"Yep. I'll get it on the warrant, get somebody to witness the affidavit, and call you. That'll probably be around five. It's the best I can do. What are you up to?"

"Some good, I hope. I'm playin' sheriff in your county, Mr. Jennings. I hope you will CYA me if this blows up."

"If what blows up?"

"Good answer. I'll wait for your call."

Freddy drove slowly on the dirt road beside the tracks and up to the gulley's top, which was beginning to fill with streamers of fog.

Both spray planes were on the apron by the runway. It looked like Drake had pushed and tugged them out of the hangar by himself. They weren't side-by-side but sat where they'd been left, discarded toys.

In their place in the hangar, Drake's car. The hood was up, parts on the fenders and on the floor. Drake was leaning into the engine well, pulling at tubes and belts. Rap music was coming from a jam box.

Freddy was sure Drake couldn't hear him driving up but didn't want to risk the reaction a horn honk might bring, so he put his lights on bright as he stopped beside one of the planes.

It took Drake a moment to notice the head lights. He stood, turned, stared at Freddy, then looked to his left, grinned, back to Freddy. He looked like a self-conscious eight-year-old, smiling into the blinding headlights. He went to the boombox on the tool bench and unplugged it.

Freddy got out and leaned on the Mustang's radiator.

Drake imitated him, leaning on the left fender.

"Drake, whatcha doin'?"

Drake picked up a crescent wrench and scratched the side of his jaw with it. "Fixin' it." wrench and scratched the side of his jaw with it. "Fixin' it."

"What's wrong with it?"

Drake giggled and looked to one side, cocked his head down as if sharing a secret. "Don't know. I'm gonna find out. Look at all this stuff. It looks like worms in here," he said, pointing to the engine well.

Freddy was relieved. The car wasn't going anywhere for a long time. It was evident from the bird's nest of hoses and tubes Drake had piled on the engine. Freddy glanced down below the fan blade. A discarded radiator hose almost hid the tracker's red light. Freddy had no reason to believe Drake had seen it.

Drake leaned up. "What are you doin' here?"

"You told me to come today."

"Musta been somebody else. Never mind. Hey, Momma," he yelled, "come meet my new friend." Drake pitched the wrench on the top of the car's battery, turned, and walked quickly toward the hangar's rear.

Freddy quickly got in his car and drove toward the crossing. Had he turned and looked back, he would have seen Drake at the hangar door, wiping away a tear and smiling the most brittle of smiles.

Mariel had promised Freddy chili before the game and—in her words—something really special after. Part of the bargain was they were taking Mariel's niece Bea with them.

As he was pulling up to Mariel's apartment house, his phone buzzed. He looked at the ID. "Mr. Jennings, what's happening? Do we have a warrant?"

"Afraid not. The judge didn't get to that city hall in time and is trying to get the local sheriff to do the e-mail. I haven't heard a word about that yet."

Freddy went over the scene at the airport in his mind. He was confident that Drake had boxed himself in for the night.

They could afford to wait. They could get to it in the morning.

By game time, the gray fog curtain had come to earth, wrapping around the grain elevator and embracing all but the top floor of the courthouse and the steeple of All Saints Episcopal. It crept through neighborhood streets and laid on the football field, swirling above the grass. It luffed and pulsed in the air, allowing the teams to be seen as if through a wet screen door.

The home bleachers were about half full. The fog all but obscured the visitor's side. Their unseen band honked and bleated into the thickening mist. Rob and Janelle were sitting with her friends on the other end of the home bleachers. Dan and LaDonna and their friends from took up a center swath of the rickety wooden structure. Wyman Costley and Ella Parker huddled together on the seats above LaDonna, enjoying the whispers the wet air carried down from the crowd.

Nearby, Freddy Espinoza sat with Mariel and Bea, starry-eyed and bubbling with excitement. She smelled her small mum, a miniature of the one Freddy had given her *tia*.

Freddy slowly scanned the crowd from the kickoff. At the end of the first quarter, he told Mariel he was going to the bathroom.

He walked behind the concession stand, had a whispered exchange by two-way with Marv Harter, who was standing at the north end of the bleachers. Freddy reminded the deputy that if he took his ball cap off, Harter was to go to the back of the bleachers and move toward him.

Freddy joined the group of men moving along the chain-link fence bordering the playing field. For Freddy, the thickening fog brought something not right. A gentle hum, just below the range of hearing.

When tension rose, it always served him well. For Freddy, the old familiar no-name warning, a demand on all his senses. Then, his cell phone. He pulled it from his inside pocket. Jennings' ID and one word, *signed.*

Freddy managed to relax with Mariel and Bea through the rest of the half. He pretended to enjoy the almost invisible halftime show where the sound grew faint when the twenty musicians turned to march across the field into the mist. The hum in his head was coming closer and closer. It was like one of the instruments they carried, not in tune but demanding to be felt and almost heard. He looked at his cell phone several times. The red dot was still at the airport. But where was Drake?

By the end of the third quarter, the fog had grown so thick that the only hint of progress was the light blooms on the scoreboard. How much time left?

Bea, snuggling up to Mariel, tugged at the sleeve of her parka. Mariel leaned over. *"Tia, ese hombre allá, tiene ojos tan grandes y negros. ¿Creas que es un insecto?"*

"No, *preciosa*, there are no men with big black eyes who are insects. What did you see?"

Bea snuggled closer and pointed toward the crowd at the fence. "I saw him *tia*. Those shiny dark things on his eyes make him look like an ant in one of my picture books."

Mariel looked to her right, gasped, and nudged Freddy. Drake was standing in the milling crowd of fence-walkers, cap pulled low over his forehead, collar up to his ears. She thought he nodded at her, then turned and walked toward the back of the bleachers. She stood and moved Bea between her and Freddy. He smiled down at Bea and looked at Mariel. She motioned with her head.

Freddy stood, took his car keys from his jacket pocket, and tossed them to Mariel. "I'll find you. Don't worry." He didn't wait to see her surprised expression. He bounded down six rows of bleachers toward the knot of fence-walkers and Drake, who was moving into the fog.

Freddy was about to catch Drake when a huge man in overalls, tattered hoodie, and sweat-stained cap moved close enough for Freddy to smell his beer breath.

"Where you goin' there, Pancho? Don't ya know it's bad manners pushin' folks aroun'? Or didn't they teach yew no manners in Mesiko? I rekin yew outta think 'bout apologizin'."

Freddy knew he didn't have time to grab the hulk's outstretched fist and take him to the ground. He retreated two steps, reached in his back pocket, retrieved the badge holder, and held it up within two inches of the man's bloodshot eyes.

"Excuse the shit outta me."

Freddy pushed past the man, walked into the fog below the bleachers. He moved forward one step at a time, stopped, listened, but heard only the crowd above him, and then, "You lookin' for me?" Freddy turned, turned again, but couldn't locate the voice.

"Look, Momma, a dancin' bear. Hey senorrrr, why don't you call for help?"

Freddy took out the two-way. "S.O. One?"

"Ten-four, comin' your way."

The voice now coming from the right. "Yeah, you got the sharpest knife in the drawer comin' your way."

Freddy stepped to the side, hoping to see a shadow against the back of the bleachers. Then, the blinding light.

"Now, can you see me, Mr. Mechanic?" The light was a blue orb blooming from a brilliant disk being waved back and forth, moving away from Freddie. He pulled his .38 from the back holster and sighted above and to the left of the light source. "I don't want to shoot you, Mr. Kilborn."

The light moved slowly away, disappeared. "Oh, it's *Mister* Kilborn now? What should I call you?"

"My last name is Espinoza. I'm a Texas Ranger. I have a warrant for your arrest. I am armed. I advise you to surrender now."

"So what?" The voice seemed to drift from right to left. "Come get me. Should be easy." Then the sound of one body encountering another in the mist. "Shit. Well, if it ain't the Deputy Dawg. Get the fuck outta my way."

Freddy wiped the film of moisture from his face and rushed forward. He put both hands on his pistol, almost tripped over Marv Harter, who was on all fours. Freddy holstered his weapon, helped Harter to his feet, nearly collided with Dan Baker.

"Can I help, Freddy?"

Freddy ran past Dan and shouted, "Make sure everybody's safe. Go back up in those stands and keep them there. Please. Come on, deputy, let's go." His voice was swallowed by the fog as he urged Harter ahead of him. "Where's your cruiser?"

Harter stopped and bent over to catch his breath. He pointed to the almost invisible white SUV. "We gonna pursue?"

"You get in the passenger's side. Gimme your keys. Let's go." Freddy started the engine. He shut his door and rolled down both front windows, concentrated, motioning Harter to be silent.

A cheer went up from the bleachers. He let the dispatcher know he was in service and moved the SUV slowly toward the street, stopped, listened. Then, the sound of a six-cylinder engine pushed to its limit, metal against brick, speeding through a dip in the northbound lane of the highway.

Freddy reached for the microphone. "Holden S.O., this is Espinoza. We're in pursuit of a red Ford Ranger pickup, northbound on 220. Any DPS in the area?"

"Negative. Nearest in Breckenridge. You want a reserve deputy? Advise location of Deputy Harter."

He slowed as he crossed the dip Drake had scraped. "Harter with me. Negative on the reserve. Out."

After Freddy drove north past the grade school, then the feed yard, the fog thinned and disappeared. At the city limits, he could see the tail lights of the pickup receding in the distance of the clear night. It had to be Drake. Freddy cinched his seat belt and floored the accelerator pedal.

When he turned toward the bleachers' back, Dan was surprised to see LaDonna walking toward him. "Donna, I got to see if I can help . ."

"Danny? What are you going to do?" She grabbed his jacket and pulled him close. "Danny? Tell me you're not going to be involved in this. Tell me right now."

Dan glanced back again and then held her by the shoulders.

"Donna, this is going to sound funny, but I owe it to Zeke, and in a way, to Drake to keep him bein' hurt or worse . . ."

She twisted her shoulders so his hands fell off and then stepped forward. "No. Damn it. No. I don't want you playing cop. You're a reserve deputy. Fine. That doesn't mean you have to get yourself shot."

Dan stepped back and said, "Look at me. Bein' a reserve's got nothing to do with it. I have this feeling, 'Donna. If I can take some of the heat out of this—Now, I gotta go. I want to try to find Drake before Freddy Espinoza does. I think I know where Drake went, out by the creek north of town." He turned to walk away.

LaDonna tried to grab his sleeve, but he pushed her hand away.

"Go back up there, to the bleachers, and tell Ella what's going on. Please get a ride with them to the after-game. I'll call you as soon as I know, somethin'. Whatever you do, don't say anything 'bout this to Janelle and Rob. I'm gonna be all right. Don't worry." He waved her protest off and disappeared into the fog, heading for his Suburban.

Glancing in his rearview mirror, Drake sped north, crossed the

Jerrod Creek bridge. He cut his lights, turned onto the creek-side road, slowed, looked over his shoulder to see the blue flashing lights tracking away to the north. He accelerated along the dirt road.

Topping a slight rise without slowing, the pickup shuddered over the washboard ripples in the road. The dramatic change surprised him. He jerked the steering wheel, hoping to get in control before colliding with two cottonwoods. He accelerated up the incline, his right front wheel lost its grip. The pickup began skidding sideways.

He jerked the steering wheel left to counter the fishtail to the right, skidded sideways down the slope, rammed a stone wall. The pickup rushed into the night air, turned on its top, and slid down the steep creek bank. His gut told him he was going to roll again. His last conscious act was to grab for his seatbelt.

31

O ld Boar raised himself from the nest he'd hollowed in the creek bank's loose soil, released a pungent stream of urine into his nest, emptied his bowels, stomped, and kicked to mix the essence with the still, fetid air.

As if on a spoken signal, the herd—two boars, three sows, four shoats, fifteen piglets—stood, stretched, and shook themselves. Some of the piglets ran under one of the sows and were butted off their feet. They righted themselves and fell in with the herd as it climbed the soggy bank and moved into the naked willows.

They threaded through. First aimlessly, then in a jagged line out onto the moonlit clearing at the field's edge. They moved a few yards, stopped, turned the muddy soil with their snouts, swallowing a scurrying cricket or trampling a frantic centipede. Some found grubs, others the still-fresh roots from the soybean harvest.

Within ten minutes, Dan was nearing the Jerrod Creek Bridge. There was no sign of flashing lights from Harter's cruiser or Drake's pickup. He slowed as he crossed the bridge, then turned right onto the dirt road that paralleled the creek.

He stopped, pulled his six-cell flashlight out of the console, activated his caution blinkers, and stepped down from the Suburban and listened. "Freddy's not here. I bet he's five miles away by now," he said to himself as he squatted in the middle of the road. He moved his light in a slow arc from the dirt track to the asphalt and back. On the left side of the road was a slight skid mark, a shallow groove heading east.

Dan stood and walked to the track. He stood over it a moment, moving his eyes from left to right. Movement caught his eye. About five feet away, a small dirt clod toppled and rolled down into the faint track. Dan ran back to his SUV. As he shut the door, threw the still-lit flashlight into the passenger seat, drove east, long-quiet tracking skills from his teenage hunts with Big Dan were unfolding in his mind.

"Wait. We gotta turn around. He can't be that far ahead of us." Freddy slowed and veered to the right, made a U-turn, and stopped on the other side of the road. He looked at Harter and pointed at the thin blue line on the map display.

"You know this country better than I do. Show me where we lost him."

Harter studied the screen, looked up at the distant lights of Jerrod, back at the display. "It's hard to say. Let's go back that way, a little. He can't be that far ahead of us."

Yeah, so I hear, Freddy said to himself. He turned on the blue strobes and started back toward the town.

The herd stopped, heads raised, snouts quivering as the wet whisper breeze rose through the mangled trees of the creek bed and puffed across the flat ground before them. The piglets clumped closer together. The sows pushed in line, waiting.

Old Boar snorted back at Young Sow. She spun, squealed, and ran past him, stopping to take the air of the Other on the freshening breeze. The salty scent was growing strong, the urine musk, pungent droppings mixed with sand and, most promising, the air of blood. Old Boar began to trot, paced ahead, quickening.

Drake woke to grinding pain from his left leg, numb from the knee down. When he tried to move it, pain cascaded upward, causing him to gasp. He waited for the numbness to crawl up to his thigh and tried to move again. He struggled to remove his revolver from his jacket pocket and put it next to him on the creek bottom.

He tried to prop on one elbow, but the move awoke a stabbing pain in his ribs. He took his flashlight from the other inside pocket and turned it on. He saw the pickup upside down, the driver's door open, top crushed. "Thrown out," he said as the pain surged and he passed out.

Old Boar grunted deeply and pawed the ground, causing all eyes to seek him. Take the air. The Other is near. He moved his head up and down, side to side, moved his ragged tongue across his remaining tusk, and grunted from his belly several times.

He peered over the creek bank. There below the Other lay. Old Boar did not recall such brokenness. He raised his head to take the air.

On it, the sweet tartness of pain. He grunted to Sow, who brought Old Boar's eldest with her. He wheeled back and forth, like Old Boar, suspicious of the Other. This Other was alone. Then the rumble noise of another coming close. Old Boar huffed, backed away from the bank. Sow and piglets followed him into the cottonwood shadows.

Dan saw the trouble as the road curved. The top of the low stone wall he and Zeke had built for one of his father's friends was missing. He stopped and aimed his flashlight beam out the passenger window at the high weeds beyond the wall. They had been smashed to the edge of the creek.

Dan got out, scaled the wall, made his way through the crumpled weeds and to the edge of the creek bank. Ten feet below, his light showed the overturned pickup, followed the stream bed, found Drake, face down in the small trickle of water.

Dan fished in his pocket for Freddy's card and punched in the number on his cell phone. "Freddy, I found him. Where are you?"

Pause. "Deputy Harter says we're about eight miles from the bridge."

"Don't cross the bridge. Turn on the road before it. Go about four miles. Look for my flashers. And, call the ambulance."

"Is he alive?" The siren could be heard through Freddy's cell phone.

"I hope so. I'm goin' down in the creek right now."

Dan pocketed his phone and followed his flashlight's beam down the loose bank and onto the gravel bottom. As he got close to Drake, he could see he was semiconscious; his lips rolled back in pain. At an odd angle, his leg was stretched to one side, a wet blot of blood seeping through the fabric at the knee. Dan kneeled and patted Drake's shoulder. Drake moaned and opened his eyes.

His voice was a raspy gurgle. A trickle of dried blood had collected below his nose. "Help me," he whispered, reaching for Dan. "Who are you?"

Dan took his hand. "It's Dan, Drake. Help's on the way."

———

As he topped the small hill above the bridge and turned off the siren, Freddy told the dispatcher to send the ambulance. He slowed, turned right, and cautiously steered in the deep sand that had drifted from the fence line. The sand was deeper as he drove away from the bridge to the west. After fifteen minutes, no sign of Dan's flashers. The road curved to the right and slightly uphill. Another mile, a barbed-wire gate.

Harter leaned forward, stared at the fence. "This ain't it."

"Well, good, deputy. That clears that up." On the map screen, the cruiser was a small red dot somewhere to the north of Jerrod Creek, west of the road that crossed the bridge. He pulled his cell phone from his pocket, called Dan. No answer.

Freddy had no choice. There was no place to turn around without going through the gate and into the pasture beyond. He wasn't going through the gate and into the pasture beyond. He wasn't in the mood to send Marv Harter to open the gate. Freddy went in reverse, watching the display as he backed toward the creek.

———

Dan's cell phone buzzed. He was about to answer and remind Freddy which way to turn when he got to the bridge. The battery message flashed, and the screen went black. "Oh shit. I should of told him to turn left." He realized the beam from his flashlight was getting weaker, the light was becoming redder as he swept back and forth.

"Havin' trouble with your dinky little light, big man? How about this one?" Blinding blue light erupted from Drake's place on the sand.

Dan drew a quick breath, raised his forearm in front of his eyes, stepped to the right.

Below Drake's light, a small red blossom followed by a sharp *crack*.

Dan dove to the right, rolled over a driftwood log as the round whooshed by four feet away. Two more shots, one finding Dan's sheltering log. *Three*, Dan thought, *five to go*.

The sand on the creek bank smelled like Iraq. He was crouching to avoid shots fired by a suicidal enemy soldier, reaching for his AR-15, then willed reality back.

The blue light wavered, clinked as it scraped in the gravel. "I know you're there Missssssster Baker, daddy's best friend. Who's that with you? Lookee there. What's that bitch daughter of yours doing here in my little paradise? Watch this, Nelly." Two more shots echoed off the sides of the gulley, one a low-pitched flutter nearby, the other stirring the sandy soil up the slope.

Three left.

Scraping sound, followed by a moan and deep cough. Dan peered over the log and saw Drake had the light again, aiming it at the top edge of the creek. Another round followed it. "Two more," Dan whispered.

He flattened and began to crawl away from the gyrating blue light and into the jumble of bleach-white wood. "Drake, I want to help you. There's an ambulance coming. Now, I want you to stop shooting. I need to show them where you are."

Coughing, pained whine. "Run for it, big man. Let's guess how many of these little jewels I have left. Hey, maybe I got another clip. Who knows?" Liquid cough.

Dan looked around the stump. Drake was writhing in the muddy trickle, banging the light against the sand and sobbing with pain. Dan felt his way backward until he bumped a tree trunk lying in the shadows.

He went over it and scurried up the bank. At the top, he rolled into the dry underbrush. "I'm goin' for help, Drake," he yelled. "Hang on. We're gonna get you outta there."

"Go to hell, big man, take your slut daughter . . ."

A distant cry against pain, another pistol shot, and then the comfortless glow of the unmoving blue light on the dry leaves above.

One left.

Dan pushed through the tall brittle reeds. The full moon was clear of the horizon, making it easy for him to see. He stepped up and over the stone wall, looked right and left. He spotted the Suburban's roof, barely visible about two hundred yards away. He ran to it, got in the driver's seat, and plugged the power cord in his cell phone, called Freddy.

"Dan. What's goin' on? You okay?"

"Yeah, where are you?"

Freddy explained his wrong turn, backward drive from the dead end, almost getting stuck in the deep sand at the corner. He was in sight of the bridge, would be across the road and on the way to Dan in a few minutes.

"Is the ambulance comin'?"

"Should be almost here. Wait. There he is, at the bridge. What about Drake?"

"From what I could tell, a broken leg. Sounds like some internal injuries."

"You with him?"

"He's in the creek bed. We'll talk about that when you get here."

"Ten minutes."

"Not soon enough. Drake's got a gun. He's been shootin' at me. I think he's used a clip, but I can't be sure. Don't let the ambulance in here first." Dan closed the call then picked LaDonna's number out of his directory.

"Where are you? Are you all right?" Her voice was strained, had a moist sound. Dan knew she'd been crying.

"I'm okay. I'm on the road north of the creek bridge. Don't worry.

I'm not in any danger."

"You sure? Everybody's worried sick about you. What about Drake?"

"Long story."

———————

Swinging his massive head from side to side, Old Boar huffed the air. He stamped at the piglet who scurried between his legs, sending it squealing. He moved slowly to the edge of the stream bank and peered over. There was the Other, being still, holding its light thing.

Old Boar scanned the creek bottom, dug his hooves into the sandy soil, slid downward, followed by Sow and three piglets. There was the smell of brokenness coming from the Other. Old Boar ventured forward, sniffing at the sandy bottom.

———————

Drake fought off the haze, summoned enough energy to raise his head. Then the ambulance sound registered. It was coming to take him home. He coughed, moaned at the hurt of his ribs and throb of his leg. Another sound made the hair on his arms prickle. He reached for the flashlight and aimed it down the creek.

Old Boar made a deep squawking sound, pitched his head up, and backed away from the light, pushing Young Sow aside. He pawed at the pebbles, splashing mud droplets up on his steaming skin. He put his head down, snuffling in the coming death of the Other.

Drake fumbled for his pistol and flashlight, rolled to his side, spat blood, took the grip with his other hand, felt the trigger. He pointed it toward Old Boar, squeezed off the last round, and fell back, staring up into the silhouettes of the golden leaves above. A bolt of pain caused him to draw a quick, shallow breath, in it Old Boar's fetid killing smell. As he closed his eyes, he felt jagged teeth crush his forearm and then knew he was being shaken like a limp corn stalk.

With a deep swallow, he cleared his mouth, made a plaintive gurgling sob. As red haze enveloped him, he saw Alberta Elizabeth Parker Kilborn being embraced by the risen moon.

-30-

~ Acknowledgements ~

My deepest thanks to those closest to me, who encouraged me to go on despite stumbles – especially:

Dr. Russell Long, Vicki Schoen, Kathi Campbell Greer - critique group colleagues

Texas Ranger Jay Foster (ret), who answered all my naïve questions.

Jessica Wikoff, for her patient help with my rudimentary Tex-Mex

Terry Vogel, Texas 69th District Court Investigator

Tad Fowler, Assistant Potter County Attorney

Jason Davis, S&D Spraying Service

Coco Duckworth, first reader

Pam Kessler, my editor,

Parman Reynolds

Richard Dee

Kerry Knorpp

Other books in the *Jerrod Series* available through Amazon:

Espinoza-book 2, The Jerrod Series
Texas Ranger Freddy Espinoza reluctantly becomes sheriff after the arrest of his predecessor on drug charges. He gets help from friendly poltergeist.

McTague—book 3, The Jerrod Series
Scotty McTague left a well-paying IT position to take over the family wheat harvesting business. It was a mistake, but deep family connections made it very difficult to undo until . . .

Year Zero—Book 4, The Jerrod Series
The Coronavirus comes to Jerrod, changing the lives of everyone in the small town. (summer, 2021)

Visit waynehughes.net

* Reviews from the critics

* Samples from each book and the work in progress

* Front pages of the *Jerrod Citizen*

* Order an autographed copy

* Join the e-mail list

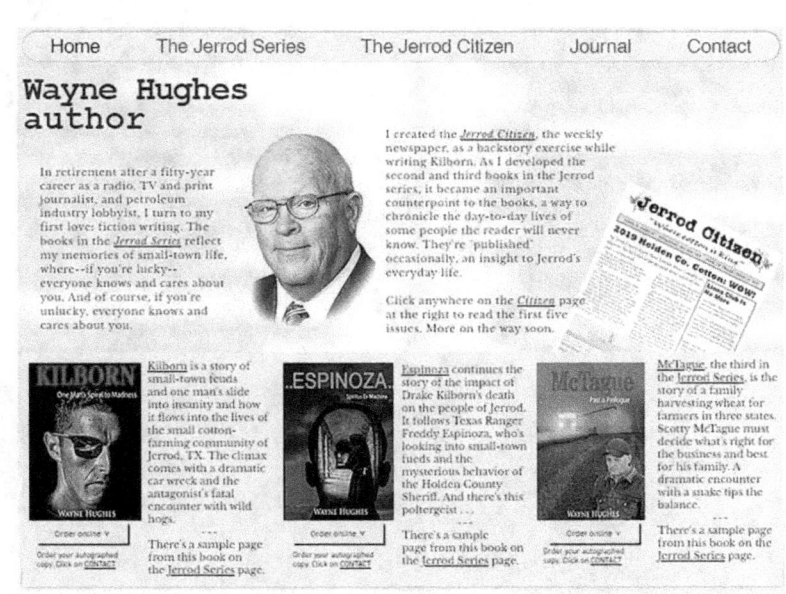

www.ingramcontent.com/pod-product-compliance
Lightning Source LLC
Chambersburg PA
CBHW070058260626
47160CB00004B/1241